A DANGEROUS DECEPTION

"Someone shot arrows at me," Audrey said, her teeth chattering. Reaction was setting in, embarrassing her. She wanted to appear brave for Harry.

"What!" He grabbed both of her shoulders and peered into her eyes as if he did not, or could not, believe her. Wordlessly she pointed to the tree.

Harry released her. Audrey watched him closely as he eyed the arrows, then tried to pry the uppermost one. It did not give easily. He didn't bother with the second, but snatched the piece of cloth from its shaft, glanced at it and stuffed the scrap into his breast pocket.

He turned to her, his eyes ravaged, his cheeks suffused with color. "Stay here. I'm going to search the wood."

"No, don't! It's too dangerous."

But he was already on the opposite side of the road, peering into the undergrowth. After a few moments he returned.

"No one's there now. I'll take a better look later. I wish you had told me you were leaving and I would have accompanied you. Don't go out alone again. Promise me."

"What did the note say?" she asked, thinking, *Either he is the greatest actor in the world, or he could not have done this to me.*

Abruptly he swept her into his arms. She sank against him in dizzy relief, feeling protected beyond reason. Surely nothing bad could happen to her now. She turned her cheek against his coat, relishing the gentle roughness of the material, the clean masculinity of his scent. She fancied she could hear his heart beating beneath her ear.

Books by Marcy Stewart

CHARITY'S GAMBIT
MY LORD FOOTMAN
LORD MERLYN'S MAGIC
DARBY'S ANGEL
THE VISCOUNT TAKES A WIFE
LADY SCANDAL
THE BRIDEGROOM AND THE BABY
A BRIDE FOR LORD BEAUMONT

Novellas in Anthologies:

"An Indefinite Wedding" in
FLOWERS FOR THE BRIDE
"Lady Constance Wins" in
LORDS AND LADIES
"A Halo for Mr. Devlin" in
SEDUCTIVE AND SCANDALOUS
"The Enchanted Bride" in
MY DARLING BRIDE

Published by Zebra Books

THE DARING
MISS LASSITER

Marcy Stewart

ZEBRA BOOKS
Kensington Publishing Corp.
http://www.zebrabooks.com

In memory of my wonderful dad,
Gordon Ray Stewart
1919–2000

And with special thanks to the best writer friends
anywhere: Faith Garner, Janice Maynard,
Jan McDaniel, Lurlene McDaniel, Leigh Neely,
Jan Powell, Susan Sawyer and Clara Wimberly

One

"Don't look now," said Miss Audrey Lassiter to her sister as she made a pretense of arranging a spray of violets in their display cart, one of many lining Saint Duxbury's crowded main street and open-air market, "but that older gentleman in brown, the one standing beside O'Toole's sausage stand, has been staring at me for the longest time. Oh, but now he is pacing toward the river; perhaps he—no, he's turning this way again. Don't look, Rebecca, I tell you. He'll see us noticing him and there's something mysterious about how he continues to glance my way."

"I don't know how I can be expected not to look when you tease my curiosity so," said the young woman seated beneath a faded parasol as she leaned outward, one hand shielding the portion of her cheek not covered by her bonnet. "He appears harmless enough. There's no mystery. Everyone stares at you because you're beautiful."

"Oh, what a lot of nonsense." Audrey, having detected a whisper of resentment in her sister's tone, frowned with regret. She should have said the man was staring at them both, even though Rebecca sat in the shadows and was almost entirely out of sight. But that, of course, was how the younger woman preferred things, always pushing Audrey forward when it was Rebecca who owned the talent for growing luscious vegetables and vibrant flowers and baking breads that put the village baker to shame.

Audrey was convinced that had their fate been left to herself, the Lassiter family would have starved.

When an elderly woman appeared to examine the cabbages and potatoes with arthritic fingers, the young lady gladly allowed her attention to be drawn away. When she thought to look again for the stranger, he had moved on.

The remainder of the morning passed without incident, the cries of hawkers growing vapid, the rows of carts gradually diminishing in number as heat beamed upward from the cobblestones. The Lassiter sisters endured longer than most; but at last, humidity coiling their hair into ringlets, they wheeled their cart homeward.

Today the journey to the edge of town and the cottage where the Lassiter family dwelled took no longer than a half-hour. Since the route forced them through some of Saint Duxbury's less genteel neighborhoods, the young women had sometimes in the past been delayed by ruffians or the occasional soldier looking for feminine sport. Once a band of children had made off with several of Rebecca's finest loaves of honey and cinnamon bread. Today no one bothered them. No one had troubled them for several weeks now.

Audrey would have been more relieved had she not suspected the reason was that Burl Ingerstand, the village smithy's son, had put it about that the Lassiters were under his protection. Thinking of his stout frame and curly red beard, his thunderous voice and unbearable ignorance, she winced. If ever there existed a mixed blessing, surely it hailed to the name Burl Ingerstand.

"The wagon looks considerably lighter than it did this morning," Martin Lassiter said from his chair, when Audrey and Rebecca parked the cart beside him in the front garden and began unloading the leftover vegetables to store away from the sun. "But you both look spent."

"We've grown used to Mr. Ingerstand's help, Papa," Rebecca said as she entered the house, apron full of potatoes. "Thankfully he'll be back from London with his mother's new table in time for Thursday's market."

Audrey sent a sharp look toward the doorway. "I'm just as happy he's gone."

"Yes, well, good use of a nuisance, I say," said Mr. Lassiter, knuckles whitening as he strained to wheel himself over the threshold. Behind him, arms awkward with two baskets of nosegays, Audrey longed to help but knew he would resist. "If he must flit around my daughters like a honeybee searching for clover, the least he can do is relieve them some little portion of the labor their father cannot provide."

His words drove through Audrey like a knife. "You're worth far more than your labor, Papa."

"That's as well then, since there's little enough of it." His voice shook with pretended humor, although Audrey knew he deceived none of them, not even himself. An attack of apoplexy three years before had left him unable to walk and with limited use of his left hand. Prior to that time he had served as vicar in a hamlet near Maidstone. Now he was fit only to tutor the few Saint Duxbury children whose parents felt an education worth a scattering of pence or, more often, a gift of meat, supplies, or labor. Had this cottage not been bequeathed them from a maternal aunt, she knew their situation would have been hopeless.

"You do what you can," Rebecca said in pragmatic tones, directing a glance in Audrey's direction that she could not fail to interpret. Rebecca did not believe she was doing her part. She still blamed her for not accepting Will Whitson's offer of marriage last winter. She believed that Audrey had neglected an opportunity to rescue them from a life of poverty and hard toil.

As Audrey fetched her mother's china from the cabinet and began setting the table, she noted gloomily that the room which constituted the main living area of their tiny cottage needed whitewashing again. What a dismal place it was! She would have her mother back if she could, but at least that good lady had not seen how far down in the world they had fallen. But perhaps if her mother had survived her bout with pneumonia, she would have found a way from the tangle. Audrey could not.

At night the sisters often discussed their predicament in their loft bedroom beneath the rafters, whispering in the dark so Papa could not hear. Audrey's education was sufficient to merit a governessing position, but what, then, would happen to her father and Rebecca? A governess did not earn enough to support a family, and Rebecca was too shy of curious comments and gazes to sell her wares at market without Audrey. That was why Rebecca believed marriage was the only answer and that Audrey must find someone to rescue them. Preferably a man with wealth.

Never mind love. Never mind happiness.

Lining the bread basket with a scrap of clean linen, Audrey watched her sister stir an unpromising mixture of cabbage and diced potatoes into the boiling pot suspended over the fire. Even Rebecca understood that they no longer traveled in circles which allowed them to meet the sort of useful bachelors for which she hoped. Therefore, when Will Whitson, a mere carpenter, proposed, she believed the compromise a tolerable one and could not understand Audrey's selfish refusal.

What Rebecca did not realize, and never would if it were left to Audrey, was that even if she had been accommodating enough to marry someone she didn't love, she had it from Will's own lips that he could not take on the care of her family, saying he had parents and two sisters of his own to support on a craftsman's wages. Moreover, when he understood she meant to refuse him, he'd sealed his fate, declaring his relief at being freed from the sound of her father's voice droning on about poets and philosophers who never did a decent day's work and the sight of her sister's wrecked face, which troubled his dreams like a curse.

It was this last memory which put her off her meal when they finally sat to eat. She picked at her vegetables until Rebecca scolded her for wasting food. *I am the older, not you,* Audrey almost retorted, but as always, a glimpse of the ragged scar bordering her sister's hairline from forehead to chin stilled her tongue. She was careful not to linger her gaze upon it, or Rebecca would put her hand to shield the old injury, so particular was she of offending even those who loved her most. Only with her family did she remove her bonnet and raise her face with a semblance of confidence, and Audrey would not have her give up that small freedom.

Life could be wrenchingly unfair. There were times when she heard Rebecca sobbing into her pillow at night, and she knew the tears were for her ruined future as much as the vanity natural to any young girl. Before the accident, Rebecca had been far more lovely than Audrey could ever hope to be.

"You are both very quiet," Papa said, reaching for one of the books he always kept at hand. "Perhaps a sonnet will brighten you?"

"Or lull Audrey off to sleep and leave me with the cleaning up," Rebecca said. "She's drooping already."

Audrey could not let this pass. Rebecca's desperation had lately taken a bitter edge, and Audrey refused to suffer it. "I'll help you as I always do," she said pertly, and stood to gather plates. Then her father's hand slipped around her wrist.

"Stay a moment, daughters. There's more to life than work. If your mother and I did not teach you that, we taught you nothing."

A look passed between the sisters and, a measure of peace restored, they returned to their seats. But Audrey disliked Shakespeare's sonnets, as they were redolent with passages about fading beauty and love and death, and she asked her father to begin one of the plays instead.

"A play, then? What shall it be? . . . We've not read *Julius Caesar* in a long time; perhaps—"

A knock sounded at the door. Audrey rose to answer it as Rebecca instantly planted elbow to table and cradled her face.

A flash of presentiment warned her their visitor would be the man from the market, the one dressed respectably in shades of brown, but it did nothing to calm the flare of alarm she felt when actually seeing him at her doorstep. And the way he stared at her, as if she were a mirage on some desert, helped less.

"Oh." She searched for words, her brain as helpful as a block of wood. "You."

"Please," the stranger appealed, as if fearing she would close the door in his face, a thought not far from her mind. "Miss Lassiter, I don't wish to frighten you. I believe you may have seen me at the market today watching you, but I mean no harm." Unassured, Audrey stiffened. "My—my name is Nathan Turner. Here is my card. I do business in Saint Duxbury every quarter with my lady's solicitors, Barnett, Hartzell, and Simpson—perhaps you've heard of them?"

"All men of integrity, I believe," said Mr. Lassiter, wheeling his chair beside her.

"What do you want?" Audrey whispered. She could never stop fretting at how vulnerable they were, all of them. The thought haunted her, especially in the small hours of the night, when groups of horsemen rode past calling to one another, often drunkenly, or the odd carriage crept by— was it going to stop *here?*—or sometimes simply when the rafters settled uneasily, creaking the changes in temperature like old bones pacing off mischief.

"Audrey," Papa chided. "Forgive my daughter's lack of politeness, Mr. Turner. We don't often receive visitors. Is there something we can do to help you?"

"Yes. That is, I believe so, Mr. Lassiter, although you may find what I have to say unusual. May—may I come in?"

And in spite of the most pointed, disapproving expression she had ever sent her father, the stranger was inside the cottage before Audrey could do more than step aside. She would not offer him hospitality, though, not a man sturdy enough to crack her father's spine with two fingers for all that he must be forty years old. Well, perhaps younger now that she saw the vitality of his skin more closely; his cheeks were ruddy as twin radishes. He must enjoy his port or work outdoors, neither of which recommended him overmuch. And, most condemningly, aside from nodding briefly at Rebecca and shaking Papa's hand, he would not stop staring at her, not even as he claimed the best rocker and felt his way into it like someone blind or addle-headed.

"I'm sorry, I know I'm making you uncomfortable, Miss Lassiter," he said. "It's only that—"

Audrey sank into her chair at the table. "How did you know my name—our names?"

"When I saw you at market I made inquiries at the solicitor's and learned that you were—*are*—a genteel family, and so I thought to make your acquaintance because of the most remarkable—"

"You made inquiries? People of *gentility* generally find such clandestine actions offensive. Or perhaps you merely wanted to assure yourself that we weren't a family of Bonaparte's spies before approaching us?"

"Audrey!" exclaimed Mr. Lassiter, torn between surprise and laughter.

"Or is it possible," she added, unable to stop herself, "you believe anyone selling produce in a public market has less social standing than a—than a speck of dirt on a flea's bottom?"

In the silence that resounded after this remark, Mr. Turner's face lengthened in dismay and loss.

"Please, Audrey," Rebecca begged through her fingers. "Be civil."

Audrey narrowed her eyes at her sister, whom she was certain was at this moment dreaming of how she would decorate her bedroom in the home of her soon-to-be brother-in-law, since Mr. Turner was the most prosperous-looking gentleman to cross the threshold of this house in their history here. Well, she would sacrifice many things for her family, even to her very life, but not her future. There must be an alternative to a loveless marriage. There simply must be.

"Even in anger you look like her," Mr. Turner ruminated, breaking her icy speculations into shards of curiosity. "It's remarkable. All these weeks I've been searching town and country for someone like you, and here you are in a village I frequent more than any but my own."

"You've been searching for someone who looks like me?" Audrey echoed. "Why?"

The visitor shifted his bearing, reminding her of a merchant bent on persuasion. She was instantly on guard again.

"I am the steward of Lady Marianne Hastings, who lives at Far Winds near Guildford in Surrey. I've served her husband's family since I was a lad, beginning as stable boy and working my way up. She is a great lady, miss, the more so since she's endured so much. First her son's early death, then Sir Hastings's passing—he was a knight, Sir Andrew Hastings, K.C.B.—and then, seven years ago, the disappearance of her only remaining child, Roxanne."

From her shadowed place at the table, Rebecca made a mournful sound. Mr. Turner glanced at her and continued.

"The girl was only ten at the time, but if she'd grown into a young lady, she'd be the spit and image of you, Miss Lassiter. Golden hair and blue eyes, and lashes dark as a crow's feathers. She was small like you, too. Fragile as a newborn calf."

Audrey was unsure how she liked being compared to crows and cows, but apparently he meant it as a compliment. "That's a very sad tale, Mr. Turner, but I'm perplexed as to why you wished us to know it."

"But that's just it, you see!" he burst, expanding his arms. "Lady Hastings lies on her deathbed convinced to the last that her child lives. If you would consent to pretend to be Roxanne for only a short while, she could die happy!"

Shock impelled Audrey to her feet. "Impersonate her child? How utterly unthinkable!"

"But why not, miss? It would make her dying blissful and peaceful, and she deserves it."

"I'm sure she does," Mr. Lassiter said, "but it would be a lie."

Mr. Turner turned toward him. "But a gentle lie, sir, never meant to harm anybody, only meant to give her joy."

Agitated, Audrey began stacking their luncheon dishes to be washed. "I could never do such a thing. Even if I were willing, our ages don't coincide. If I've added correctly, the child would be seventeen. I am twenty-one. There is a marked difference between those ages."

"But you look younger and no one will know. I'm willing to pay well for your trouble." When she made no answer, he cleared his throat. "You would have to wait until my lady passes, for I only have a little laid by at present.

But she is leaving me a great sum, miss, enough to buy my own farm and more. I'm willing to give you half of it. Ten thousand pounds."

"Ten thousand pounds!" Audrey exclaimed, rattling the plates back to the table.

"Ten thousand pounds?" Rebecca shrieked, raising her head and forgetting her disfigurement for the moment. When shock, then compassion, passed through the stranger's eyes, she turned angrily, almost defiantly, to her sister. "Audrey?"

"You cannot seriously expect me to play such a role! Not for any amount of money. How do we know he's who he says? Perhaps he sells gullible young females to—to harems, for all we know!"

"A rational fear, Miss Lassiter," he said humbly. "You may ask the firm of Barnett, Hartzell, and Simpson, and they will speak for me as I've known them these many years."

"Ten thousand pounds," Mr. Lassiter mused. "The two of you would never have to work another day in your lives if we managed carefully. But I'm not so certain as to the morality of impersonating someone, even though Mr. Turner's motives appear pure. I must say he does speak persuasively, as if doing this would be an act of Christian charity . . ."

Audrey looked from her father to Rebecca and back again. "Whatever his motives, I can't do it."

"You *won't* do it, you mean," the younger woman said loudly. "You *can* but you *won't,* while I *would*—but I *can't!*"

"Oh, Rebecca . . ." Audrey had never felt so wretched.

"It must be your decision, of course," said their father.

"It's wrong. And even if it were not, I could never deceive anyone properly." As the silence lengthened with the tension of conflicting wills, Audrey's eyes grew wet with the injustice of it. This was *her* life they were discussing, and couldn't people be thrown into prison for such acts if found out? She was no actress. She had not even made a convincing shepherdess when cast in a Nativity play several years before at chapel, and all she had to do then was stand in the background and utter "Hark."

"I cannot—no, I *will* not, do this scandalous thing."

Rebecca charged from the room with a cry. Looking sharply disappointed, Mr. Turner made his bow.

"I remain in town until Saturday, should you change your mind."

"Don't delay your leaving for me," she said, her voice thick. "I won't change my mind."

Rebecca scarcely spoke to Audrey during the next two days, and only the dawn of market day brought a semblance of normality to their conversation. But, Audrey reflected unhappily as she tied the last spray of bluebells together before placing it into the cart, that was only because Burl Ingerstand had arrived, and Rebecca apparently wished to maintain the illusion of a happy family. All part of the effort to charm him into making an offer of marriage to Audrey, a thing she dreaded to confess to her family she would never accept should the event arise.

Best not to worry about *that* discussion until—and if—it became necessary, especially after her refusal of Mr. Turner's scheme.

The trip into town was as uncomfortable as always. Mr. Ingerstand made a great display of pushing the cart, remarking on how easy a task it was for a strong fellow like himself, and didn't the two of them straining together take twice as long to get it to market? Half running to keep up with his pace, Audrey longed to inform this red-haired bear of a man precisely what she thought of his boasting, but she dared not stir Rebecca's displeasure again if she could avoid it.

Once they had set up in the usual place across from O'Toole's, a flurry of customers streamed toward them, most of them intent on purchasing loaves of Rebecca's bread, and Audrey stayed busy for many long minutes. Unfortunately, she was not too occupied to note how Mr. Ingerstand, stationing himself between their cart and that of a scissors-grinder, watched her constantly while making loud comments to passersby. She wanted to believe his remarks were meant good-naturedly, but that was not how they were often taken.

"In the family way again, Mrs. Busby?" he was saying now to the cobbler's wife, who stood selecting a sack's worth of potatoes. "No? Well, you could have fooled me! Best guard that figger or your mister'll be turning his eyes to a lass he can reach his arms around, won't he? Ha!"

"Isn't your father expecting you at the smithy?" Audrey cried as Mrs. Busby flounced away without making her purchase.

"Oh, Da can do the work of five men," he assured her.

Rebecca's sharply indrawn breath and pointed stare drew Audrey's attention to a figure across the street. It was Mr. Turner. Meeting her indignant eyes, the steward turned guiltily and strolled a few paces further into the crowd.

Noting the exchange, Burl Ingerstand scowled. "Who's that?"

"No one of importance," Audrey said.

"He is Mr. Turner," Rebecca said, her voice tinged with dawning excitement. "He works for a great lady and has an excellent income. He saw Audrey in the market this week and was so smitten he paid her a call. It strikes me he can scarcely keep his eyes from her, don't you agree, Mr. Ingerstand?"

Aghast, Audrey stared at her sister. There could be no

doubting she meant to make the smithy jealous, but this twisting of facts left her speechless.

"He keeps eyeballing her all right," he said, looking murderous. "I go away a day or two and they circle like hawks." Moving his jaw back and forth, he stood in thunderous quiet for a moment, then abruptly seized Audrey's arm. "Do you aim to be mine or not?"

"What?" she exclaimed, slicing a wild look at Rebecca, who watched her hopefully.

"You know I been courtin' you these past weeks, and I want to know if you aim to say yes to marryin' me or go off with some other cove? Because I don't want to be wastin' my time iffen you do."

Several market-goers began to show a sudden interest in their direction, but the smithy waved them away.

"You've been courting me?" Audrey could not believe this man was proposing to her over a wagon full of cabbages.

"What did you think—that I was carryin' your trinkets for me health?"

"I'm sorry, I didn't realize. I—I can't marry you, Mr. Ingerstand." She deliberately turned her eyes from Rebecca's frantic signals.

"And why not?" he roared.

"Because I don't love you."

He released her arm with a jerk. "Verra well, then. There's them what ain't too high and mighty to have me." Turning to Rebecca, he added, "If you'd be wantin' an example, I'm thinkin' Miss Rebecca here wouldn't mind me payin' court to her. Her face may not be much to look at, but the rest of her is mighty fine indeed, and she's a good cook, too. What say you to that, missy?"

"How dare you speak to her so!" Audrey exclaimed, but Rebecca flung up a restraining hand. With fascinated horror, Audrey watched her sister gather composure.

"I shall be happy to receive your visits," she said, finally.

"There, you see!" He grabbed a nosegay from the cart and thrust it into Rebecca's hands. "Some people don't know a good thing when they see it," he pronounced with a triumphant glare for Audrey, then strode away.

Silence reigned between the sisters for an eternal moment until Audrey could no longer contain herself.

"You cannot mean you'd consider him, Rebecca. He's not worthy of you!"

"Who else will ask me, looking as I do?"

The familiar pain resounded in Audrey's heart. She wished to comfort her sister but knew Rebecca considered reassurances about inner beauty and other such things to be utter rot. And then a horrible thought struck.

"You don't have feelings for him, do you?"

Rebecca gazed downward, her hand going to her face. "He disgusts me as much as he does you, but someone must see to our future. Since you will not."

Next to them, metal screamed as the scissors grinder turned his wheel sharpening a set of knives. On their other side, a woman sang out the merits of her fresh scones and muffins. The familiar sounds of the market gradually faded from Audrey's ears until she heard only the thumping of her own heart.

"You're giving me little choice," she said at last.

"There aren't many choices for such as we," Rebecca said sadly.

Without another word, Audrey untied her apron and went in search of Mr. Turner.

And thus she found herself at sunset four days later alighting from a hired gig in the drive of Far Winds, her head spinning with carefully rehearsed histories of the inhabitants within as well as her own fabricated one. As the driver drove off, she watched him until he disappeared around a line of elms, then gripped the ancient valise that contained her pitiable wardrobe and walked on trembling legs to the door, where a brass lion's head knocker dared her to lift its fierce maw. She scowled back, then exercised it four resounding times. She could pretend confidence with inanimate objects, at least.

As she waited, she decided the butler would probably send her to the servant's entrance as soon as he laid eyes upon her. She was wearing her best gown, the ivory muslin she saved for chapel services, but that was not saying much. It was three years old, and the lace trim needed replacing. There was a spot near her back hem that she had never been able to get out. Mr. Turner had waved away her concerns about her clothing, saying that, given the story he had devised, it was best she didn't look fashionable. That would doubtless be the only requirement she would be able to get right.

Scanning the three-storied, golden-bricked structure before her and its immaculate grounds, Audrey had never felt so alone. *I can't accompany you,* Mr. Turner had said, *because that would give away our plan. The visit must seem to be your idea alone. As far as anyone else knows, we have never met.* Hearing this, her father had objected, but Mr. Turner assured him he would be nearby if needed, that he would in fact be present when she arrived. Miss Lassiter would at all times be safe.

Well, she didn't feel safe now. And where *was* that steward? A surge of foreboding flowed through her. What if she had been engaged in an elaborate prank of some sort? To what end, though, she could not imagine.

By the time the butler admitted her with a doubtful glance at her attire into a hall wide enough to contain their entire cottage, she knew she was more afraid than at any moment in her life.

Before she could mutter more than a few confused words to the servant, a young gentleman emerged from the salon to her right. The confidence of his bearing and the elegant dishevelment of his clothing seemed to shout that he felt at home here. From the descriptions she had memorized, he must be one of the lady's nephews; surely Lord Harry, not Thornton, for this man had auburn hair, not blond. Or was it the other way around? *Think quickly!* she told herself. Trailing him was Mr. Turner, and she was so grateful to see a familiar face that only his warning frown prevented her from running toward him as to a long-lost relative.

Recalling her mission, she returned her attention to the younger gentleman.

"Harry?" she ventured, stepping forward to meet him in an attempt at surety. "It has been so long, and we have all changed so much."

"You are speaking to the Right Honorable the Lord Hastings," the butler corrected severely. She of course knew Harold Hastings had inherited his late father's title of baron, but Mr. Turner had informed her that the family never used titles amongst themselves.

"Easy, Tidwell, or you will frighten the young lady." To her relief, the servant bowed and walked stiffly away. Looking at her from a daunting height, the baron added with interest, "Have we met, Miss—?"

"My n-name is Roxanne." She had never stuttered before, but then she had never lied before, either, at least not to this depth. Besides which, his commanding good looks and manner were making her extremely nervous. "I've been lost a long time, because I was injured and forgot who I was. But my memory, or parts of it at least, has returned, and I very much wish to see my m-mother, if you please."

The pleasant light in his eyes had steadily faded during this speech. Now his gaze flamed to hellish life.

"You little liar," he said.

Two

What a disappointment she was.

Upon sight of the pretty chit in the hall, Harry had hoped for an evening's diversion, for she must have an interesting story to appear all by herself at Far Winds at nightfall. A broken-down carriage, he had fleetingly conjectured. Perhaps she had been traveling on foot to visit a relative and had lost her way. Something of that nature. Something innocuous to bring a young lady alone into a dangerous world. And lady she was, he had decided in an instant, for all that her clothing and bag bespoke hard times. A lady stood in a certain way, spoke civilly, and conducted herself with refinement, all of which could not easily be imitated. Or so he had believed. Now he must revise his thinking, for lady she certainly was not.

Ladies did not lie, especially in this cruel, conniving, shameful manner.

His gaze roamed insolently over her from head to toe. She was a delectable morsel but not to his taste, now that he saw her game. And she wasted her time turning pale and shrinking away like an innocent maid, trying to appeal to his sympathy. Why was beauty so often paired with perfidy? He would go to his grave wondering.

"Whatever your game is, I have no patience for it," he

said. "Take your lying tongue and leave my house at once. And be grateful I don't call the magistrate."

She fairly leapt for the door, but Nathan surged after her, surprising him—and the girl, by the look she gave his steward—by clutching her arm and returning her to him.

"Perhaps you shouldn't be so hasty, my lord," he said.

"I beg your pardon?"

Splotches of red blossomed around the steward's cravat. He had overstepped himself. Yet still he spoke."Well, Lord Harry, just look at her. She does resemble Roxanne a great amount, or Roxanne as she would appear all grown up."

"As do half the young women in England," Harry snapped.

"No, my lord, I must disagree."

His brows lowered. "Must you, indeed?"

"I mean—look, my lord, at her eyes. How often did we remark at that color, and those dark lashes so uncommon with a headful of golden hair?"

So now even Nathan had turned into a fool, deceived by a pair of beautiful indigo eyes. Everyone he knew disappointed him, save one, and she lay dying upstairs. To think this fresh-faced imposter would take advantage of his grief was past bearing.

"Paint, Nathan. Paint and artifice can change anyone."

"I do not paint my face or my hair!" exclaimed the chit, driven back to life by the suggestion of this lesser crime. "I never would!"

"It's comforting to know there's something a wench like you wouldn't do. Now go, or I shall truly lose my temper."

"My lord, I—" Nathan began.

"A wench like me . . ." interrupted the girl, her tone growing strong. "No one has ever spoken to me like that."

"No?" Harry challenged. "How would you know? I thought you had lost your memory."

She appeared to ignore this jab. "I can understand why

you might have difficulty believing me. What I cannot understand is why you won't give me the opportunity to explain what happened."

He gestured expressively as if to an audience. "Could it possibly be that I have better ways of spending my evening than listening to hurtful fabrications? My cousin Roxanne is dead. She has been dead for seven years. No matter what color your hair, you won't make me think otherwise."

"Then you have a remarkably closed mind. Precisely what *would* it require to obtain an unprejudiced hearing from you?"

"It would require appreciably more than a false-hearted slip of a girl appearing at my doorstep without so much as a note of preparation or an ounce of proof." He moved threateningly forward while motioning toward the door. To his increasing ire, she refused to retreat.

"Lord Harry, listen to her, please," Nathan begged.

Was the fellow besotted by this creature? He was deuced persistent in her defense.

The impertinent lass actually waved his steward away. "If I have been dead these past seven years, then I should like to see my grave," she said. "It's a reasonable request, I think."

He came within a hand's-span of her desirable body, forcing her to step back at last. "There are no reasonable requests for criminals." He paced forward again, and again she shuffled backward. It was wise of her. If herding had not worked, he would have lifted her bodily over the threshold and thrown her back into the larcenous world from which she came. "I'm sure you know as well as I do the body was never found."

"Of course it was never found, because"—she appeared to struggle for a moment—"because here I am."

In spite of his certainty she lied, he found himself growing more disillusioned. "Are there no limits to what you will say?"

Tears sprang to her eyes. "I have come to see my mother, and I refuse to leave until I've done so!"

Almost, almost she moved him. Idiot! Best get her away before he fell under her spell as Nathan had.

"What's all this commotion, Harry?" came a voice from the head of the stairs.

He exhaled an oath. All this two-penny opera needed was for Thornton to appear. He watched the young man's smooth descent with an irritated eye. Dressed to the nines as always, he was wearing yet another new waistcoat by the look of it. But what was to stop his extravagance when their aunt footed the bill? The closer he came, the more intrigued Thornton looked. Yes, there was that carnivore's gleam as he took in the intruder's charms.

The baron's lids lowered in disdain. "You're too late, Thornton. Our uninvited guest was just leaving."

"That seems a shame. Must you hurry off, Miss—"

The chit took advantage of his divided attention and scurried past him, running toward Thornton as an arrow to its target. "Thorn, it is you!" she chattered. "Surely you recognize me. I followed you around like a puppy for all that you were six years older, and sometimes you would become impatient with me; yet mostly you were kind. You were always my favorite." Glancing at Harry, she added, "Some things I have forgotten, but never that."

A puzzled smile crossed Thornton's features as he lifted a questioning gaze to the baron.

"It claims to be Roxanne, returned from the dead," he told him.

Thornton paled, his smile dissolving. "What did you say?" he whispered through bloodless lips.

"Not from the dead," she assured him. "I'm no ghost,

Thorn. I've been lost all these years, my memory gone. But now it has returned, and so have I."

The baron had never seen Thornton so nonplussed, and had the circumstances been different he would have enjoyed it. His primary duty, however, was to remove this deceitful girl from the premises. He was done with threats, which had accomplished nothing. She was further ensconced in the house than when he began, trembling at the bottom stair with a heart-rending look of appeal for Thornton.

Without another word, the baron advanced purposely toward her. Her panicked stare conveyed her understanding of his intention. And then, between one breath and the next, she pushed past Thornton and raced up the stairs.

"Catch her, you block of stone!" shouted the baron. "Don't let her get to our aunt!"

Audrey, running faster up the steps than she thought possible, her body calling on all her resources to escape the men chasing her, believed she had never heard a more hateful voice. The devil himself could not sound worse. What a terrible waste of a man, to have so much and yet act so spiteful.

She could hear the two of them growing closer but dared not look back. Their boots were pounding the marbled stairs in a rhythm almost as quick as her heart.

Hopefully Mr. Turner followed, too, and would not permit them to kill her.

Tucked away in a tiny part of her brain, a voice cried out, *What are you doing?*

Quiet! she answered it. Somewhere during her conversation with the baron, timidity had turned to anger. How dare he not give her a pennyweight's benefit of the doubt? Was she so untrustworthy?

Yes, answered that annoying little voice.

But she had never been untrustworthy before, she reasoned back, and she would not be doing so now if it weren't for the needs of her family. Besides that, Mr. Turner had convinced her that she would be doing a kindly deed, and this ill-tempered baron should not be treating her as if she were someone . . . *common*.

She reached the top of the stairs and could almost feel their breaths on the back of her neck. She would never succeed, but she must try. Lowering her head, she sprinted across the balcony, the balustrade and shimmering chandelier a blur to her right.

When she reached the hallway leading to what she trusted was the eastern bedroom wing, she darted left and circled a linen cart just in time to avoid stumbling. Glimpsing an open-mouthed maid making a bed within the chamber, she sent the cart spinning toward her pursuers.

When the detestable baron plowed into it with a growl, and Thornton fell over the baron, she could not contain a smile of glee.

But she had no time to gloat. He would be on his feet in an eyeblink, and the rage on his face had increased tenfold. She plummeted toward the end of the corridor.

Let me remember which room belongs to Lady Marianne!

The layout of the house was one of the things Mr. Turner had taught her, saying it might help convince the family that she was Roxanne. Now it was her only hope.

Surely, surely he said her room was the last chamber on the right! Or was it the left? She had time for only one choice, and it had better be the correct one. She hesitated, then veered to the right.

"No!" shouted that awful voice behind her. "Don't go in there!"

Taking this as confirmation, she boldly swung open the door. To her horrified dismay, she found a young woman of approximately her own age napping on a chaise lounge in a sitting room.

The girl's eyes opened dreamily, then sharpened with confusion. "Who are you?"

Audrey turned desperately, but her hunters had arrived to block the doorway, their angry breaths stealing all the air from the room. Panting, Audrey stepped back. How she longed to fade into the wallpaper, just another rose among blue ribbons! And where was Mr. Turner?

"What is it?" the girl demanded. "Harry? Thorn? Who is this person?"

"Hush, Lucy." The baron clutched Audrey's arm in a bruising grip. "I'll explain later."

So this was the niece, Lucille Brown, Thorn's sister. But wasn't her chamber in the other wing? She was solicitous of Lady Marianne, or so the steward had said. She spent a great deal of time with her. . . .

Even as Audrey was being pulled from the room, she gave a last desperate look around. It was an anteroom, she discovered; not just a sitting room, for another door, slightly ajar, led from it. Surely this was the lady's bedchamber?

"I demand to see my mother!" she cried loudly.

Lord Harry immediately crushed her to him, his hateful hand covering her mouth as he dragged her backward. She could not breathe; he would suffocate her in front of these witnesses, and they were letting him do so! She clutched at his fingers with all of her own, scratching at the unyielding flesh, kicking backward until he grunted and then swept her into his arms as easily as he would a sack of straw. He was a monster!

Writhing in his arms, she could not speak because he would not let her, but she told him her thoughts with her eyes. It was a good thing God did not give power to thoughts or he would be reduced to a lump of twisted tin, for that was how cold his heart must be.

"Who's there?" asked a frail voice beyond the door.

The baron's eyes burned into hers. "No one, Aunt. Only Thornton and Lucille and myself."

"But I thought I heard someone ask for her mother," Lady Marianne called weakly.

"That's odd," Thornton said, giving Lord Harry a look of complicity. "Perhaps you were dreaming."

Audrey let herself go limp. Reflexively, the baron relaxed his grip on her mouth, and she managed to bite the edge of his finger. Hard.

"You little wretch!" he shouted.

A great silence fell after this remark.

"Harry, I want you to come in here this instant," said Lady Marianne, sounding firm despite the quiver of illness. "Bring everyone in that room with you. And I do mean everyone."

The fury in his eyes could have spawned a forest fire, but she matched him spark for spark. Finally, he released her, but not gently. She shook herself away from him, smoothing her gown and patting her hair and rubbing the awful taste of him from her lips. She was startled when he jerked a handkerchief from his pocket to bind his finger. He was bleeding! But only a little; there was no need for him to make such a commotion over a tiny wound, not a great hulking fellow like him. Not after he had manhandled her so. Come morning, she would find bruises all over herself, beyond a doubt, and she would not spare a second's regret for her actions of self-preservation.

"Now see what you have done," he said bitterly, and, waving his bandaged hand in a most arrogant manner, motioned her forward.

* * *

The imposter's voice droned pleasantly on, building castle upon castle in the air. Sitting apart from the others, Harry studied the petite beauty with cool eyes. She looked convincing, he had to admit, seated beside Marianne's bedside and speaking with increasing confidence, as if she were persuading herself even as she tried to persuade them.

The life-size portrait of a ten-year-old Roxanne above his aunt's four-poster did bear a startling resemblance now that he compared the two, so remarkable that the imp herself had stumbled upon seeing it.

It had been the only flaw in her charade so far, but there would be others.

Still, she had done her research well. If what she was doing weren't so evil-hearted, he could almost admire her.

"But why did you steal away in the egg-man's wagon in the first place?" Lucy was asking. "The last any of us knew, Roxanne had gone for a walk."

"As I said before, many things are still vague," said the girl. *And many things will remain so,* Harry added with silent scorn. "But I believe I meant it as a jest, or perhaps I wished to go into town and no one would take me. I'll probably never know."

"Probably not," he said, unable to keep quiet any longer. "Probably none of us ever will, and probably we wouldn't believe it if we did."

"Harry, let her speak," said his aunt.

Immediately he fell silent. Marianne was white with emotion, her hands clenching at her bedcovers. He knew how much she longed to believe that her child had returned to her. She had always said Roxanne lived, that she would know if it were otherwise. He held no belief in motherly prescience, but he'd always understood her need to hold on to such a fantasy.

Allowing her to do so had now proved to be a mistake. He blamed himself. Long ago he should have claimed he found Roxanne's bones and held a burial service. The grief would have been a sad blow, but a final one she could put behind her. At least she would have been spared this mockery.

They would be fortunate if shock did not kill her tonight.

"I don't know why I didn't alight in Guildford as I'd planned," the girl continued. "Possibly I fell asleep, for we were some miles beyond town when I jumped off the farmer's cart."

"And that was when you hit your head against the rock," Thornton supplied, his tone as skeptical as Harry's would have been. He gave him a humorless smile of acknowledgment.

"Evidently so, for that is where the gypsies found me." Harry snorted.

"They did," she said acidly, without looking in his direction.

"Of course they did," he returned. "Poor gypsies. Blamed for everything from thievery to kidnapping to murder. How convenient they are to our society. Without the omnipresent gypsies, we might have to shoulder the blame for our sins ourselves."

"But their reputation was earned somehow," Marianne said. "Such things do happen."

Lucy stirred, green silk rustling. "You must admit it sounds unlikely, though."

"There have been many stranger things which have occurred," said the golden-haired liar, returning Lucy's stare with a force that surprised him. Lucy's will was not an easy one to balk. He knew that well enough.

Marianne reached a frail hand toward the imposter. "Go on with your story, my dear."

My dear. He could not believe this. His aunt was succumbing already, and to a tale not fit for a chapbook. To his disgust, the girl hesitated—such a *touching* affectation;

it was an actress, wasn't it?—then wrapped her fingers around Marianne's.

"When I awoke, I found myself in a gypsy's wagon bound for Bournemouth. They were kind enough to me, but after discovering I couldn't remember where I lived, I lost all usefulness to them. I suppose they had hoped to return me to my home for a reward. At any rate, I was a burden to them, merely another mouth to feed. Therefore, when we arrived at Bournemouth, I was taken to a land-owner they knew, one who allowed them to camp on his small landholding. This family was kind enough to take me in, the wife being barren and having always wanted children."

"How very convenient," said Harry. "And what were the names of these angels of mercy? Oh, but perhaps you've forgotten with your memory in the condition it is."

"Of course I haven't forgotten the man and woman who are as dear as true parents to me. George and Elizabeth Hill are their names, and although they didn't have much in the way of possessions, a more gentle, generous couple cannot be imagined." The look she gave him had the flavor of victory in it. "You may find them at Thistle Hill House in Bournemouth, if you want proof."

"Contacting them will only prove that you have partners in your lies."

"Harry!" Marianne fixed him with stern gaze, then softened as she turned to the girl. "How is it your memory came back to you?"

"I began to have dreams several months ago," she said. "Tiny fragments of my life here would surface. I would see myself riding a black pony—"

"Tigret!" Marianne exclaimed. "How you loved him!"

"—yes, and sometimes I would dream of Thorn, too—"

"I'm flattered." Thornton looked grim, however, not pleased.

"—but of course I didn't know it was you at the time—"

"You always had a weak spot for Thornton," Marianne said. "I once overheard you telling Lucy that you wanted to marry him when you grew up, do you remember that, Lucy?"

"No," Lucy replied. "No, I do not."

The imposter ignored her. "Sometimes I would see this house and portions of the grounds, such as the rose garden and its brick walls, the iron gate, things such as that. These dreams troubled me greatly."

"Because you didn't know what they meant," Marianne supplied.

"That's exactly it. I didn't know."

My God, Harry thought.

"But one morning two weeks ago, while I was walking down the lane to deliver a basket of bread and preserves to a sick neighbor, I became faint and stopped by a flat rock beside the road for a few moments. A wave of vertigo passed over me, and suddenly I remembered everything. Or almost everything, I mean."

"And then you ran straight home to tell your kindly guardians, I suspect," Harry said solicitously. "No, I retract those words. You're the kind of exemplary person who would have finished her mission to the ill neighbor first, aren't you? No matter how dizzy you might become, no matter how ill, no matter what momentous discovery you'd made about yourself, you would hurry on to do your duty. I can see you scurrying down the lane, arms burdened with baskets full of good deeds, in my mind right now."

This time the girl said nothing, only leveled him a look that might singe his eyes were they not so heated already.

"There is no reason to be mean, Harry," Marianne said. "How did Mr. and Mrs. Hill take the news that your memory had returned?"

"They were saddened to know I must leave them, but

they were happy for me as well." She threw a glance at
Harry, then turned back to Marianne. "I think that is the
true measure of love, don't you? That you want the best
for the ones you love, even when it means something painful for yourself?"

Her voice trembled the slightest amount on this last. Despite his anger, Harry felt a responding dip in his emotions.
He steeled himself. She was a master at artifice. One had
only to look at the stars in his aunt's eyes. He would not
fall victim to her wiles.

"Well, well," Marianne breathed, her gaze consuming the
girl. The older woman slowly lifted a hand to the imposter's
cheek. "You are so very beautiful."

*No, Aunt. Don't let your preoccupation with perfection
lead you astray.* That the girl was perfect he could admit
beyond a doubt. A perfect fraud.

A turbulent quiet stretched in the room. Thornton and
Lucy exchanged worried glances, then looked to him. He
shook his head helplessly and returned his gaze to the girl.
For all her wickedness, she fascinated him. How carefully
she kept her vision centered upon the lady in the bed, but
he sensed her awareness of them all.

"I believe you," Marianne said.

Thornton and Lucy immediately cried out, but Harry said
nothing. He had known this was coming for some moments
now.

"You can't mean to simply take her word for it," Thornton said.

Marianne gave him a fierce look. "This goes beyond
that. A mother knows her child."

Tears welled in Lucy's eyes. "Please don't misunderstand
us. We want her to be Roxanne, of course we do, for your
sake, because we love you so much. But how do we know
she's not an imposter? If someone took it into mind to
impersonate your precious daughter, surely she would be

well prepared as this person is? I'm only asking, Aunt Marianne, how can we know for certain?"

"I know, that's all. But if it will make you happy, I'll send Nathan to verify her story. And before you say anything, Harry, there are more people in Bournemouth than Mr. and Mrs. Hill. Nathan can interview their neighbors, their merchants, whomever. You cannot involve an entire town in deception. We'll be able to learn for certain if this young lady came to the Hills as she said. Would that satisfy you?"

"But even if she's telling the truth about being found by the gypsies and then adopted by that family," Lucy said, "does it necessarily follow that she is our Roxanne?"

"If she's not, then why did she start having dreams about Far Winds and Tigret and Thorn?" Marianne demanded.

"We have only her word for that," Thornton reminded her.

"Are you suggesting that this young lady, all the way over in Bournemouth, would hear about my daughter's going missing years ago, then decide to pretend to be her? How ludicrous, Thornton. My husband may have been a knight, but I don't believe we are *that* famous."

"It's not beyond possibility, and a certain kind of person might want to take advantage of such an opportunity," Harry said, thinking of his aunt's fortune, which, unlike his uncle's estate, was to be left at her discretion.

"Complete foolishness," Marianne said. "I haven't enough for anyone to go to such lengths."

While this remark could be debated, she sounded stronger than Harry had heard her in a very long time. Her color had improved as well. He briefly considered the possibility that believing this girl might be *good* for his aunt.

But not when she discovered the truth. It would finish her.

"Perhaps I should leave the room," ventured the imposter, sounding uncomfortable, as indeed she should. "I believe you have much to discuss."

"No, my dear," Marianne said, lifting both arms. "Pay no attention to these doubters. Come to me, my beautiful Roxanne. Welcome home, dearest child."

Harry watched them embrace with a cynical eye. The minx even managed to work up a relieved sob and a creditable sprinkling of tears, but this game wasn't over yet.

Having lost the battle, Lord Harry began to plot the war.

Three

On her first morning at Far Winds, Audrey awoke in Roxanne's fairy-tale bedroom with its yellow-and-white flocked wallpaper, its carefully preserved golden silk canopy and matching counterpane, French Provencial furnishings with a glass-fronted bookcase containing porcelain dolls wearing brightly colored dresses fit for princesses, a large window which overlooked an inspiring view of the rear of the estate, and a set of French doors opening onto a small balcony from which she knew could be seen a courtyard and the opposite wing of bedrooms, and wept a storm of tears.

Of all the scoundrels in the world, she was the worst.

She was truly, *truly* an awful person to raise Lady Marianne's hopes in this manner, even if she did, as Mr. Turner said, make her dying hours happier. The tragedy of Roxanne's death—for death it surely was—it could not be such a silly story as she herself had told—was nothing to be treated lightly. Not that she meant to treat it lightly, but such would be the perception of her role when the truth came out.

And come out it would, eventually. After the lady's death, she would have to confess to everyone and slink away like a beaten dog with her ten thousand pounds. The entire

household would congratulate themselves on how they'd
been right, how they had known all along she was a liar.
Especially Lord Harry, with his scornful green eyes and
spiteful tongue. She could easily imagine the baron sending
her off to gaol even as the steward, explaining the merit
of his intentions, begged him against it. Perhaps they would
send their servant of many years to gaol as well. Nothing
would surprise her.

How she rued the day Mr. Turner saw her at market!

And now that gentleman had been dispatched on his own
mission of deception, gone to investigate her story in
Bournemouth. Only he would not be traveling there at all,
he had told her in a whispered conversation long past midnight, his knock on the bedroom door almost frightening
her out of her wits. After she had scolded him for abandoning her to the angry nephews and niece—he had been
just outside in the hallway, he'd assured her, ready to perform a rescue if needed—he'd explained his intention of
visiting her father and sister to inform them of her success.
He promised to bring them funds enough that they would
not have to work while she was away. After a realistic interval, he would return with the confirmation that all the
Bournemouth neighbors agreed with her story. Lady Marianne and the family believed him without question in all
matters.

After this they won't, she had wanted to say, but didn't.

So now she was not even to have the small comfort of
Mr. Turner's presence. Everyone in this household was
against her, save Lady Marianne. Even the maid who turned
down the bed last night looked doubtful and introduced
herself almost inaudibly, as if she didn't want to waste
breath on a charlatan.

It was that same maid, Lyddie, who knocked on her door
a few moments later and entered with a cup of hot chocolate and raspberry-filled scones. Audrey had never thought

to be served breakfast in bed, had only read about the experience in novels. Instead of being delighted at the privilege, the scents of chocolate and sugar seemed cloying to her, as if mocking her treachery.

"This was always your favorite, Cook said. You do like your sweets, don't you?" The maid noticed her tears, and her expression sharpened. "Something wrong, miss?"

"No, I—I'm just happy to be home," Audrey answered.

Lyddie shrugged and left the room. After taking a tentative sip of the chocolate, Audrey forced herself from the bed, poured water from a delicate ivory pitcher into its matching basin, and washed her face. Splashing water on her skin served to prime her tears again. In the midst of this sad christening, another knock sounded at the door, and a woman entered without waiting for her answer. Without a second glance for Audrey's distress, she introduced herself as Mrs. Charlotte Prate, the seamstress.

"The lady wishes me to fit you for a new wardrobe," she said.

"Surely not an entire wardrobe," Audrey said, sniffling, and allowed herself to be turned and prodded about. The servant with the tape measure intimidated her. She was a very tall woman, tall and moderately thin, and her close-set, blackberry eyes and pointed nose put Audrey in mind of a beagle. "Maybe a gown or two, just ordinary day dresses, that should be all I'll require for now."

"That's not what the lady says. You're to have everything."

"Oh, *my*. But that will take you a very long time."

"I'm to hire helpers from Guildford. My sister has a shop there."

"Oh, *goodness*." A fresh wave of despair washed over Audrey. Lady Marianne was trying to make her daughter happy. Wasting money on *her*. This charade grew worse by the moment.

At last Mrs. Prate finished her measurements, a task done largely in silence—a disapproving silence, Audrey believed. Hardly had she gone when Lyddie re-entered to help her perform her toilette, a thing she had never required assistance with before. She felt foolish sitting at the mirror in her lavender-sprigged gown, faded by many washings, while Lyddie arranged her hair. But she had to admit her curls profited by the objective hand and told the servant so.

"Thank you, miss," Lyddie said in her whispery voice, beginning to rummage from one dresser drawer to the next. "Ah. I knew they'd be here somewhere. A purple ribbon to brighten up your gown and set off your hair real nice."

"No!" Audrey cried. Long ago, little Roxanne had worn that ribbon. Seeing the maid's shock, she added, "I shouldn't take the time, I mean. Mother will be waiting for me, and I must hurry."

She jumped from the dressing table and left the room, not daring to look another time at the maid or the ribbon for fear she would weep again. Not since the death of her mother had she shed so many tears in such a short period of time.

Lady Marianne's room lay across the hall from her own. When Audrey knocked, the lady's maid answered and led her through the anteroom to the bedchamber. Her heart somersaulted as she saw Lord Harry seated at Marianne's head. He was the last person she wanted to endure today.

Entering the room hesitantly, she could not help noticing how grave he looked as he held one of his aunt's hands in his own. If the memory of his rough treatment of herself had not been so bitterly fresh, she could almost believe him capable of tender emotions. That notion dissolved, however, as soon as he became aware of her. His gaze growing icy, he lowered the lady's hand and viewed Audrey as he might a leprous beggar. She sent him a look of similar disdain, then averted her eyes.

"Your visitor has returned, Aunt," he announced in an ugly tone.

"My daughter, you mean," said Lady Marianne, beaming and extending her arms.

Audrey, taking care to approach on the side opposite the villainous nephew, rushed into her embrace, wishing her a good morning and trying to steady her emotions. The lady appeared wan in the light streaming through her windows, and deep shadows lay beneath her eyes. Even so, her beauty was striking for one above a certain age, with only a slight crinkling of skin at the eyes and neck; and her bones were fine, elegant even, her chin strong. Illness had not dimmed the sheen of her gray-streaked, light brown hair, either, which fell in waves across her apricot peignoir. Yet Audrey wondered if her arrival had not worsened Marianne's health.

Marianne eventually released her and begged she sit on the edge of the bed. Peering at her more closely, she stroked Audrey's cheek. "My darling, how tired you look."

"Perhaps she had trouble sleeping," the baron suggested nastily.

"I slept very well," Audrey lied, her gaze fixed on the lady.

"Never mind then," Marianne said. "No doubt you have been missing your guardians, and the adjustment must be stressful. Take a nap after luncheon. It will help. You look lovely anyway, even in that old thing you have on. We'll soon have some decent gowns for you to wear. Charlotte visited you this morning, I believe?"

"Yes, and I had wanted to talk with you about that. She spoke of making far too many dresses. I won't need very much."

"Why, my dear, whatever can you mean? You will require everything. The Hills may have been wonderful with you, but they certainly could not afford the kind of apparel a knight's daughter is expected to wear, especially at social functions."

"Oh." Social functions? "I meant for now, while you are ill." Quickly she added, "When you're better, *that* would be the time to become extravagant."

"I don't regard dressing my child properly as an extravagance," Lady Marianne said kindly but definitely, and Audrey understood she must give way. Despite the lady's frailty, there was a firmness to her lips that bespoke a strong will. "Besides, child, I cannot depend on my sickly heart growing stronger, I fear. No, don't let me alarm you, either of you, but I've learned from my physician that I should not postpone things that I wish to do. Not if I hope to do them in this world instead of the next."

"Aunt, don't," pled the baron in such broken tones that Audrey thought anew that he might not *always* be horrendous. The grief in his expression could not be fabricated, and for an instant, an instant only, she vibrated with sympathy not only for Lady Marianne, but for him as well.

"Harry, there's no use pretending. Denying the truth does no one any good, least of all myself. And I'm not dismayed by the approach of death, or not terribly so. At least I shan't experience the indignity of becoming a sagging pile of bones—"

"You would be beautiful if you lived to be ninety," he said.

"—or losing all good sense." She smiled at him, a special smile that hinted at years of camaraderie. For a fraction of an instant, Audrey felt ridiculously forgotten. "And that is why I've decided to give a celebratory ball for Roxanne's return."

"What!" he exclaimed.

"Oh, *no*," Audrey moaned.

"And why shouldn't I?" the lady demanded.

The baron glared at Audrey. "Because she is no more Roxanne than I am."

"Harry, I've heard your opinion, and I don't want to hear it anymore." Marianne squeezed Audrey's hand reassuringly, making the younger woman feel even more low. "I shall give her a ball because I wish to honor my daughter."

"But you aren't healthy enough," Audrey protested. "You wouldn't be able to enjoy it. If you waited until you're better, though—"

Marianne made a gesture of restraint. "I shall enjoy the celebration even if I'm not well enough to make an appearance. This is a time for happiness, my dear, and I'm eager to share my joy with all my friends and neighbors." Audrey dared not glance in the baron's direction. "And now I'm tired, so off with both of you. Harry, I wish you to take particular care of my daughter and stop treating her like an interloper."

"But she is," he said with conviction.

Audrey thought he must be the most stubborn man ever to live. It did not matter that he was right about her. He should keep his thoughts to himself.

"Do you care nothing for my happiness?" Lady Marianne cried with sudden vehemence.

"I care for little else."

"Then do as I ask and be kind to your cousin."

Lord Harry met the lady's gaze for an interval of time, then lowered his eyes. "I only want what is best for you."

"I know." She patted his hand. "It's early yet and not too warm outside. Why don't you take her for a ride?"

Audrey's eyes widened with dread. She didn't want to be near this man, not to mention she had ridden a horse only a handful of times in her life. "Please don't ask him to do something that plainly would be distasteful to him."

"He wants what is best for me," Marianne said with the pertness of a young girl. "You heard him say so yourself.

And at this moment, what is best for me is that the two of you become reacquainted."

Audrey waited for him to protest again, but this time he said nothing. Sudden inspiration struck. "But I don't own a riding habit."

"You may wear one of Lucy's. She is only a little taller than you."

The lady had an answer for everything, it seemed. Audrey made an attempt at interjecting lightness into her voice. "Well, riding . . . we had only a plow horse at Thistle Hill House. Do you know how long it's been since I've been on horseback?"

Immediate interest sparked in her opponent's eyes. "How very strange. Riding was always your favorite activity. You certainly have changed . . . *Roxanne.*"

"It couldn't be helped," she told him, then turned to Marianne. "What I want most, why I've come here, is to spend time with you, M-Mother. I mean, I want to enjoy every moment with you that I can." This sounded so like a reminder of approaching death that Audrey hurried on, "So that we can catch up on our lost years." That was no good either, for the longer time she spent with any one person, the greater the chance she would be caught out rather than caught up. "I should be happy to read to you," she finished with desperation.

"You are a good child," Marianne said. "No mother could wish for more. But run along so that I can sleep. Enjoy yourself and visit me again this afternoon. Harry, be certain to send Bertha in on your way out. There's a spot of tea on my coverlet, and she must bring me a fresh one."

Conscious of the nephew's deadly eyes on her, Audrey rose, feeling as if she had turned to stone, and walked from the room, every step shadowed by the leaden paces of a man who distrusted her to the bone. Yesterday's judgment of the baron's character had been modified somewhat by the gentleness he showed his aunt today, although she would not go so far as admitting to being hurt by his opinion. He truly could not detest her any more than she detested herself. Yet somehow it still amazed her that anyone could hate her so deeply.

Well, no matter, no matter, she didn't care for him, either.

Lending clothing to the imposter did not sit well with Lucy, Lord Harry was not surprised to discover a quarter-hour later in the breakfast alcove off the morning room. Here, where a large round table curved into a bay window papered with strawberry vines, the family took many of their meals. None of them liked the austerity of the formal dining room unless it was populated with convivial guests.

The pretender Roxanne—how he hated giving her his young cousin's name, but he must call her something other than the devil, for his aunt's sake—had gone to dress. He had told her to meet him at breakfast when she was ready.

"I cannot countenance that Aunt expects me to do such a thing," Lucy said, shivering with distaste as she spread butter on a cranberry muffin. "I told Lyddie to give that woman my old fawn-colored velvet and then to burn it afterward."

"A little harsh, don't you think?" Thornton said from the sideboard, scooping sausages onto his plate.

"What, do you believe I should accept her with open arms? She is the lowest kind of criminal."

"Don't forget that our aunt believes her."

Lucy shot her brother a surprised look. "Are you defending this person?"

"Not at all. I'm only suggesting we defer to Aunt Marianne's wishes, since she's so ill."

Thornton slid into his chair and began to eat, each movement fastidious and restrained, yet hinting at a primal enjoyment. He did enjoy his food, or rather, his aunt's food. He enjoyed everything in his own sly way. Harry sometimes thought of him as a well-trained beast. A fox perhaps. A lazy one willing to live off the work of others and offer nothing in return, other than a stale kind of charm. He was sick to death of him and wished the man would find something useful to do with his life. Thornton was twenty-three years old and a boy no longer. Harry had been shouldering the responsibility of his uncle's estate for eight years now, since he was nineteen.

Lucy watched her brother for a moment, then leaned toward him, her eyes burning. "You weren't so accepting of her last night. What has changed? Did you dream about her? I suppose she is attractive in a coarse sort of way."

"Not coarse at all, sister. She's very lovely, really. And amusing. She led us quite the merry chase last night, didn't she, Harry? How's the finger, by the by?"

"You mean to pursue her, don't you?" Lucy exclaimed. "How disgusting. She is little better than a cyprian. Perhaps she *is* one, for all we know."

Harry was surprised at how much their conversation irritated him. He slammed his cup into its saucer. "That's quite enough, both of you."

Thornton raised one eyebrow. "You should calm yourself as well, Harry. The conniver can do us no real harm."

"You may think that imposter won't do any harm, but she has wormed her way into Aunt Marianne's heart already," Lucy said. "Even though I have attended her faithfully all these years, she sent Bertha to me this morning saying I needn't visit her until this evening."

"She was very tired," Harry said, meaning to comfort.

"But not too tired for *her*," Lucy said, voice cracking. "I have tried to be like a daughter to Aunt Marianne. More than anyone, I've understood how deeply Roxanne's loss affected her. I've done everything I could to make her

happy, sacrificed my own youth to do so in fact, and goodness knows she can be difficult at times—I'm sorry, but I
must say so—and now in a moment a stranger has walked
into my place."

As Lucy was only twenty and had relished his aunt's
bounty as much as any of them, Harry had to clamp his
teeth to refrain from dispute. He could not doubt her tears
were genuine, and she had been devoted.

"Don't worry," he told her. "The *faux* Roxanne will
make a mistake soon enough, and all will return to normal." The same dull, normal drill of overseeing the estate,
enduring her brother the parasite, and fending off ambitious
young ladies in pursuit of a title and wealth, the chief of
whom was Lucy herself.

"Do you really think so, Harry?"

He should not have sounded so warm, for Lucy was
melting toward him, her eyes softening like heated chocolate, her hand reaching for his. As he was in the act of
cutting his beefsteak, he could only pause awkwardly and
give her a strained smile.

It was into this scene the interloper appeared. She
marched into the morning room with head held high, although the flush in her cheeks revealed deep discomfort.
The fawn-colored habit which suited Lucy's darkness so
well was all wrong for her, leaching vitality from her skin
and making her appear ill. On her, the garment hung like
a feeding bag and was far too long. At the doorway she
stumbled over the hem, then pulled up the material with
an irritated little cry. He had to stop himself from laughing.

Thornton stood and offered the seat beside him. She told
him she had already breakfasted and would await Lord
Hastings in the salon.

"Sit down and eat something," Harry commanded before
she could make her exit. "No one regards a morning cup
of chocolate as a true breakfast." He could not tell her that

Lyddie, whom he had engaged for a few shillings as his spy, had reported Miss Roxanne had partaken of nothing on her morning tray. "I'll not have you fainting in hunger while riding with me."

"Oh, very well," she said, and without looking directly at any of them, took a plate from the sideboard and began lifting lids from the warming trays, seemingly at random. No one spoke as she dotted her plate with food, and the silence grew heavy.

She took the seat beside Thornton. Eyes lowered, she scraped a morsel of egg toward her mouth. Harry knew she was intensely aware of them watching her. She chewed the tidbit of egg as if it were leather, then sighed and chewed some more. When she swallowed at last, a difficult operation from the look of it, he thought for an alarming instant that she would choke.

"Would you care for a cup of tea or coffee?" Thornton asked, sounding the perfect host. "As you see, we serve ourselves at breakfast, having decided it's preferable to have at least one meal without the servants hovering and reporting every word we say back to the kitchen."

"I'm sure she remembers," Lucy mocked. "We've always been progressive at Far Winds, haven't we?" She flicked Harry a knowing look, then back. "Roxanne?"

"Please," the girl said, ignoring Lucy entirely. "Tea."

Another silence fell as Thornton filled a cup of the required beverage and served Roxanne. As she sipped, her hands trembled slightly. Harry was very nearly moved to compassion. She made a face.

"Something wrong?" Thornton asked, all concern.

"It's a little sweet, but I do thank you."

"I'm sorry. Three lumps of sugar. That's how you used to drink it, but I suppose your taste has changed now that you're almost an adult."

Harry, his gaze fixed on her, caught the fleeting dip of her brow.

"Yes," she said. "Sugar was not so easily come by at Thistle Hill."

"That must have been a trial," said Thornton.

"Eggs!" cried Lucy, surprising the girl so that she dropped her fork. "Roxanne always hated eggs except when they were buried in cake!"

"If you are hungry enough, you can learn to eat anything." She tugged maliciously at the expanse of material at the waist of Lucy's riding habit. "But what do you know of hunger? Obviously nothing."

Harry covered his mouth with his napkin. Thornton caught his eye and exchanged a rare look of amused, masculine brotherhood. The baron felt led to applaud her return of spirit. He must be bored to find himself aligning with this female, even for an instant.

"Are you calling me *fat?*" Lucy screeched.

Roxanne considered her. "Not at all. You look quite nice, to say truth. I have always wanted to be a larger woman myself."

This did not appear to mollify Lucy. "We were in want before Aunt Marianne took us in," she said heatedly. "We knew hunger. Without her, Thorn and I would be destitute. We're not truly her niece and nephew, you know, or you would know if you really were Roxanne, but only the children of her brother's second wife. Her brother, our stepfather, was no better a father to us than our own, gambling what little money we had until we were penniless. When he died, our mother brought us here and abandoned us to Aunt Marianne's generosity, which I'm grateful to say has never failed. That's why we'll not allow an upstart like you to hurt her!"

"Easy, my sister," Thornton said gently.

Roxanne looked stunned. Lucy's breaths were coming

fast and uneven. Harry covered Lucy's hand, knowing he shouldn't, but wanting to steady her. His cousin, or rather almost-cousin, did not often speak of those old, humiliating days, and he understood how much it pained her. He was not too occupied to view an intriguing series of emotions running across Roxanne's face. She remained quiet for an interval as though searching for words. Probably contriving more stories. Her glance fell upon Lucy's and his linked hands, moved up to his eyes, then quickly away. He fought a ridiculous impulse to release Lucy at once.

"Hurting her is the farthest thing from my mind," she said at last. "I only want to make her happy." Almost as an afterthought she added, "Especially now that I know she's so ill."

"Bah." Lucy's mouth turned downward. "You wish us to believe it's not her approaching end and the promise of restoring Roxanne's inheritance to yourself that has brought you running?"

"Inheritance?" she murmured, as if she had never heard the term.

Her innocent look was too much for the baron to ignore. "Perhaps you've forgotten, but your mother has a considerable fortune to leave, at least half of which she intended to leave to you, until you died. Disappeared, I should say."

She studied each of them in turn, her expression becoming opaque. "I see. And when I disappeared, she changed her will."

"Naturally she did." Lucy reached for an apple in the silver bowl at the center of the table. "Anyone would."

"And named you as beneficiaries."

"We were already beneficiaries, as were a few of the servants. But our portions increased after your—whatever it was that happened. She is very open about her desires for the ones she loves. We're all she has now."

If Harry had not known what an actress she was, the

disappointed, lost look in the stranger's eyes would have disturbed him. She certainly was believable. She should be on the stage.

"I have no interest in disturbing your plans," she said slowly. "I only want to make my mother as comfortable and as happy as possible."

"So you have said." Lucy carved a wedge from her apple. "You'll understand if none of us believe you."

"The morning's getting on," Harry said, suddenly tired of their baiting, and his own. "We'd best go, Roxanne, if you're finished."

"Would you like company?" Lucy asked, looking at him hopefully. "Thorn and I haven't ridden in days."

He glanced at the girl, but she was staring pensively ahead at nothing. Her plate remained almost untouched. "Not this time," he told Lucy. And then the chit did meet his eyes, and the disillusionment he saw there shook him to the marrow. Why did she appear so crushed? Was it because they had her inheritance? Didn't she guess Marianne would change the will back to her? Surely that was why she came. It could not be that she regarded *them* as vultures waiting to pounce on his beloved aunt's holdings, waiting for her to die.

Surely not.

Perhaps she only worried that Marianne would expire before changing her will.

He led the way from the room feeling an odd heaviness in the vicinity of his heart. Although the girl renewed her struggle with Lucy's gown, trying valiantly not to fall as she walked, her predicament failed to amuse him this time. After a moment he offered her his arm, and, after a moment, she took it.

Four

An hour later, perhaps two—Audrey had no way of measuring time during her uncomfortable journey across the estate other than the plodding, upward circuit of the sun—she fought her impulse to demand a return to the stables. Roxanne had liked to ride, the baron had said, and ride she would. Even if Lucille Brown's velvet habit seemed to grow larger and heavier by the moment, the morning's moist heat serving to expand it into a clinging blanket.

Her back and bottom ached from the side saddle, too, but she would not be the one to cry enough, no, not even were he to lead her all the way to London. He should not have that satisfaction from *her*.

She must admit the outing could have been worse. Given the hostility the nephews and niece held for her, and Lord Harry in particular, she half expected to find her mount to be an untamed stallion bent on galloping across a ravine and killing her. Instead, the groom, a man hardly taller than herself and exceedingly grumpy, had assisted her upon a calm, sleepy mare that seemed no more inclined to hurry than she did. She imagined the dawdling pace must bore Lord Harry dreadfully. Since he was given to long silences this morning, she was unable to tell for certain. Not that she would care if she could.

She had far deeper things to worry her.

The beauty of the estate's grounds was almost, but not quite, enough to distract the spiraling of her thoughts. As they rounded a path between rows of beech and ash trees, she caught her breath as the ground fell away toward a glimmering pond. On its far shore, a white, six-sided pavilion with a pointed roof and waist-high latticework nestled closely to the water. Artfully placed trees, shrubbery, and flowers gave the scene an air of controlled wildness. She had never seen anything so lovely in her life.

"This place used to be one of Roxanne's favorites," he said, watching her.

She remembered. It was one of the things Mr. Turner had thought to tell her, although he'd not prepared her for how compelling was the scene. There were many things he'd forgotten to mention in his preparation, such as the fact that Lucille and Thornton were not truly Lord Harry's or Roxanne's cousins and had been as impoverished as her own family, and worse. At least she and her sister had enjoyed kindly parents disposed to love and treasure them.

Nevertheless, she thought, frowning, Thorn's and Lucy's upbringing did not excuse their ill treatment of her. She had no intention of stealing their inheritance. Of course, they could not know that. But all their objections to her she now saw in a new light, and not a favorable one. Were they truly concerned about Lady Marianne's feelings, that she might be duped by a false Roxanne—for when one thought about it, what did it matter if the lady died happy?—or did they fight her to defend their long-held stake in the lady's pocketbook? She could not help believing the latter.

And while she could almost excuse the siblings, how it stung to think of Lord Harry as the most opportune among them. As the closest surviving male in Sir Hastings's family, the baron had inherited Far Winds by the laws of primogeniture. As he also held his deceased father's title of baron, one must assume he owned another estate as well, perhaps four or five for all she knew. How much could one man require?

Such greed surprised her, although she had no reason to be surprised at anything he would do. She had known him less than twenty-four hours, and during that time he had grilled her with insolent questions and chased her down like a rabbit. And she could still blush recalling how he'd grabbed her in his arms in a most familiar way. Truly he was unspeakable. That his tender treatment of his aunt might be spurred by mammon should not depress and disillusion her, but somehow it did.

One fear lowered her thoughts even further than these.

What if Lady Marianne *did* change her will in favor of herself? What would she do? There was no possibility of her accepting it, even if such a deception did not land her at the hangman's noose.

There existed only one solution. If the lady made even a hint that she intended changing her will, Audrey would have to disclose her true identity. But then she would lose Mr. Turner's promised reward, and her family would be no better off than before. Rebecca would do something foolish, like marrying Burl Ingerstand or insisting Audrey do so.

It was a dreadful muddle. She had known this charade would be difficult, but never had she imagined such complications.

She could not think of it now, as he was waiting for her reaction to the pleasant scene before them, and she must carry on her assigned and hated part.

"There were swans, as I remember," she said. "I fed them crusts of bread."

"The swans have been gone for years. No one comes here anymore except the gardeners."

As he led the way around the pond, she wearily brushed

a curl from her forehead, then exhaled in irritation when it fell back into her eyes. Awkwardly keeping her reins in hand, she worked at forcing the curl beneath her bonnet. The mare ambled to a stop. Successful at last, she looked up to find the baron watching her, his lips twisted in mild amusement. Did he find her so laughable, then? She averted her eyes and urged her mount forward, eager to continue this eternal ride, for surely it must end at some point.

"Would you like to rest at the pavilion for a moment?" he asked.

"I don't need rest; I am fine, thank you."

"I can see that, but I'd like to stop, if you don't mind."

She felt a tug of nervousness. He could not mean her physical harm, for the groom trailed them in the distance, as was proper for an unwed man and woman alone, even if they were cousins. She eyed the cane-backed rockers within the shelter. How comfortable they looked beneath the shade. He meant her to relax, no doubt, and would ask many questions with the intention of tricking her. Well, let him try. If she did not get off this horse soon, she would expire.

With a reluctant graciousness she could not help admiring herself, Audrey agreed to break their journey. She had forgotten this would mean his hands would be upon her again, helping her slide from the saddle. He took his own time about it, too, releasing her far more slowly than she would have liked. She blinked her irritation at him, his strange green eyes only inches from her own, her heartbeat accelerating painfully. Finally, he stepped back and offered his arm. She felt very peculiar walking up the shallow stairs and waiting as he dusted one of the chairs with his handkerchief. He indicated she was to sit, then performed the same duty with the chair beside hers.

A thrush took flight as the baron sat. The prospect of

water and nature could not be more pleasing, Audrey thought, except for the disapproval of the man beside her and the groomsman sitting stiffly in the saddle on the far side of the pond. Despite the tension which had not left her since her arrival at Far Winds, she leaned back her head and closed her eyes.

"Comfortable?" he asked quietly.

"Mmm." *Please don't say anything more.* She had enough to plague her, with that hugely worrying fear nagging at her brain.

"You looked ready to fall from the saddle a moment ago."

She opened her eyes. "Years of little practice."

"Yes, I know. You had only the plow horse."

Not even that. The inquisition was beginning again, as she knew it must. Was she not to have a moment's peace at Far Winds? For the first time, Mr. Turner's ten thousand pounds seemed too little for her assignment.

"Life has been difficult," she said.

"Yes. It often is."

She sent him a burning look. What did he know of deprivation and hard work, of wondering if your family would have a roof over their heads or enough to eat?

He held her gaze. "Are you thinking I have no reason to say so? Roxanne would know better."

Audrey's eyes fell. To what was he alluding? Had something happened to him, something terrible? It could not be so unfortunate as what her own family had endured, surely. He looked too well-favored, acted far too confidently, to have suffered. She wondered, though, and was suddenly consumed with curiosity to know more about him. But she dare not ask!

"There—there are many things I still can't remember."

"Oh, yes." He tapped a finger to his temple, smiling cynically. "The memory problem. How useful it is. Don't

speak of your accident too often, will you? The servants
will start using it as their excuse when they neglect their
duties. We do have a few on staff who would prefer hitting
themselves on the head with a rock than doing their work,
I'm afraid."

She pressed her lips together. "You don't believe me."

"That surprises you? What surprises me is that anyone
would."

"But *why?*" The question rang from deep within. He
was not acting angrily with her as he had before; he seemed
merely sad, or disappointed, which troubled her far worse.
"Why do you refuse to even admit the possibility?"

He thought a moment. "Because you're nothing like
Roxanne."

"Of course not," she said, daring a smile. "I have grown
up."

"No one changes his or her given nature, no matter how
long he lives."

"That sounds rather limited, my lord. Surely you believe
that circumstances can influence one's development?"

The baron regarded her gravely. "Do I believe a pauper
can be raised a king? Perhaps. But if that pauper is born
with an angry, unruly temperament, I believe he will make
an angry, unruly sovereign."

"How dismal, if that were true."

"In my life I've seen it proved over and over."

"Then you have my sympathy." Into the ensuing silence,
she moved her rocker into gentle motion. "So you believe
I have changed. In what manner, if I may ask?"

"Why? Do you wish to improve your performance?"

She fixed her eyes on the faraway groomsman, who was
stretching himself without ceasing to watch them. The
baron's persistent disbelief dismayed, even hurt, her. "Perhaps we had better return," she said, beginning to rise.

He captured her wrist momentarily. "No, sit down."

When she slowly obeyed, he went on, "When I came to live at Far Winds, Roxanne was eight years old. I was eighteen. We had nothing in common, and I took little notice of the child. But there were other reasons than our age difference to keep us apart."

She waited, then prompted, "What reasons?"

Still he hesitated. There were more things about this man that maddened than she had originally believed. He certainly understood the art of making someone interested in him; she was insatiable with curiosity. If only she dared, she would shake him did he not speak soon.

At last he answered, "She was a difficult child."

Audrey flew to her feet. This was not what she wanted to hear. She strode to the rail and braced her hands against it, her gaze raking the bullrushes, the trees, anything but him.

"I suppose you think flattery might work where bruises did not," she said, forcibly controlling her ire.

He joined her at the rail, looking surprised. "Your pardon?"

"You've tried to do nothing except get me to say I am not Roxanne since I arrived. When pushing me about didn't work—"

"Did I bruise you last night?" he interjected, sounding shocked.

He appeared so genuinely worried that she could not lie to him, not about this. "No, but you might have. I don't know why you didn't, because you were quite rough."

"I'm very sorry." He stepped uncomfortably close, his eyes deepening to emerald and reflecting concern. Lightly he ran his hand down her velvet-covered arm. She was surprised enough to allow it, although his fingers burned trails through the fabric before coming to rest beside hers on the banister.

"You were very upset, I suppose," she excused. "You

couldn't have expected your cousin would return so suddenly." *And wreak havoc with your inheritance,* she reminded herself, lest the baron's considerable charm have her telling the story of her life during the next moment. Resolve strengthened, she added with growing heat, "But I don't appreciate your calling me a 'difficult child.' All children have their moments, need I tell you. But of course you were trying to say that I—that is, the imposter I, which you keep insisting I am—you want to say that I am different from Roxanne, which would be a compliment in reverse. If Roxanne is difficult, and I am unlike Roxanne, then I am *not* difficult. That is what you meant, isn't it? And now I suppose I'm to grow faint with gratitude and tell you that yes, yes, you're in the right of it, I'm not Roxanne, since you have reminded me that my character is so much better than hers?"

Breathlessly, she glared at him. To her fury, she saw a distant look come into his eye, a look she was beginning to associate with amusement in this frustrating man.

"Well?" she demanded.

Fortunately, he did not laugh. As she watched, a shadow seemed to fall across his features.

"You have misunderstood my meaning," he said. "Last night I watched you and my aunt embrace as lovingly as any mother and daughter might upon ending such a long separation. I would have expected that of Marianne. Her love for Roxanne could not be doubted, no matter what the child said or did."

Audrey watched him, transfixed, her heart stirring in a dreadful prescience, as Lord Harry's expression grew more forbidding.

"But there was one element amiss in the reunion, Cousin Roxanne. Precisely when did you stop hating your mother?"

* * *

Unable to endure more shocking statements or derision from the family, Audrey insisted upon taking luncheon in Roxanne's bedchamber upon returning to Far Winds that afternoon, but no peace could be found there, either. The cheerful yellow walls, every stick of furniture, each toy and joyful painting reminded her of a dead child she never knew and robbed her of enjoyment.

In famished exasperation she collected her tray of cold ham, turtle soup, and bread and moved to the balcony where she ate every morsel despite the hazy sunshine and a rising wind which sailed her napkin over the wooden balustrade onto the grass below. She watched the rectangle of white linen bounce eerily from gust to gust until it snagged itself on a well-manicured shrub. The napkin appeared to struggle briefly, then flew free and out of sight. Feeling an odd satisfaction, she lifted her face to the breeze.

If only she could escape so easily.

Reluctantly her gaze lifted to the opposite wing of the house, where she knew the baron had his quarters. Behind one of those fanciful balconies he slept each night, if such a one could find sleep. She determined never to think of where he rested and dressed again, and resentfully turned her eyes back to the landscape.

Was it true, what the baron said? Did Roxanne hate her mother? It couldn't be so. Undoubtedly mother and daughter had had their little spats; many did. Lord Harry misinterpreted, that was all. How deep could be the dislike of a ten-year-old, anyway? Children's emotions were notoriously short-lived. Perhaps he'd fabricated the whole thing as another trick.

But his words did not have the sound of deceit in them. *You are wrong,* she had answered his pronouncement in reflexive shock, and said no more about it. What could she say without revealing further ignorance? As if taking his cue from her, the baron had fallen into a heavy reverie on their return to the house. She could only surmise he'd pondered his own words, or regretted them. He could have been plotting how he intended to spend his inheritances, for all she knew. Rubbing the arm which he had caressed so casually, she found herself doubting that. Wanting to doubt it.

She shivered, but it was not the wind that cooled her skin.

The baron would not leave her thoughts. She wondered about the mystery of his past, wondered if he hid a dark and terrible secret.

But what did it matter, really? Audrey had been employed to bring joy to Lady Marianne, not to satisfy her curiosity or anything else.

Narrowing her eyes to slits, she blinked against the wind.

It was too soon for Mr. Turner to return, but when he did, she had much to say to him about his feeble preparations. She intended to corner and batter him with questions, and she would accept no more of his hiding beyond doors and thin explanations. Something was not right about this family, and she was coming to believe the steward deliberately omitted telling her things which he knew would have discouraged any thinking person from accepting his offer.

Into these fiery reflections, a red rose flew to the balustrade, teetered a moment, then fell backward. Audrey had almost convinced herself she had seen a bird when the rose again arced into the air, this time landing a few feet away. She moved from the diminutive glass-topped table and went to pick it up. Rising, she caught sight of Thornton Brown standing beneath the balcony with his head cocked, a winsome grin on his face.

"You've forgotten your lines," he called up to her.

"I beg your pardon?"

" 'Romeo, Romeo, wherefore art thou' and all that," he said. "Don't you remember?"

Trying to match his smile, she shrugged and shook her head.

"Then I shall remind you."

A determined light danced into his eyes. He dashed off his blue jacket and lay it carefully over a bush. Rubbing his hands together and eyeing the brick wall, he walked to the immediate left of the balcony, settled his fingers into tenuous holds, and began to climb.

"I do remember the play, if that's what you mean," she hurried to exclaim, realizing too late what he meant to do. "What are you doing? You're going to hurt yourself!"

With a determined light in his eyes, he kept climbing, his boots digging into the rough surfaces between bricks, his fingers carefully searching for broken spots in the mortar. Audrey, too afraid to speak another word, pressed her hands to her temples anxiously as he climbed higher and higher. The moment when he arrived at the edge of the balcony floor was the most tense, for a fall from this height could break a leg or worse. As though heedless of danger, he flattened his body against the wall and ventured one hand to the bottom of a baluster, where he scrabbled for a purchase and took hold, his body swinging free for an instant. Grunting a little, he walked his hands up the spindle until he reached the top. As his grinning face peered over the rail, she moved back, disbelieving his foolhardiness. Next, he swung one leg over, then the other, and jumped to his feet, crossing one arm across his chest and bowing triumphantly.

"Your servant, Juliet," he said breathlessly.

"My goodness, you could have gone inside and knocked!"

"And where is the adventure in that? You used to love

my balcony visits, and you know how much I enjoy climbing. Or perhaps you don't."

"That's as may be, but I'm older now, and I understand the possibility of broken bones."

"True enough," he said, sounding winded. "I've grown older and duller too, and it's been a long time since I tried that performance. Fortunately for me, the mortar is in no better repair than it ever was. May I sit?"

Audrey gestured reluctantly to the white iron chair opposite her own. She could not escape these people it seemed, not even in the supposed privacy of Roxanne's bedroom. There was no use whining to herself, though; she had come here to work. She determined to match his playfully condescending tone.

"To what do I owe the honor of your amazing visit?"

Thorn gave a pointed glance at her empty plate. "We missed you at luncheon."

"You did not. You could not have. You and your sister and Lord Hastings all believe I'm a liar, and I'm certain you relished my absence."

He crossed one well-shaped leg over the other, his acrobatics having not mussed his buff pantaloons or white linen shirt in the least. "Actually, I found the meal quite boring without you."

"I can imagine. The diversion I offer as a supposed imposter, ready for the eating, was not there for you to sharpen your teeth upon."

"Hah! You're hard upon yourself, Juliet. I'm willing to give you a fair chance and came to tell you so."

Sending him a dubious look, Audrey believed the handsome blond gentleman meant to charm her. He used a more practiced edition of the art than the baron, but she felt herself softening in spite of herself.

If Rebecca could see how she had traded sallies with the two examples of masculine beauty and grace living at Far

Winds since arriving here, how ambitious she would be for her. The irony was that Audrey realized the situation for what it was. Lord Harry and Thornton played wolves to her lamb. They were both determined to learn the truth in their own way. It was a good thing Mr. Turner had forbidden her writing letters or keeping a journal for fear her words would fall into the wrong hands. Rebecca would never have to know details like these.

"You didn't seem so willing to believe last night," she said.

"I beg your forgiveness for my actions and words. You startled me."

"But now that you're no longer startled, you're willing to believe me?"

"I won't venture as much as that," he said, responding to the doubt in her voice. "You can't expect instant acceptance, especially with an explanation of lost years like yours. Say for a moment you did enact a role. No one can study everything about a person, and the forgotten past does provide an easy escape, you must admit."

"Such memory losses do occur," she said firmly.

"I have no doubt. But I must admit to being discouraged that our balcony scene was one of the things which escaped your memory, since Roxanne—you—delighted in them so much." His gaze wandered sadly away, following a dove sailing in the wind. "It pains me to remember how much."

She could not be certain, but she regarded his emotions as false. "I'll tell you what discourages me, and that is a young man playing Shakespearean love scenes with a ten-year-old."

He laughed, but Audrey was certain his cheeks reddened. "No, you misunderstand. Roxanne—you, I should say—may have had a childish admiration for me, but—"

"I wanted to marry you, so Mother said last night."

"—perhaps in your little girl way, yes, but that was because I paid her—you—attention. Only as I would a little sister, you understand."

"You already had one younger sister," Audrey reminded him.

"True, and we were exceptionally close, all three of us. We bonded in the early years, long before Harry came to live here. Lucy and I were six and nine when Lady Marianne took us in, and you a toddler. Like many young children who are isolated from others, we enjoyed playing together. Our little age differences didn't matter. My aunt didn't wish to send me away to school, so I suppose that kept the three of us unusually close."

"She didn't wish you or Lucy to go to school?"

His mouth twisted. "We were tutored well at home. She said she couldn't bear losing any of us for months at a time, but Lucy and I felt differently." He began to spin the edge of her butter knife. "Lady Marianne was ashamed of her brother's treatment of us, and I believe she thought we would be reminders of his notoriety in Society."

"Oh, surely not," she protested.

He gave her a direct look. "Think what you will, but my aunt is a proud woman."

She bristled and glanced away from him, not wanting to hear anything negative about the lady who had treated her so lovingly. But he was not done. "Now, when Harry came, that was a different matter. He was already a young man and had been to school." He picked up the knife and studied his reflection. "Our aunt thought the moon rose in him."

Thorn appeared thoughtful, and Audrey quickened with excitement. Perhaps she could discover the baron's secret. "And you and Lucy and I . . . we had difficulty accepting him?"

"I don't know about you and Lucy, but I admired him greatly. He had the air of the world about him, I suppose you'd say. At least it appeared that way to me. We were only a few years apart, and I wanted to be as self-assured as he, to know what he knew. When he first came, I attached myself to him like a shadow. But he had no interest in me or in Lucy or yourself. He could have been from another generation, for all the time he spent with us."

"Why did he come here?" She proffered the question in as nonchalant a manner as she could, but her heart pounded in anticipation.

"To help Sir Hastings, for one." With a wry look he added, "As for the rest that you don't remember, you'll have to ask Harry. His history is not mine to tell, as I've learned painfully from earlier days."

Disappointed, Audrey gave a slight nod to indicate she understood. She had known already of Sir Hastings's slow, wasting demise after Joseph, his son and Roxanne's brother—who had been much older than she, Mr. Turner had said, so she wouldn't be expected to remember him—died in a riding accident. That was the reason Lord Harry had taken the reins of the estate for his uncle. But there was something more to the baron's story, and Thorn had just confirmed it by his silence.

"It is a history he expects me to know already," she said with regret.

His slight smile and lifted eyebrows seemed to indicate that he thought so, too. She had known she could never trick anyone with her impersonation. Why had no one at home believed her? Why had she come?

"Speaking of Harry, how went your ride this morning?" he asked. "Forbidding, I should imagine."

The sensation of the baron's fingers upon her arm flew unbidden into her mind, and she felt a blush creeping upward from her collar. "It was tolerable, I suppose. I enjoyed seeing the estate." Lifting a cup of cold tea toward her lips, she paused. "Seeing the estate *again*, I mean." She sipped, hoping he hadn't made anything of her error. Gesturing with her cup, she added, "I was reminded of what a trying child I used to be."

Unexpectedly, he did not laugh but took on an annoyed expression.

"Is that what Harry told you? I'm not surprised. He never got on with any of us, and Roxanne especially. I often wondered if he wasn't jealous of the relationship between mother and child. Even though Sir Hastings and Aunt Marianne embraced him almost like a son, I think he wanted more. I think he meant to usurp her in their affections." Grimly he added, "And perhaps in their purses as well."

She could not like what Thorn was insinuating, that the baron would act in deceit to attain his purpose. But who was she to moralize? she reminded herself with a thud. Nevertheless, this version of the baron did not sit well, although she did not care to speculate why not.

"But I thought my mother and I didn't get along."

"Did he say that? As though he would know how to please a parent!" His anger cooled as he viewed her startled eyes. "Of course Roxanne and my aunt had their disagreements. You don't remember Marianne from those days. Her manner might be considered harsh upon occasion. But I perceive you don't want to hear untoward words concerning her. Ah, well. Mayhaps you are too young to know it, but people are complicated beings. None are totally good or totally bad. Not the ones I've observed, at least. Perhaps your experience has been different. But you will understand that Roxanne had a will of her own, and sometimes the two of them clashed."

"But is it not the duty of the child to obey the parent?"

"In most cases, I should say so. And Roxanne did, at least most of the time, but no child can tolerate being told over and over how to walk and stand and speak as if she were a puppet or having dictated what gown to wear at every moment of the day, every day of the year. She chafed under the restrictions of her mother's desire for perfection, but Roxanne a trying child? Oh, no. She was more alive and vibrant than any creature I've ever known." Seeing her astonishment, he softened. "I should say *you* were all those things, shouldn't I? For I am coming more and more to believe you are my long-lost friend, if only for how enchanting you are."

Returning his warm stare with a disbelieving one, she could not countenance such a ready display of charm, no matter how much she might like it. Either he meant to disarm a foolish imposter into confessing or use her as practice for seducing the village girls.

Another more insidious thought occurred. Perhaps he hoped that, in the event Lady Marianne did change her will back to Roxanne, he would still receive the fortune by virtue of marrying it.

Did these people have no scruples at all? she wondered. And what kind of girl had Roxanne truly been? Whose interpretation of her character could she believe? She was determined to find out.

For the moment, she dared trust no one.

When the brooding image of Lord Harry drifted immediately to mind, she bid it firmly to go away.

Five

Before dinner that evening, when the girl he must call Roxanne entered the salon, Lord Hastings stood and bowed politely, as did Thornton. The baron hoped he did not look as moonstruck as the younger gentleman, for the beauty was clothed in a pink silk gown which set off her face and form to distraction. Amid the gold and white furnishings of his aunt's salon, she put him in mind of a delicate, pale rose set within a gilded frame.

He did not like to think he'd waited for this moment since parting with her that morning, especially after she had failed to arrive at luncheon. His disappointment then had been ridiculous, even though his motives in spending time with her were lofty—discovering the truth, for his aunt's sake.

He narrowed his eyes in irritation. Before he could form a word, Thornton had edged toward her like a champion after the prize. Evidently, the younger man could forgive criminal behavior so long as it hid behind an innocent, beguiling face. He cautioned himself not to be a similar fool.

"You look lovely," Thornton was exclaiming. "Your gown becomes you, and I like how the ribbon sets off your hair. Lyddie's work, is it?"

With a graceful curtsy, Roxanne said, "Yes, thank you. This afternoon Mrs. Prate delivered several gowns from her sister's shop that required only a little alteration." After a fractional pause, she added with what seemed unnecessary detail, "She brought new ribbons to match them all."

"She is making even more gowns, someone said," Lucy said from a chair beside the fireplace, her expression hard.

"Yes, although I wish Mother wouldn't have her do so."

The girl appeared chagrined, and the baron recalled her protesting Marianne's extravagance that morning. He wondered if her conscience was beginning to work, or if she wanted to impress them with her humility. No woman could be believed, not entirely, not at every moment. Even his aunt had not been able to change that conviction.

"She is far too generous," Roxanne added.

Lucy's lips turned downward. "A waste."

"How was our aunt today, Roxanne?" Thornton asked, giving his sister a warning look. "You were the only one allowed in the inner sanctum this afternoon, or so I hear."

They had been hearing little else since the moment Lucy joined the gentlemen in the salon, thought the baron with a subdued sigh.

"She seemed well," Roxanne said, her eyebrows pulling together briefly.

Recalling his duty as host, Harry led her to the settee and was irritated beyond measure when Thornton quickly sat beside her. Keeping his expression neutral, he took a chair across from them, beside Lucy.

"What did the two of you talk about?" Thornton asked, and leaned toward her with an avid expression.

Roxanne appeared taken aback, and Harry tried and failed to push away his anger. "A rather personal question, don't you think?"

"Don't act as if you aren't salivating to know as well, Harry. A mother and daughter separated for seven years—

who wouldn't long to hear what tender memories are being exchanged?" Turning from the baron to the girl, he added with a surprisingly intimate glance, "Besides, I simply have to know if your conversation with your mother was even *half* so interesting as ours this afternoon."

"Conversation?" Harry asked no one in particular, looking bored.

"Mother and I spoke of many things," Roxanne said, choosing to act as if she hadn't heard either his query or Thornton's final one, although she must have. She folded her hands in her lap and appeared to study them. "We talked of the changes she and Lord Hastings—Harry, I mean—have made to the estate since I went away. We are now planting barley as well as wheat, and the stables have doubled in horseflesh. She has refurbished the house—"

"Her own rooms twice," Thornton said.

"No, five times," Lucy corrected. "You have probably forgotten the Chinese motif and the phase when everything was very clean and simple with no color brighter than pale green. Oh, and the Southern plantation theme, of course."

Thornton shuddered. "I have never seen such hideous magnolia flowers in a wallpaper design. I have never seen *any* magnolias in wallpaper before or since, and I hope never to do so again."

Unfazed, Roxanne continued, "She also bought new beds for the help, and new linens as well, and a painting for every room in order to edify their taste."

She spoke as if reciting, Harry observed. He wished she would stop looking so uncomfortable. Upon reflection, however, she should be uncomfortable.

When nothing more seemed forthcoming, Lucy said, "Aunt Marianne cares deeply for her servants; everyone knows that." She discreetly crossed one ankle over the other, taking care to keep her gown from creasing. "Did she require you to change her pillow coverings? She likes them fresh every few hours and insists they be rinsed in rose water."

"The maid did that."

"Hm. Generally she likes me to do such little tasks for her. She has told me more than once that no one adjusts her pillow exactly as I do."

Hearing jealousy in Lucy's tone, the baron regarded her with weary compassion. She tried very hard to please and yet had never been able to carve a special place in Marianne's heart. Nor in his. Tonight, for an example, she wore a gown he had not seen before, so he supposed it to be new. Like many of her others, it was made of an emerald color. Some months ago he had admired a similar dress, telling her the shade complimented her dark coloring, which it did. Since then most of her new gowns were of that hue or included it in a pattern. He hated thinking she searched for his approval in her selections, for in truth he did not care one way or the other.

"That must be so," Roxanne said with sudden gentleness, as if sensing her distress. "The maid tried several times before she arranged it precisely right."

"Bertha always was ham-handed," Lucy said, her tone not softening at the girl's generosity, although she gave her a curious glance.

At that moment, the dinner bell sounded, and Thornton stood and offered his arm to Roxanne. "Don't be surprised at my aunt's requirements for her own comfort. She can be exacting to say the least."

"No more so than any other invalid," Roxanne defended, accepting Thornton's escort from the room. Following them with Lucy at his arm, Harry felt mixed pleasure at the girl's support of his aunt, for her expression betrayed doubt. As they filed down the hall toward the dining alcove, he heard her add stoutly, "If I were too weak to rise from bed, I would want everything as I liked it, too."

Thornton chuckled. "Yes, but would you expect it at the expense of everyone else, that's the question."

"You forget yourself," Harry said. They had arrived at the intimate bay in the morning room, and as he assisted Lucy into her seat, he gave a pointed look at the butler, who waited to serve them.

"I know, I know, not before the servants, and we are dependent upon her generosity and have profited by her graciousness and so on and so on. But I would be more grateful if she would ever once let me forget it."

"Stop it, Thorn." Lucy, accustomed to her role as hostess in Marianne's absence, nodded angrily at Tidwell, who turned impassively to the sideboard and began ladling fragrant onion soup into bowls. "What does it matter if Aunt Marianne is demanding at times? It is her right, and she never asks for more than she gives. Our own mother did far less for us, as you well know."

"Our mother was penniless, thanks to Marianne's brother. How do we know what she would have done if she'd had funds?" Impassioned, he leaned across his empty plate toward his sister and punctuated the air with one hand. "Where was Marianne when our stepfather died, Lucy? Did she offer to assist our mother so that she could raise her children on her own? No, she did not. The only way open to our parent was to abandon us here, to shame Marianne into performing her duty."

"A caring mother would have found a way," Lucy said huskily, her compelling eyes growing moist.

Temper rising, Lord Harry was momentarily transfixed by the stricken look in Roxanne's eyes as she observed the exchange between siblings. She appeared as disturbed as he felt, and he could not believe her emotions to be pretended.

"What do you know of Mother?" Thornton lashed. "You were too young to remember how well she loved us."

Beautiful lips trembling, Lucy said, "I shall never forgive what she did."

"You're too harsh. Things would have gone differently had Marianne played her proper role."

"That's enough," Harry said sharply. He could not stomach Thornton's ongoing anger, which he regarded as a major weakness of character. "If you believe my aunt has treated you so shabbily, why do you continue to inflict her hospitality upon yourself?"

"Yes, Lord Hastings, of course, milord; it is my duty to obey." Thornton closed his eyes momentarily and sniffed in a quick breath. Gradually the flush receded from his skin. He glanced around the table, flashed an apologetic smile toward Roxanne, and, becoming aware that Tidwell hovered at his elbow with a bowl of soup, leaned back to allow the servant room. "Sorry, sorry. Oh, what perfectly wonderful soup. Forgive my outburst, everyone. I'm famished, and you know how obnoxious I become before a meal."

Roxanne lay a hand upon the table in Thornton's direction, as if she meant to touch him. Harry looked from the hand to her face and saw standing tears in her eyes. Sympathetic tears, which Thornton also did not fail to notice. His cousin's smile became pensive, appreciative. Harry watched them both and felt alarm flowing through his blood, followed by ice.

The remainder of the meal passed as if the four of them were caught, tableau-like, within a glass bauble. Time itself slowed to a crawl. The baron fancied that even the clock in the hall had slowed its ticking.

No, that was not precisely right, he thought. Only he appeared affected by the aberration, as if he viewed the others from a faraway vantage point and outside the normal flow of events.

Roxanne, *faux* Roxanne, was working her magic upon brother and sister, and only he remained untouched. The candlelight loved her, flickering admiration and enhancement upon smooth pink cheeks and animated, albeit troubled, eyes. Thornton, if he had not completely accepted her as Marianne's daughter, appeared swept away, although he kept a part of himself distant as always. Lucy's surliness toward her had thawed a trifle as well, he believed, and it was something he never dreamed to see. She had almost smiled at one of the imposter's stories—something about viewing a proposal of marriage in the middle of a marketplace wherein a loutish fellow had, upon being refused, immediately offered for the market girl's sister—but Lucy had prevented herself just in time. A highly unlikely scenario, that story, but Roxanne had made it sound realistic. She must practice fictions in her sleep.

It was good at least one of them remained objective. He could not wait to remove *Roxanne* from this room and off to himself. There remained a multitude of questions to ask, of discrepancies in her lies to discover, and he did not want to do so before witnesses. A public disclosure held no appeal whatsoever. He did not wish to humiliate her, no matter how wrong she might be.

When they had finished dinner at last, Harry hastened to pull back Roxanne's chair, then proffered his arm. "A stroll around the grounds, Cousin?"

She could not politely refuse, although she darted a glance in Thornton's direction as if for protection. The look infuriated him. "The sun appears ready to set," she said, almost timidly, as if she were afraid of him. He grew warmer.

"Don't worry, I know my way back. We won't become lost."

"Mind if I join you?" Lucy asked, silks rustling toward them before they crossed the room's threshold.

He had been afraid of this and had prepared. "I think you should look in on our aunt," he said. "I've never known her to go an entire day without seeing you, and she will be missing you by now."

"Oh, do you think so?" The pleasure that flared in Lucy's features made him feel like the worst kind of manipulator. "I'll see if she's still awake." She passed them and headed for the stairs.

Thornton followed, his face expressive of nothing. "I'm to the village, then." To Roxanne he added, "A little business I must attend to."

Female business, Harry thought. Or gambling. He didn't care so long as Thornton left them alone. Before he knew it, Roxanne had abandoned him as well, claiming she had to fetch her wrap. He didn't bother to remind her the season was early summer and uncharacteristically warm. The bewildering, fluctuating requirements of ladies for certain temperatures had long ceased to amaze him. Within the same room, one woman could be freezing, the other hot, while the gentlemen declared perfect comfort. It was a fact of life he had grown to accept, as common as the crowing of a rooster or the brooding of a hen.

When she returned to him, the girl clutched her gauzy wrap around her shoulders as if it were a shield. What did she fear, that he would embrace her with passionate kisses? He imagined such a scene, his lips tracing along the line of her neck and down her shoulders, her soft body yielding, clinging to his.

His pulse raced to life.

God help him. If this beautiful stranger spoke the truth, she was his cousin and only seventeen years old. Whatever the case, he could not let her distract him in this manner.

"Is anything the matter?" she queried, searching his eyes worriedly.

He could not look away from her. "Nothing, other than I'd like to know who you truly are." At this, she colored and stared straight ahead. He wished he hadn't said it.

Tidwell held the door for them as the baron led the girl outside and down the shallow steps of the portico. A walking path, paved with flat stones, meandered from both sides of the house and curved to the nearest attractions of the estate. He chose the one to the left, as it led most immediately to the rose garden, his decided destination. The entire circuit wandered for three miles at least, a decent evening's exercise, but they could not finish it tonight, not without lanterns, and he would not have her stumbling and twisting an ankle. The sun was already disappearing behind the trees.

"You seem to be winning friends in this household," he said after they had walked silently for some time. "First my aunt, and now Thornton believes you. A decent number of conquests in a short time, I think. I must congratulate you."

"Just because you have taken me in dislike is no reason to be rude," she said with a resentful sideways glance. "You may return me to Far Winds if that is how you mean to speak."

"Forgive me," he said. "I become protective when outsiders try to harm my family."

She dropped his arm and swerved to face him. "I would never knowingly harm your family—*my* family—or anyone else."

The sincerity of her declaration made him ache. "I can almost believe you mean that."

"I wish you would believe it."

Against all reason, he wished he could, too. A sweet breeze began to blow, lifting the curls lying against her forehead. She seemed oblivious. Again offering his arm, he said, "Come. Let's sit awhile in Camelot."

"Camelot?"

"The rose garden." He nodded toward the structure ahead, a large square of shoulder-high brick topped with ornamental spikes that curved outward. She hesitated, then accepted his escort. "Camelot is what you used to call it. The ironwork reminded you of spears and armor, you said."

"Oh, yes. That is, I can almost remember."

He gave her a skeptical look but said nothing as they crossed to the garden. Abandoning her for the moment, he took his time swinging open the gates, enjoying the creak of stiff hinges and the sense of drama he inevitably felt when displaying the area to first-time visitors, of which she was certainly one. Roxanne had spent far too much time here to have forgotten, and the *faux* Roxanne's gasp of pleasure was one of discovery, not remembrance. Of that he was almost entirely sure.

He strolled her within and imagined seeing the garden for the first time through her eyes. Islands of healthy, groomed roses were placed artistically throughout the bricked surface, spaced well enough to allow peaceful prospects for visitors. White stone benches and round tables were scattered about in convenient groupings for such viewing, and for conversations as well. In the center lay a small, circular pool bordered by several courses of bricks. To one side a cherub appeared to pour water from a stone pitcher into the reservoir.

"How utterly delightful!" she exclaimed, stepping away from him and extending her arms as if to embrace the garden. She whirled, her eyes drinking in every aspect as if parched. "Camelot indeed!"

As he watched her, smiling, she seemed to come to her senses and with a half-shamed look took on the posture of a young lady once more. He felt sorry to see it. But though her exuberance had calmed, her enthusiasm remained, and for a few moments he followed her lead as she examined the varieties and colors of roses throughout the outdoor room. When he finally suggested they sit, she ignored the benches and went directly to the pool, where she sat sideways on the bricks, removed one glove, and combed her fingers through the water. He joined her, one leg bent beneath the other so that he could see her better. Study her reactions, he reminded himself, half-intoxicated with the scent of roses and her unbearable freshness and beauty in the softening light.

"This spot truly is enchanted," she said, her shawl now lying at her feet, apparently forgotten. "I named it well. Camelot." She closed her eyes, opened them slowly on him, and he felt her gaze pierce his heart. "Although Camelot was not always this peaceful."

"Neither was this garden, when Roxanne was small. Thornton and Lucy and she would charge through it with toy swords flashing, often lopping off the heads of our gardener's best roses as they fought."

Her expression cooled. "How you must have hated me."

"No, I never hated Roxanne." For an instant he wondered if he spoke truth. "She was only a child when I knew her, a very spoiled child who didn't appreciate the golden life she'd been given. I am very sorry for her tragedy, especially for my aunt's sake. Perhaps the girl would have changed."

"All you seem to remember are the bad things I did."

He studied her until she lowered her gaze to the water. "The only bad thing I know about you is that you're pretending to be someone you aren't." Gently he turned her chin, bringing her eyes back to his. In an urgent whisper, he said, "Tell me your true name."

She regarded him soberly, and for an instant he thought she might break. When she leaned back from his touch, he felt his heart crack. "I have told you my name. And as to my degree of naughtiness . . . After you and I spoke this morning, I asked my mother about how she and I used to get along when I was little. She said that our relationship could not have been better, that no mother and daughter loved one another more."

"And you believed her?"

"Is there a reason I should not?"

"Only that time and loss can color one's memories drastically."

"True enough. The question is, whose memories are the accurate ones?"

She had him there, or thought she did if the light in her face was any indicator. He smiled wryly. "You will have to decide that."

"Others beside my mother have told me favorable things about my early years."

"What others? Not the servants, surely. She thrived on playing tricks upon them."

"What kind of tricks? I challenge you to remember even one."

"Too easy. Once she tied the bed linens into long ropes and dragged them across the estate. I think she and her cohorts used them to explore a cave. The servants couldn't remove all the earth stains, and Aunt Marianne ordered them thrown out."

Her lips twitched. "Does that seem evil to you? It sounds like the normal actions of a high-spirited child to me."

He considered. "If that were an isolated incident, perhaps, but trouble followed wherever Roxanne went. She was a fierce leader for all her tender age. Thornton and Lucy obeyed her demands like lackeys, though they seemed willing enough. Of course it was to their advantage to do so."

"You think they played with me in order to please my mother, to insure their places here," she said bitterly.

"They knew Aunt Marianne indulged the child—"

"But she was strict as well. I could not even select my own gowns to wear; she insisted upon doing it." Her eyes sparked. "Perhaps she means to do so again, for she had me stop by her room before dinner tonight to see my new apparel. I had chosen an interesting gown which Mrs. Prate had sent, one with brown and yellow sprigs. It was truly quite nice, but Mother bid me change as it didn't suit my coloring." Thoughtfully, she added, "I haven't had the luxury of considering colors in a long time."

This last he felt had the ring of truth in it. "My aunt has a strong desire for things to be run properly and well."

"Yes, but . . ." The preoccupied look came to her face again, the look he had noticed all evening. "Do you not feel she tends to be a trifle . . . controlling?"

His back stiffened at the word. "She has had to be. Sir Hastings became incapacitated long before I came to Far Winds, and she was responsible for running the estate as well as raising three children and caring for an ailing husband. She did remarkably well. She's a strong woman."

"You admire her very much."

"I both admire and love her. I have little patience for criticism of her. She was not too hard on Roxanne. She wanted her daughter to grow up to be a dignified lady, a small enough price to pay for unlimited security and love."

The girl remained quiet for a moment, drawing designs in the water. "You sound envious."

"Perhaps I was, a little. When I came here as a young man, it was the first time I could remember being happy. Roxanne astonished me with her lack of appreciation for her good fortune."

"But your father was a nobleman. Surely you enjoyed your own family . . ."

"I wish I could say so." It was all he intended to say on the subject, no matter if she did pin him with bright, intelligent eyes. "All right, Roxanne, since you say I must believe you, tell me about your life after leaving Far Winds."

"I had far rather speak of *your* life *before* Far Winds."

"As I've told you, Roxanne already knows my history." He splashed a pebble into the water, then cut her a sideways glance. "I'm sure it will come back to you in time. But you, now. You've only told us the major happenings since you left. It's much more to the point that we talk about your recent history, since none of us know it. Except you, of course."

"Oh, well. There's not much to tell, truly there isn't. Long days full of work."

"Milking cows, plowing fields, planting corn?"

"You make light of my misfortune. It's really too bad of you."

"Perhaps I can't help myself." She could be evasive, but there were other ways to discover the truth. "Give me your hand."

"Give you my—why?"

He nodded toward the hand still dabbling in the water, and she lifted it doubtfully toward him. Shaking his head, he patted her skin dry with his handkerchief, then rested her fingers in his, palm upward. He stared. Blood began to pound at his temples. Such a pretty, dainty hand it was, were it not for its heavy calluses. With one finger he traced the hardened skin at the base of her thumb, his mind caught in wonder. He had thought to disprove her story with the easy evidence of a lady's hands, but this girl had worked at hard physical labor for a long period of time.

Was it possible she was telling the truth?

No. He would never believe it. She could be a farm girl or a milkmaid or work in any of a dozen other hardy occupations, although he could not fathom why an educated young woman would do so, but she was not his cousin.

Roxanne could never have grown into this sweet, compelling creature. Sweet, *lying,* compelling creature. His gaze fell into hers.

She snatched back her fingers. "Are my hands ugly enough for your approval? Mother doesn't like them, either. She ordered Bertha to make a special ointment which I must wear at night, wrapped in two sets of gloves to protect the sheets. I'm sorry they look so coarse. It was the price of avoiding hunger."

When she averted her head, he realized with a start that she was crying. He hadn't planned for this reaction. "Don't," he said quietly, and peered to find her eyes. She turned her head farther, her breath catching on a subdued sob. "No, I didn't mean . . ." He had meant something, but at this moment he couldn't recall what. Before he could stop himself, he patted her back and found it wasn't enough. Cursing their awkward positions on the brick wall, he stood and pulled her into his arms. After an initial resistance, she nestled her cheek against his chest and wept silently for a moment or two. He lost all sense of time. Never had he known a woman who cried without sound, though her trembling shoulders signaled him of the storm within.

Gradually she grew still. Seconds later her arms loosened, but he would not release her entirely. For the second time he brought forth his handkerchief, this time patting the tears from her cheeks.

"I'm sorry," he said. "I didn't mean to make you cry."

"But you can't help yourself." She blinked, her lashes moist. "I know you only wish to protect your aunt. Please believe me when I tell you that I intend no harm. I'm not trying to steal anyone's inheritance. Not yours, not Thornton's, not Lucy's. If she should change her will back to me, I'd refuse the money. I only want to make her last days happy."

"You seem to be doing that," he said.

How he longed to believe this bewitching girl, that the glow of sincerity in her eyes was unfeigned, unrehearsed. And for a single moment he allowed himself to be pulled in, her mesmerizing power drawing him helplessly toward her mouth. Shock flared in her face, then faded to dreamy acceptance, her lips softening against his. Had he not heard Lucy singing out his name as she walked down the path, her voice drawing nearer, he could not have let her go.

"I'm sorry," he said, his pulse pounding in his throat. "I shouldn't have done that."

"Oh," she said in a thin little voice as he released her. Her pupils had grown large as a cat's, and her mouth was rosy from his kisses. "Oh." She looked adorable. The urge to grab her was nearly impossible to resist.

"We'd better get back, it's almost dark. Lucy is looking for us." He tugged on her hand. Several strands of hair had fallen loose from their pins, but she apparently had not noticed. "Come, now. This meant nothing." The words cut him, but he couldn't have her thinking the wrong thing. "The approach of night, the scent of roses, and a pretty girl." He gestured helplessly, as if to say kissing a lady he had known for only a day was an everyday occurrence.

Slowly her expression focused on him. With a strength that surprised him, she pulled her hand from his and refused to move. "The approaching night. The smell of roses. A girl. Thank you. What a lovely description of my first kiss to remember when I am old and wrinkled."

"Your first kiss?" He did not attempt to disguise his doubt, although his spirit soared foolishly to imagine it.

"Yes, but why should you believe that? You believe nothing I say." Having so said, she brushed past him and walked briskly toward the gate.

He hurried after her, feeling twisted inside, as if he had crushed delicate flowers beneath his heel or drowned kittens. "Wait. I am deeply sorry for what I said. Allow me to walk with you to the house."

"I don't need you to walk me to the house; it is just over there," she said without looking at him.

He caught sight of Lucy hurrying toward them. He hated to think what she would make of this scene. She would make too much of it, that was certain, just as Roxanne had. "Please. I didn't mean to hurt you."

She whirled on him, and he heard the faint clang of a pin striking the pavement as another lock of hair fell loose. "Hurt me? Don't concern yourself, Harry. As you said, it meant nothing."

Six

"What an excellent hand you have, child," said Lady Marianne from her bed, holding an envelope at arm's length and squinting her eyes at the flowing script written upon it.

Audrey glanced up from the desk and thanked the lady with a wan smile. It was her fourth afternoon at Far Winds, and she had been assigned a stack of invitations to address for her upcoming ball to be given in less than a fortnight. She eyed the tower of cards and forestalled a sigh. All of this was being done under protest. The baron had protested, Lucy cried, and Thorn rode off, declaring he must visit London for a few days. The servants were no happier. She noticed their lowered eyes whenever she passed by them. They did not want to decorate and clean and cook and bake for a girl everyone except Lady Marianne believed was an imposter.

Audrey had objected more than anyone, but *Mother* remained set. A celebration must be declared; Roxanne must have her ball. Friends and neighbors were already stopping by to become reacquainted with Marianne's prodigal, to hear all about the miraculous turn of events which had brought her home. Audrey found her lies increasingly hard to maintain, her smiles more and more difficult to summon.

"Your script has greatly improved from your girlhood," Lady Marianne said reflectively.

Fear blossomed within. "Yes, ma'am. I practiced whenever I could."

"Excellent. You always were a good child."

Audrey, relief trickling through her veins at once again avoiding exposure, discreetly lay aside the invitation she had ruined in her moment of panic and began another. She didn't know how many more of these tests she could pass before crying out the truth. The burden of lies did not rest easily upon her shoulders.

If she did not have her father and her sister to consider, she thought while blinking away tears, she would confess all at this very moment. Even the prospect of the baron's reaction would not stop her. She should not care a fig about *his* reaction, anyway, not Lord Lofty Hastings, he of the *this means nothing* school of manners in letting down young ladies in the worst possible way. But she did care, and that was the trouble.

At least he had had the decency to avoid her over these past few days, even to the point of absenting himself from the table now and then. As for herself, she often took her meals in her room. With Thorn away, the strain of facing the baron and Lucy, or Lucy alone, was simply too much to bear. Although she suspected Thorn of being a trifle frivolous, he did make an entertaining companion most of the time. At the very least, he did not force her to guard every word lest she betray herself as some did in this household.

Lying nearly upright upon a mountain of pillows, Lady Marianne slowly raised her arms in a luxuriant stretch. The movement was unusual enough to capture Audrey's eye.

"Do you know what I should like to do?" asked the older woman. "I would like to sit outside on the balcony and feel the sun on my face. How long has it been since I last did that?"

Audrey had no idea, but the lady had not been outside since she'd arrived, not to her knowledge. "Do you think—I mean, should you? Won't it overtire you?"

"Oh, humbug. I'm always tired anyway." She reached for the porcelain bell lying atop her bedside table and rang it. "Tired of this bed, tired of this bedroom, tired of being ill." Seconds later, the maid scurried into the room pulling a pair of spectacles over her ears. "Bertha, bring my chair. I'm going outside."

"Oh, yes, milady!" cried Bertha, happily clapping her hands and running from the chamber. Within an eyeblink she returned pushing an intricately carved chair made of rosewood. "This is what you've been needing for many a day," added the little round maid as she assisted the lady into the chair. Audrey, who had much experience in such matters, rushed to help. "Fresh air is good for the soul and good for the body, I always say."

Bertha's enthusiasm shamed Audrey. During the past days, the lady's appetite had improved, her cheeks had begun to look less hollow, her skin appeared more vital, her eyes sparkled. In short, Lady Marianne seemed to be improving rather than declining. This was felicitous news, wonderful news. Audrey had come to feel a certain fondness for the older woman, although Marianne's forceful personality did not allow her to grow overly close, not nearly to the level which Lord Harry seemed to have attained. Of course, that was because he had the advantage of many years' acquaintance. But fond or not, she was not so low as to wish anyone's demise to hasten along, yet she had been led to believe such an occurrence was imminent and that her time at Far Winds would be minimal. If circumstances continued in this manner, she would falter, she knew she would.

"You must join us as well, dear," Lady Marianne said as Bertha pushed her chair onto the balcony. "You're working too hard; your eyes are red."

Audrey followed meekly; it was, after all, what she was being paid to do. Or not being paid to do, as was becoming more likely, since Mr. Turner could not afford the promised ten thousand pounds if he did not inherit it, and he could not inherit if Lady Marianne did not die. And she did not want Lady Marianne to die!

"Mr. Turner," she said aloud, shocking herself. It sounded like a curse.

"What's that?" Lady Marianne asked.

"Hm?" Absently, Audrey sat in one of the cushioned iron chairs while Bertha claimed the other. "Oh, Mr. Turner. I was just . . . Will the steward be invited to the ball?" she improvised.

The lady tilted her head and peered at Audrey. "Not in the usual course of events. Do you wish him to be invited?"

"Oh, not particularly."

Marianne made a sound somewhere between a snort and a chuckle. "What made you think of him, then?"

"Only that, well of course I only met him briefly, but he seems efficient at his work, and I've been wondering when he might be coming back." It was merely one of a list of things she wondered about him. He had promised to stay close by, but she had not seen him since the first night. The increasingly dreadful conviction that the steward could not be trusted was beginning to keep her awake nights.

The older lady leaned back her head, and Bertha jumped to adjust the pillow lining the chair. "He is efficient. If I know Nathan, he will be knocking at all the doors in Bournemouth, intent upon bringing every dollop of truth back to me. I hope you don't worry that he'll bring a false report concerning that nice couple who took you in."

"Not at all." She knew he would bring a false report; that had been the plan.

A late afternoon breeze ruffled the women's gowns, sending a chill down Audrey's arms, one that spread to her spine as she thought of other possibilities: Mr. Turner run insane and decrying all knowledge of her, Mr. Turner lying unconscious or dead in a ditch. *I am in very great trouble,* she admitted to herself. She met the lady's concerned eyes. "I do worry that he's taking so long."

"Nonsense. He's thorough, that is all. Bertha, bring my blanket, will you? I'm cold." The maid hastened to obey, fussing over the lady as she tucked the corners of the covering beneath her shoulders and around her feet. "All right, stop," she said crossly. "You're worse than a mother hen." Bertha beamed as if she had been complimented.

They sat in silence for a while. Marianne's balcony overlooked the rear of Far Winds, and from here a green expanse stretched far into the distance, where it was broken by a line of trees. A paved walkway—a portion of which she had tread with the baron on that disastrous evening in the rose garden—curved from vista to vista: here a porcelain statuary surrounded by topiary boxes, there a fountain nestled among patches of sweet williams, columbines, and syringas. . . .

Audrey surveyed the grounds with longing, the peaceful beauty of her surroundings mocking the agitation within her heart. Everywhere she looked reminded her of the baron. From here she could see a portion of the bricked garden where he had kissed her, then spoken to her so cruelly. Beyond the trees, she could imagine the pavilion where they had stopped awhile during their ride. She recalled how his hands had lingered at her waist when helping her from the saddle and how concerned he appeared. The image of his strong, pleasing features, his tall strength, the clean, masculine scent of him—she could not dismiss these from her mind. How contradictory he was, a contradiction shown most plainly in his eyes, which could turn from amusement to censure within a heartbeat.

It was becoming very plain to her that, were it not for the baron, her work here would be much easier. She closed her eyes and prayed for sleep.

"Why, I believe we're to be entertained," Lady Marianne said a few moments later.

Audrey's lashes lifted. On the lawn below, one of the footmen had begun the process of setting up archery equipment with Lucy supervising, her voice a commanding murmur from this distance. Indecision seemed to be the order of the day. Lucy would point to an area, and the servant, the ends of his cravat flying from his gold satin vest, would move the target and its stand there, after which the young lady would sight the spot down her arm as if drawing an imaginary bow, then shake her head with displeasure. This scene was repeated several times, the footman's posture growing more stiff at every move. Finally, Lucy commanded him toward the rose garden, and the footman responded with respectful but dissenting tones. The young lady's voice grew higher with argument.

"Lucy, Lucy," mumbled Lady Marianne despairingly.

With a turnover of her heart, Audrey watched the baron approach the commotion at a lazy pace. He appeared to side with the servant, pointing with a sweeping gesture toward the largest uninterrupted expanse of green and leading Lucy closer to the house. As the lackey scurried in the opposite direction with the target, Lord Harry spotted the ladies sitting on the balcony, his gaze pinning Audrey for one taut instant, then moving to his aunt's. A smile broke across his face, a smile so sincere and beautiful and so markedly not meant for her, that Audrey felt even more woefully alone.

Oblivious to them and looking crossly over her shoulder

at the retreating servant, Lucy could now be heard to complain that the sun would be in her eyes.

"Better that than piercing the gardener as he tends the roses," Harry said carelessly, still intent upon Lady Marianne. His voice rising, he called, "Aunt, it's good to see you outside. You're looking well!"

At this, Lucy turned quickly, her eyes brightening. "What a wonderful surprise! You do look very well! Are you feeling better?"

They had now walked closely enough to make yelling unnecessary, and Lady Marianne waved and related that she was feeling fine enough. "But go on with your practice," she added. "I want to see who has improved the more since last time. We like competitions, don't we, Bertha?"

"Oh, indeed, milady," Bertha said eagerly.

Lady Marianne turned to Audrey. "You should join them, my child."

"Oh no, I had much rather sit with you," Audrey replied, heart sinking as she looked from the baron to Lucy and back again. She could not judge which of them appeared more dismayed.

"Oh, humbug. Go down and play, girl. It will be good for you."

"You used to enjoy it so much!" Bertha added.

Audrey's pulse began to fly. "I-I really don't remember."

"That's right, she did like it," Lucy said, her expression sparking unpleasantly. "You were almost as accurate as Thorn, I recall, and ever so much better than I. Do come down, Roxanne!"

"It has been so long I doubt I still know how to hold a bow," Audrey told her.

"One never forgets *that*," Lucy said, her encouragement exaggerated to a degree which set Audrey's teeth on edge. During this exchange, the baron stood quietly and detached, his eyes set upon nothing.

Desperately, Audrey appealed to the lady, "I truly should return to the invitations. Only imagine if they are late."

"They won't be late. Now off with you and enjoy yourself."

That will be impossible, Audrey thought; even more impossible than avoiding the situation altogether. Glumly she trailed into the lady's bedroom and through the house, then outside, her slow steps bringing her to the back in time to see Lord Hastings release an arrow which pierced just right of the center of the target. Amid the applause which followed, she hung back beneath the balcony with the vain hope of going unnoticed.

Lucy was the first to see her. "There you are at last. It's your turn. Harry is in the lead with an almost perfect shot, but mine landed only inches from his. See if you can best that!"

As if moving through deep water, Audrey approached the pair watching her. She found herself captured by Harry's solemn eyes and reached unthinkingly for his long-bow.

Surprisingly, he did not release it immediately. "You might want to use Lucy's as it's smaller and more suitable for females."

"It makes no difference to me," Audrey said, her voice trembling.

Lucy laughed. "If it makes no difference, then let her use your bow, Harry. No doubt all that farmwork has made her strong as a man."

"Lucy, mind your tongue!" Lady Marianne cried from the balcony. "You're being devilish unkind!"

"I'm sorry, Aunt Marianne," the girl responded in contrite tones, though her eyes glinted heat at Audrey. "I meant nothing."

Moving impatiently, Lord Harry reached for Lucy's bow. "Give over, Lucy. Her arms aren't long enough for mine."

"Oh, very well," Lucy muttered ungraciously and, by-passing the baron, shoved her bow in Audrey's direction with such force that one of the ends jabbed her upper arm. A burst of pain rayed outward from the spot, and Audrey bit her lip to prevent crying out.

"You cat!" the baron said to Lucy between gritted teeth.

"Lucy, be careful!" the lady exclaimed from her perch. To Audrey she added worriedly, "Are you all right, child?"

As Lord Harry was at that moment examining her arm with gentle fingers, Audrey nodded mutely, her mouth too dry for speech. When he stroked the capped sleeve of her gown upward, his palm smooth and cool against her skin, she felt a pleasant dizziness. She could feel his breath on her skin, he was that close. She could almost forgive him everything.

"This time you will have a bruise," he said, his eyes mere inches from hers.

"I don't care," she said, and meant it.

Lucy walked nearer to them, her gaze shifting back and forth. "You are all making a great fuss over a little accident. Much worse than that happens to me all the time, and I don't make faces and act as if I'm dying."

"You grow tiresome," the baron said to her.

Reluctantly, Audrey shifted her eyes to the young woman, a great coldness forming within. She reached for the bow, which now lay at her feet.

"You don't have to do this," Lord Harry told her quietly. "You've been injured."

"But much worse happens to Lucy all the time," said she, her gaze locked with the other woman's.

"Allow me to show you how to hold the bow," he whispered, moving nearer in preparation to guiding her.

She could not have his hands upon her again or she would falter. Worse, she might lose her anger. She stepped a pace away from him. "I watched you a moment ago. That's all the instruction I need."

Audrey accepted an arrow from Lucy and set it in the bow, positioning her hands and body. Sighting the target with one eye closed, she pulled and released. The arrow cut the air, swift and true as a hawk.

"Dead center!" cried the footman in disbelieving tones.

"Astounding!" the baron pronounced, his smile threatening to thaw her, as did the happy applause and congratulations sounding from the balcony. "You've beaten both of us!"

Lucy folded her arms. "A fluke."

It was no fluke. She had been reluctant to join the pair on the lawn because it necessitated proximity to Lord Harry, not because she lacked skill. One of the things Audrey's mother and father had insisted upon was that their daughters be schooled in as many accomplishments as were affordable. Archery fell within that designation, and she and Rebecca continued to practice almost every Sunday afternoon. It was an outing their father insisted upon and anticipated, as they must journey past the boundary of Saint Duxbury to an empty field allowing safety. The field's privacy offered relief for their father from the crowded cottages and noisy children which often grated on his nerves, and Rebecca's. They ordinarily took a picnic lunch and made an afternoon of it.

Thinking of the family now lost to her—*God forbid it be forever*—Audrey coldly demanded and received another arrow. Again she stretched the bow and sent the arrow sailing across the green.

"The center again!" cried the lackey, teeth showing in a wide grin. "Only a hair away from splitting the other in half!"

"I don't believe it," Lucy said, her posture a portrait of frustration. "How did you become such an expert if you spent all these years toiling on a farm from morning 'til night?"

"As you said," Audrey responded with unabashed enjoyment, "some things you don't forget."

That evening before dinner, Harry reported to his aunt's bedroom as ordered, having received a message relayed by Bertha. He felt pleased to see Marianne's color remained high after the afternoon's exertion, although her preoccupied expression stirred him to uneasiness. He made the usual pleasantries as he pulled a chair next to her bed.

"You always say I am beautiful, but I'm not," she said in a glum voice. "My mirror tells me how I look. My skin has grown loose, and I have lines at my eyes and mouth. I am an old hag."

He had to laugh at this and did so, heartily. "You are not old. You're barely past your fiftieth birthday."

"Thank you for the reminder!"

"But you look fifteen years younger."

She shook her head irritably. "Many people are dead by my age. I was beautiful once, though. It is the province of the young." Her eyes slanted toward his. "One has only to view my daughter to see that."

This made him instantly uncomfortable, and he merely inclined his head. When she continued to study him, he blurted, "You asked to see me. Was it a visit you wanted, or is something troubling you?"

She glanced away briefly. "What a display Lucy made of herself this afternoon." Smoothing a wrinkle from her sheets, she added, "But Roxanne vindicated herself well, don't you think?"

"The girl has an excellent eye." He could not prevent a smile, thinking of her and Lucy's well-deserved comeuppance.

Moving her legs restlessly beneath the coverlet, Marianne asked abruptly, "And where is Thornton all these days? What is he doing?"

She already knew he had gone to London, and he could not understand why she was asking him. These abrupt subject changes and her perturbation increased his concern. He hoped her illness was not taking a turn for the worse just when he thought she might be getting better.

"You know how often he goes away. I never know what he's doing. Nor do I care, quite honestly."

"Well, perhaps you should. I want you to look after her, Harry," she said with sudden energy, pushing herself higher against the pillows. "Don't let anything happen to my child."

"What are you talking about? Your—the girl isn't in danger."

"Isn't she? How do you know?"

The possibility struck him with brutal force. His heart rate increasing, he demanded, "What makes you think she might be harmed? Has she received a threat?"

The lady stared at him. "Harry, we are speaking of Roxanne. You know I have always suspected someone stole her away or worse, perhaps for fear of losing their inheritance. I had made no secret that I was considering leaving everything to her instead of the bequests I'd originally planned. It was foolish of me, wondering out loud as I did, never thinking that someone would take it in their head to prevent me. Roxanne was to get half anyway, you might recall, but she had begun to complain it would not be enough to support her. Thus I was contemplating the change to please her.

"Or it may have had nothing to do with the money. Perhaps the deed was done for some kind of revenge against the family. And now that she has come home, I still wonder. You might recall that she has no recollection of climbing into the wagon which drove her away from Far Winds. Why is that, I ask you?"

He hesitated. "I can give you no answer which will please you." *Or myself,* he silently added, blinking away a vision of the unnamed girl who was coming to occupy his thoughts with uncomfortable frequency. *The fair pretender.*

"Well, think a moment. What if someone had drugged her or struck her so that she was unconscious and put her in the back of the wagon? Anything could have happened, and what is to prevent the same thing happening again? Oh, Harry, don't give me that skeptical look. I know you think she's lying, but if so, why fabricate so poorly? With a little thought, she could have designed a much better story."

"Perhaps she was clever enough to realize that too neat an explanation can't withstand close scrutiny," he said slowly. "But with the history she has told, all kinds of excuses may be made for her. As you have just proved."

Clutching the fabric of her coverlet in her fists, she said in harsh tones, "Would you please for just one moment lay aside your prejudice and entertain the possibility that she *is* my daughter? And that she might have been forcibly removed from me seven years ago?"

Against all reason, but anxious to soothe, he said, "All right. But allow me one question. If your suspicions are correct, whom do you suspect of this terrible crime?"

"If I knew that, I wouldn't need your help, would I?" Seeing she had offended him, she softened her tone. "That does remain the question. I can only guess first those who would profit most."

He contemplated her for a long moment. "That would mean Thornton, Lucy, and myself."

"Well, I would sooner suspect myself than you. But don't forget certain of the servants who know they're receiving large bequests: Bertha, Tidwell, Nathan, and James, I suppose, as I've promised him a farm of his own instead of his rooms above the stable. And naturally *all* of the servants would inherit something."

Harry had always thought it a mistake that she told everyone the contents of her will, but nothing could be done about that now. "I can't believe you would suspect any of them." Thornton did not strike him as having the energy or ambition to concoct such a ridiculous scheme, and Lucy was a female and a child herself when Roxanne disappeared. He wanted to find it easier to consider the servants, but as their aging, and for the most part kindly, faces passed through his mind, he could not accept them, either. "You haven't changed your testament in the girl's favor already, have you?"

"No! I'm honoring your doubts by waiting until Nathan's return with the confirmation of her identity. Until then, Roxanne will probably be safe enough, but she could use your support even if she's not in physical danger. I saw Lucy with her today and was appalled at her unkindness and obvious dislike."

Anger flared as he recalled how Lucy had intentionally—he was certain—struck the girl with her bow. Lucy's behavior had appalled him as well, but there was a long walk between jealousy and murder. Somehow he must make his aunt see reason. With compassion in his eyes, he placed one hand over hers.

"You've spent many hours, years even, thinking such things, Aunt. You've worn away your good health with such worries. Don't you understand that if someone abducted Roxanne, he would have sent a ransom note rather than wait for an inheritance far in the future? Yet nothing of the kind was ever found. You have also mentioned revenge, but what would be the reason when you have no enemies? No, my dear, as difficult as it is, we must accept that she met with an accident."

"She did *not* meet with an accident; she is alive and well and living beneath this roof!"

Florid patches bloomed on her cheeks and down her neck, alarming him. "All right, all right. Don't disturb yourself."

"I *will* be disturbed until you agree to look after Roxanne. You can do this for me, can't you? Simply because I've asked you to do so, whether you believe my fears or not? It will be only for a little while until Nathan returns, when he can take over the responsibility. I expect him any day now."

She could not know what she was asking. "Ordinarily I would do anything for you, gladly, but the girl and I . . . we don't get on well together."

Marianne gave him a shrewd look. "No, you get along *too* well. I watched you with her this afternoon. I'll remind you I was young once, and I recognize attraction when I see it. No, Harry, don't bother to protest. I know you don't think she is my daughter, and I'm certain your feelings are guided by that. We will know for certain—that is, *you* will know, for I'm already convinced—when Nathan returns with the information from Bournemouth. But until then, you must think of her as your cousin, do you understand me? *Cousin,* Harry."

His breathing quickened to discover how transparent he was to her.

"And if it turns out she isn't?" he said.

"Impossible."

"But if it does?"

"In the very unlikely event that she is an imposter, that would make her a criminal. Even setting aside the illegality of her act, what kind of person would raise a dying woman's hopes in such a manner? Such a one could have no moral sense and no character at all. Even if she is lovely and charming, she would be beneath our notice. Wouldn't you agree?"

He sat silently, his gaze fixed on an interesting knot in the pine wainscoting on the opposite wall, which resembled a man's head lifted in an open-mouthed scream.

"Harry?" she demanded.

Coming to himself, he smiled briefly, kissed her hand, and stood. "I'm guided by your wisdom in all things," he said.

Seven

On the afternoon following the archery competition, Audrey spent her spare hours searching Roxanne's room, hoping to find clues about the young girl she had been engaged to impersonate. At odd moments on previous days, she had made stabs at discovery but allowed the demands of Marianne to distract her. Today the lady had declared she needed rest and directed Bertha to forbid all visitors excepting Nathan Turner, should he arrive. As that arrival seemed increasingly unlikely, Audrey's desperation to understand Roxanne multiplied by the hour.

After locking the bedroom door, she began at the dresser, opening one drawer at a time and removing its contents, being careful to keep each item in the same order as it had lain within. After examining each toy, article of clothing, book or item of jewelry, she turned to the drawer itself and glided her fingers along the corners and behind the back. A child could be very clever about hiding things. Old letters, notes, drawings, perhaps even a diary—these could easily be overlooked by grief-stricken adults when cleaning a missing girl's room. She did not seek any article in particular but hoped to find anything which might shed light on Roxanne's character.

Not only did she long to find a clue that might divulge

what had happened to the child, she prayed such a discovery would soothe the feelings of Lady Marianne when the truth came out about *her.* For Audrey's own unmasking could not lie far in the future; she was certain. Nathan Turner notwithstanding, she could not bear her own continual lying. Every time she met the baron's eyes, every time she stepped into Lady Marianne's bedchamber, the weight of her deception threatened to render her speechless.

She would not allow herself to consider how unlikely it was that she would be the one to find the missing piece of the puzzle after all these years, for that would be admitting defeat before she began. Slowly and methodically she made her way around the room: dresser, bookshelves, chiffonnier, bedside tables, wardrobe, window seat, even the slats beneath the bed.

After tedious hours, with only splinters to remove for her troubles, she had to admit defeat. If ever there had been anything to find, it was gone now. The disappointment was crushing. She plopped facedown across the bed and racked her brain for another solution. She must find a way out of her unthinkable dilemma. Her mother had taught her the virtue of persistence, but that dear lady could never have imagined her in this larcenous position. Tired and heart weary, she lowered her lids sleepily, her glance falling upon the floor. What if wooden planks were beneath the carpet, and one of them was loose? She drifted off to troubled dreams contemplating it.

When Lyddie came to prepare her hair before dinner, Audrey asked about the floor.

"It's been carpeted for as long as I've been here, and that's five years now. Seems like it was carpet before then, too, because I've heard others talking of how milady has them done every ten years if not before."

Audrey sighed and handed Lyddie a pin. The servant was fascinating to watch in the mirror; her face reflected every emotion. At this moment she appeared determined and earnest as she twirled Audrey's hair into smooth curls. In her eyes, it was magical how the servant made her unruly hair obey.

"What do you know about me when I was little, Lyddie?" she asked. "There's so much I can't remember from those days."

"I wasn't here then, miss."

"Right, so you've said, but perhaps you've heard something from the other servants who did know me."

"Oh, I can't say as they ever talk about Roxanne. You, I mean."

Can't say or *won't say?* thought Audrey, not failing to note how Lyddie's lips were set straight and hard. The maid didn't believe her, either. Audrey had never felt so friendless and alone. How she missed Rebecca.

Several minutes later Lyddie finished, having anchored a silver comb at the back of Audrey's hair. Surveying the maid's handiwork with Roxanne's hand mirror, Audrey broke the silence. "I've never known anyone who could manage hair as you do, Lyddie," she said sincerely, her voice reflecting her sadness.

The servant thanked her and moved to the door, then hesitated. "You know, miss, if you're wanting to find out about yourself, you ought to visit your old nurse, Adelaide Spencer."

"My nurse!" Of course, of course! She should have realized there must be a nursemaid. Naturally she would know more about Roxanne than anyone. "Did I also have a nanny?"

"Somebody told me they never could keep your nannies long, but your nurse stayed until she was pensioned off to one of the servant's cottages a year or two before you went missing, or so I've heard. You take the road in front of the estate and go about a mile west, then turn right on the lane. She dwells in the third cottage to the left, in case you don't remember."

Audrey could barely restrain herself from embracing the dour maid and was effusive in her thanks.

"I don't know how much help she'll be," Lyddie added warningly, her mouth grimacing downward as if in spasm. "She's forgetful too."

Sometime that afternoon Thornton had returned, as Audrey discovered when she descended to the salon before dinner. He wore a gray jacket and trousers with a waistcoat lined in blue and gray stripes that drew the eye, yet she could not help thinking the baron looked far more distinguished in black and ivory. Lucy was lovely and lush in a mint green muslin trimmed at neck and hem with darker green, though her features were marred by a look of coldness at Audrey's entrance.

Audrey refused to allow Lucy's attitude to make her feel small. She had worn one of her loveliest new gowns, a peach-colored silk, in defense of her eroding sense of self-worth, and felt an instant's gratification when the gentlemen regarded her with admiration. She had also timed her arrival carefully and was satisfied to hear the dinner gong sound a moment after she entered the room. The shorter her time spent with the family, the better, she believed fervently.

Thornton was brimming over with news from London and monopolized the first two removes. By the time Tidwell began serving the roast duckling in wine sauce, Thorn had discussed every relative and friend known to the family—or so Audrey imagined; no one could be acquainted with more people, surely—and had moved on to Court news.

"The princess was presented at last, poor dear, with the

duchess of Oldenburgh as her sponsor. She arrived in her own carriage with three footmen and a coachman. And Prinny was hissed by the disapproving masses who think he should be better to his wife, if you can imagine."

He paused to fork a large morsel of duck into his mouth and chewed quickly. Although bored, Audrey felt grateful that nothing in the way of conversation had been required of her thus far. Lucy, apparently transfixed by her brother's gossip, had been interjecting comments and questions in excited counterpoint. The baron remained as silent as Audrey.

Becoming aware of his gaze resting upon her, she saw a companionable look of exasperation in his eyes and smiled, her cheeks flushing. *Steady,* she counseled herself. This was a man of which she knew little. He was the kind of man who kissed a girl one moment and told her it meant nothing the next. He had a mysterious past about which no one would speak. It was possible that greed motivated his actions and manner, even to his admirable devotion to his aunt.

But she could not believe he hid such evil. Even though he had hurt her, she could not lose the notion that his character was good.

"Speaking of domestic devotion," Thorn continued after a hurried gulp, "there have been several reports of husbands selling their wives at market."

"That's unspeakable!" Lucy exclaimed. "Slavery is illegal."

"Don't judge too quickly," Thorn said teasingly. "In these cases the wives seemed willing enough. Perhaps they believed they could do no worse."

"That only proves how woefully few options are available to women," Lucy said.

"On that we can agree," said Audrey, whose present situation would never have occurred were other opportunities open. Lucy appeared surprised and not very pleased to have her support.

Thornton grinned. "Never fear, Lucy. No one plans to auction you off. For what you'd fetch, it wouldn't be worth the trouble."

"Thank you very much, Brother!" she said with indignation.

"Oh, you look well enough, I suppose," he bantered on, "but you can't *do* anything—can't cook or bake or clean or haul water up from a well."

"You are too amusing for words," Lucy said, her eyes like dark ice.

He turned his smile upon Audrey. "Roxanne, though, would attract the gold, for not only is she beautiful, she's mastered all the domestic arts from her years as a farmer's daughter."

Lord Harry set down his fork. "That's enough, Thorn. You're babbling like a child."

"And you're speaking like a parent, which you are not," Thorn returned, his expression growing sharp. "I'll say what I wish to say."

"That's fine, so long as you speak with civility."

"Yes, my lord. Of course, my lord." Thorn waved his fork as though directing an orchestra.

Audrey sent the baron a swift glance of gratitude, his defense swelling her emotions beyond all reason. Thornton, looking back and forth between them, became suddenly contrite.

"How go the plans for your ball?" he asked her in solicitous tones.

"All of the invitations are sent," she said. She could think of nothing else good to say about it.

Thorn leaned aside as Tidwell removed his empty plate. "Marianne must have absolute confidence that you're the true Roxanne to have planned the ball in your honor.

Nathan Turner hasn't yet returned with the evidence—not that I doubt you, mind—and a fine mess it would be if you *were* tricking us."

"I said the same to Aunt Marianne," Lucy interjected with a grimace. "She remains certain that she's correct."

"Still, it all seems so hurried. Our aunt isn't giving much time for guests to respond."

Lucy said, "Oh, they'll respond all right. Acceptances have already started to flood in." After a few moments she added sardonically, "This is going to be the event of the year. Everyone will cancel any other plans they might have had, because they want to see Marianne's daughter. Oh, there are going to be so many people!"

While Audrey's heart chilled imagining it, Thorn chuckled. "You speak as though the entire county was invited."

"Very nearly, even to that horrid Captain Berkbile."

"Thank you, Tidwell," Harry said to the butler, who had exited briefly and was now serving the baron an apple dumpling dripping with caramel sauce. "What's wrong with Captain Berkbile? He seems a nice enough fellow to me."

"That's as may be, but that kerchief he wears over the lower part of his face makes me ill. I keep imagining what's beneath it." She gave an exaggerated shiver. "Ooh!"

Solemnly, Harry said, "He was wounded defending our country at the Peninsula. We should celebrate his heroism, not shy away from him."

"That sounds very noble, but I believe someone who's maimed or very ugly should be mindful of normal people's feelings and stay home. And then if anybody wants to visit that person, they are perfectly free to do so. That seems the solution to me. I cannot believe Aunt Marianne invited him, not with her sensibilities. Of course, she'll probably only put in an appearance, if that, so she won't have to look at him as we will."

The pressure in Audrey's temples had steadily increased

during this speech, and she could not keep quiet an instant longer. "I hope he does come. I should like to be the first to dance with him." She placed her fork next to the remainder of her dessert, which she could not finish, not with her stomach tied in knots from Lucy's heartless words. "Please excuse me, I need to take some air."

She strode from the room before her tears blinded her, leaving behind a great silence.

"You're becoming an absolute witch, are you aware of that?" Harry said to Lucy, crumpling his napkin and throwing it beside his plate. He scraped back his chair and walked angrily away.

"I was only saying what everyone thinks," Lucy called after him. "I didn't mean to sound cruel and she knows it. She's being melodramatic to get your sympathy!"

"Be quiet, Lucy," Thornton was heard to say in a stern voice.

"You're both besotted!" Lucy cried.

Harry had reached the front door by this time and flung it wide. Already the girl had disappeared from sight. Would she have taken the same path the two of them walked the night he kissed her? He wagered not and turned to the right, breaking into a jog. As he cornered the wing of the house, he saw her on the walkway ahead. Within seconds he overtook her and was shocked to find her sobbing uncontrollably. Immediately he put an arm around her waist. After an initial resistance, she relaxed against him as they walked to the nearest bench. As soon as they sat, he offered his handkerchief.

"This threatens to become a habit," she said after a moment, when she grew more calm. "I burst into tears, then you give me your handkerchief. If I'm going to be such a waterfall, I'd better start carrying my own."

"You shouldn't pay attention to Lucy," he said in consoling tones. "She doesn't mean half of what she says."

"Perhaps not, yet I know many people who agree with her about disfigured persons, that they should stay out of sight." Her fists knotted in her lap. "I can't help wondering how *she* would feel if something like that happened to her."

Even with a pink nose and swollen eyes, she was adorable. He scanned her face inquiringly, searching for an answer to the mystery she embodied. "It's kind of you to feel so passionately for the unfortunate."

"It's not kindness," she said fiercely. "I know someone, someone very dear to me, a very beautiful young lady who was injured in a fall. Her perfect face is marred forever." She stroked the side of her cheek as if to illustrate. "And it was my fault," she added in a whisper.

Helplessly he watched her struggle again for control. "I find that hard to believe. Surely it was an accident."

"It *was* an accident, but I had been put in charge of her. Rebecca was nine, and I eleven. We were waiting in the pony cart while my—my guardians shopped at the greengrocer's. Rebecca was adventurous and bored and began climbing all over the cart. I told her to stop—at least I think I did, but perhaps that's only what I hope. After all this time I can't recall with certainty, the whole morning is like a dream to me. A nightmare."

She paused, twisting his handkerchief in her lap. Whatever untruths she had told since her arrival, she spoke truth now. He would stake his honor upon it.

"Whatever I did or didn't do," she continued in tones of self-disgust, "Rebecca continued to climb. We had already made a few stops that day, and several crates of supplies lay in the back, because we seldom came into town and so bought in quantity. Also, there were some kegs of ale we carried for one of our neighbors who ran an inn. I tell you this so that you can visualize there were many items to explore, a fairy-tale land full of caves and mountains and dragons for an imaginative young girl. Watching her, knowing I was helpless to stop her, I became irritated." She lowered her head. "Worse, I felt ashamed."

"Because she wouldn't obey you?"

"How I wish that was the reason." Her eyes lifted, taking in the landscape and the gray, overcast sky. Harry had the feeling she saw nothing. "Across the street from us lay a jewelry shop with a window display that never failed to fascinate me. For as long as I could remember, a collection of music boxes lay behind that dusty window upon a black velvet cloth. Some were very elegant, ormolu on white, with beautiful ladies looking into mirrors. I recall several colorful ones with horses prancing. The box which caught my interest most was a castle set beside the sea."

Darting a sideways glance at him, she came back to the present. "One would think I was starving and the boxes were delicious pastries, the window enchanted me so. On this particular morning, a mother and her two children stood before the shop. From their clothing I perceived they were more prosperous than we, so it did not surprise me that when the jeweler spotted them looking, he wound several of the boxes. I could barely see the tiny figures moving from where I sat, but the little boy began to demand that his mother buy him a horse. As he did, the daughter caught me watching them. 'Who are those dirty children and why are they playing in that pony cart?' she asked loudly. The mother looked at us, shushed both of them, and moved her family inside.

"With them gone, my view was a little better, but I couldn't hear the music, not across the street. So, knowing this might be my only chance for a long time—the jeweler would not indulge penniless children like myself, I had already tried—I slid from the cart and ran to the window."

Sighing, she put her hands to her temples and rubbed.

"I wish it was only my desire to see the boxes that pushed me over there, but I had some ridiculous notion that by doing so I would earn the girl's respect, that she would understand I was part of her world, the world which appreciated beautiful things and wore bright new dresses that matched shoes and hair ribbons should I so desire. I burned for her to understand that I was not ordinary. What foolishness, and all to prove something to someone I never saw again, who never even noticed me outside the window."

She shook her head and continued, her tone darkening, "But Rebecca did. When I left, she decided to follow. In her hurry, she missed her footing on one of the crates and fell head first from the cart. The side of her face was torn deeply by a protruding nail."

The quietness of evening began to spread around them. Harry did not speak for several minutes, feeling her need for a healing space. Her tears had ceased, but he sensed the heaviness of long-held guilt. More proof to him that she was not, could not be, Roxanne. To feel responsible for an unfortunate accident after so many years conveyed integrity, as did her honesty concerning her reasons for leaving her charge. In telling him this, she had opened herself to possible censure. How could she be so honest at one moment and such a liar the next?

Even as his aunt's warnings about flawed character drifted through his mind, he extended one arm across the back of the bench, enclosing but being careful not to touch her. He dared not so much as brush her creamy skin or he would lose control as he had before. No matter how wicked she might be, she entranced him completely. Try as he would to remain objective, a part of him persisted in admiring her despite her lies.

"I am very sorry about what happened to Rebecca," he said. "But you were merely a child and not to be blamed. You should release yourself of sorrow and guilt."

"How can I?" she asked in a ragged voice. "How can I live freely when Rebecca must forever wear the mark of my neglect? There's no release for her. Not that she blames me. No one has ever blamed me. That makes it worse, I think."

"You are your own worst judge."

"Perhaps, but it's deserved. There's nothing I can do to make it up to her. Whatever little things I attempt, it's never enough to compensate for the loss of a normal life. You cannot imagine how lovely she is, Harry. She should have beaux lining up at the door. Were it not for the scar, she might be married by now with a babe in her arms."

"Motherhood at fifteen sounds frightfully young," he said, regretting his words the moment they blurted from his mouth. He could not help his incessant suspicions, but now was not the appropriate time.

Her eyes immediately became guarded. "What?"

Cursing himself, he tapped his fingers on the back of the bench. "You said she was two years younger, I believe. Since Roxanne is seventeen . . ."

"Oh, I see. You never stop, do you?"

"Forgive me?" But he knew exactly what she meant.

"My tongue slips during a weak moment, and you pounce upon my words hoping for proof that I'm not Roxanne."

"I'm sorry for mentioning it, and I do apologize. The mathematics suddenly jumped at me, and I spoke before thinking."

"I was speaking metaphorically. Not that I consider age important anymore, now that I've grown up."

"You do seem unusually mature for seventeen."

She continued as though he had not spoken. "And I think of Rebecca as more of a contemporary now."

"You continue to see her, then? She remains part of your life?"

The intelligent, assessing look she gave him made Harry feel suddenly ashamed. It hurt how much he craved her good opinion when he knew she was untrustworthy herself.

"You're not the only one who can keep secrets," she said, rising.

He accompanied her back to the house, both of them walking in silence.

Eight

For the next two days a deluge stranded the inhabitants of Far Winds indoors, and Audrey, when she was not visiting Marianne, kept to her room as much as possible. While she longed to see Lord Harry, every encounter brought a surge of conflicting emotions which she did not wish to inflict upon herself. As if sensing this and determined to thwart her at every turn, he managed to be present whenever she came downstairs. If the salon was empty and she wandered into it for a respite by the fire, within moments he would arrive. If she entered the music room to stare through the windows at the rain, she could be certain he would be there in an instant. It was as though he followed her, although he inevitably acted surprised at finding her within the room. She could not understand it, for much of the time, other than an initial greeting, he hardly spoke, not even to parry with her verbally; or if he did speak, it was in the way of one stranger passing the time of day with another. Did she not know better, she could almost imagine the night he kissed her so passionately had been a dream.

She found his omnipresence maddening yet endearing. Increasingly she dreaded the day when he discovered the truth about her. How easy it was to imagine the look of contempt that would fill his eyes.

There were other reasons to secret herself upstairs. Fielding barbs and questions and accusations from Lucy held no appeal, and Thornton's casual flirtation, while occasionally amusing, meant nothing to either of them she was sure, but somehow disturbed her.

Thus she hid herself away with books borrowed from the downstairs library. Lady Marianne required her no more than a few hours a day, so she had much time for reading. Sometimes the lady herself asked Audrey to read aloud to her, often bits of poetry or whole chapters from the Bible. She felt relieved to do so, for truly it was difficult to think of things to talk about with the older woman, who seemed bent on recalling past days when Roxanne was small and nothing else. To Audrey's mind she displayed a surprising lack of interest in her missing years, but she felt glad it was so.

Early on Sunday morning, a vicar from Guildford held a worship service in the salon. According to Lyddie, the service had become a tradition since the lady's decline had sharpened some months before. Even with his regular congregation to attend to later that morning, the clergyman was more than willing to perform double duty, the maid said, because the Hastings family had always been generous to the church. As the daughter of a former vicar, Audrey hoped that Christian charity motivated him as well.

Everyone at Far Winds was expected to attend, including the servants. With a degree of pomp, two liveried footmen carried Marianne down the stairs in her chair and set her gently in the center of the room. Lord Harry and Audrey were directed to seats on either side of her, and Thornton and Lucy completed the row. The servants sat behind them in a number of lightweight chairs moved into the room for the occasion. The vicar, still damp from his drive through the rain, stood before the fireplace and led them in prayers and hymns in mellifluous voice.

The Reverend Foggerton seemed a kindly man but a nervous one, as if the grandeur of his surroundings intimidated him. If so, Audrey could not blame him, but as he stumbled through his homily, she began to suspect it was more than that. Again and again his glance returned to Marianne, as if seeking her approval. Curious, Audrey slid a covert look at the lady. With her head leaning back against the chair, the older woman viewed him beneath heavy lids, her aristocratic profile tense and forbidding. Audrey averted her eyes, feeling she had seen something she had rather not.

Perhaps she was being unfair; perhaps it was pain which made Marianne look so imperial.

Audrey's thoughts shifted to the hours she had spent with the lady over the past week. How little she understood the complex woman sitting beside her. At times she seemed benevolent, as Mr. Turner had first painted her and Lord Harry insisted she was; at others her demanding nature made Audrey sympathize with the child Roxanne's dislike—not hate as Lord Harry had suggested; she would not believe a child could hate its parent. The girl must have felt smothered, penned in for her training like a prized colt.

Was it Thornton who had said people were complicated, neither totally good or bad? She was seeing the truth of that more each day in everyone, including herself. It was not a novel thought by any means, but she had never grafted it into her philosophy about others, not truly. Now she wondered about old enemies, people she had considered hopelessly wrong in the past, such as the ones who decided the paltry amount of her father's pension and forced them from the vicarage. The chapel leaders did after all have to provide a place for the new vicar and his family, and there was not much money in the coffers.

Perhaps the smithy, the awful Burl Ingerstand, even had a softer side. Most of all, she wondered about Lord Harry, but he seemed impenetrable. As did Roxanne.

With every passing hour Audrey's curiosity about Roxanne grew stronger. Her frustration at not being able to visit the nursemaid almost drove her mad. Thus when Monday dawned with a heavy mist that burned away by midmorning, she rejoiced as she donned her walking boots and a sturdy carriage dress and prepared to set out.

After informing Lyddie of her destination in case Lady Marianne wanted her, she descended the servant's stair in hopes of avoiding notice. Unfortunately the entire kitchen staff saw her as she slinked through, dodging a strong-looking woman carrying a platter of ham, skirting the pastry table just as the cook scattered a handful of flour over its surface. Holding in a sneeze, Audrey waited until she was outdoors before smacking the white dust from her skirt.

At least Lord Harry hadn't seen her. Her greatest fear was that he would insist upon accompanying her, and she wanted to question Adelaide Spencer alone.

Walking around the west wing of the house, she ignored the drive and cut directly across the side lawn, frightening a pair of birds from the yew hedge into flight. Turning west at the public road as Lyddie directed, she held her skirts above the puddles and hurried as if the devil were at her heels.

In hardly more than a quarter hour, she arrived at the cottage she believed to be Nurse Spencer's. Breathing deeply to calm her racing heart, she viewed with pleasure the little house's thatched roof, narrow mullioned windows, and ivy-covered walls. That Harry and Lady Marianne would provide such pleasant housing for their servants, even a pensioner, spoke well of them. A wooden gate marked off the cottage's boundaries, and simple flat stones led to the front door past a garden rioting with wildflowers. Immediately she wished for such a place for her family, something warm and comfortable and lovely. How happy they could be.

When a diminutive woman admitted her a moment later, the interior did not disappoint. The front parlor was roomy enough for several overstuffed chairs of various patterns and colors, and wooden beams lined the walls and ceiling. Hardly an inch of wall or table space was not covered with paintings, plants, or ceramic figures of children holding toys, removing shoes, shepherding sheep, reading books, studying a globe. Audrey felt dizzy with so much to look at, and it was only when she realized her hostess was weeping that she recalled her mind back to the business at hand.

"I knowed you would come back one day, Miss Roxanne," she was saying, her pink, shriveled cheeks wet with tears. "They couldn't tell me anything would happen to *you.* I knowed you could take care of yourself. Naddie din't raise no birdbrains, I told them, but did anyone listen? No, of course not. Not to the likes of me, they din't."

Heart constricting, Audrey put an arm around the tiny woman's shoulders—she was not accustomed to seeing people smaller than herself and felt very protective and wicked for raising false hopes—and assisted her to the chair nearest the fireplace. Sitting in the chair opposite, she scooted to the edge of the cushion and drew so close that her knees almost touched the nursemaid's.

"You don't doubt that I'm Roxanne? Everyone else does." She winced. "Excepting Mother, of course."

"Huh. I've heard all the talk." The nurse pulled a flowered handkerchief from the sleeve of her bombazine gown and blew her nose. "Nothing gets past old Naddie. Never has, never will. And what's good enough for milady is good enough for me. I heard how she knowed you at sight. I can see why. You're the image of my little Roxy. You look just like I knowed you would."

Smiling painfully, Audrey said, "Thank you, Nurse Spencer."

"Why don't you call me 'Naddie' like you used to?"

"Of course . . . Naddie. Did you also hear that I was in an accident and am having trouble remembering my past?"

The old woman laughed, her faded blue eyes nearly disappearing in a web of wrinkles. "Who don't have trouble remembering! 'Course with me, it's the past I recall and today that I have trouble with!" Worry crinkled her eyes as she looked at a dainty, rose-covered teacup sitting on the table beside her. "Did I offer you tea?"

Audrey begged her not to bother. "I'm glad you can remember the past, because I was hoping you could tell me what I was like as a child."

The nurse stared at Audrey for one suspenseful instant, then glanced away. "How about a hot toddy if you don't want tea?"

After refusing, Audrey watched in surprise as Naddie lifted a gin bottle from a basket beside her chair, filled her teacup to the brim, swallowed several times, and smacked her lips.

"You're right, hinny. Forget the tea, forget the hot, go straight to the toddy, and you will want not." She cackled and struck her knee.

Audrey's eyes widened. "Can you tell me anything, Naddie? About my past?"

"You was a terror, my bairn. Just like your mother before you. She brought me with her from Land's End when she married Sir Hastings. You might have forgot that, but I raised her and many another child. Oh, you both cut out my work for me, that's written in stone, but especially you. You used to put leeches in my bed." The bottle gurgled more clear liquid into the cup. "Now your brother was a dear child. Like his father he was, and it liked to broke my heart when he died. It did break your papa's heart, you know. Just as your going broke milady's."

"Then my mother and I were very close?"

"As close as two cats fighting in a gunny sack." Craftily

she eyed Audrey over her teacup. "You was all she had left by that time. Both of you was too proud to own you cared for each other, and too stubborn in wanting your own way. Just too much alike, that's all. But I knowed you cared."

Fighting despair, for she was not learning anything useful and not likely to with Naddie's eyes beginning to glaze, Audrey asked, "Can you think of anything I might have done the last day I was here?"

Naddie hiccupped and appeared surprised. "I heard you climbed in a wagon and got hit over the head by gypsies."

"Yes, something like that, but much remains vague. I wondered if I came to see you near to the time I disappeared, or if I said anything about running away." Desperately she added, "Maybe I had some habits that were dangerous and you warned me against them. . . ."

"You did plenty of dangerous things. Climbed on the roof of Far Winds once. Was always exploring the countryside with those other two. There's caves around here that you had no business in."

"Caves . . ."

"Yes, that was the first thing they looked into." She blinked in confusion. "Something you said just then . . . what was it?"

"About caves?"

"No, no, before that."

"We were talking about dangerous things. . . . I asked if I'd said anything about running away—"

"That's it! You *did* come to see me not long before you went missing."

"And I spoke of running away?" she asked, hope stirring.

"No. Least I don't recall as you did."

Audrey leaned back in frustration. She could not expect help from this dear little gin-preserved woman, though by the look of concentration on her face, she was trying. Naddie's lips were moving silently and her fingers pointing this way and that as she attempted to relive a conversation seven years ago. It was hopeless.

"You said you were afraid!" Naddie pronounced.

"Afraid?" The colors in the room appeared to fade for a moment. "Of what?"

"I think it was—no, no, that couldn't be."

Audrey slid to the front of the chair, her gown rising to mid-calf in her haste. "Who, Naddie?"

"Oh, I'm an old woman and don't have half my mind left. You were always going on like some actress in a play anyhow. Most of what you talked about was make-believe."

"Who, Naddie?" she repeated, fighting an urge to shake her. "Who?"

She threw back her head, giggling. "You sound like an owl, girl. Now I'm not going to say out loud what this old brain thinks it remembers, but you must have writ it down in that journal of yours or you wouldn't have brought it to me and made me swear on the blood of my head that I would never show it to anyone until you came back to get it."

She wanted to shout aloud her excitement. "Do you still have it?"

"Of course I do! You knowed you could always trust old Naddie! It's . . . now, wait a minute, I'll think of where I put it, just give me time . . . the attic!"

Nearly mad with joy, Audrey was led to the kitchen, where she found a narrow, steep stair leading to a sloping second floor crowded with dusty wooden boxes, broken furniture, piles of rusted tin soldiers, and old stuffed animals that looked as if someone, or something, had gnawed their innards. Did the woman throw nothing away?

Remembering Naddie's admonition to search the trunk first, Audrey held her candle as high as the roof line would allow and half-crouched her way through the maze to an ancient, heavily carved box. She lifted the lid with guarded anticipation. As she feared, the trunk was filled with items, most of them old letters in childish handwriting. Tokens of love from many long-ago charges, Audrey guessed, and was struck with sadness.

After some time of riffling through documents, she found a small diary tooled in red leather. Her hands trembled as she opened to the first page. There, in large, rounded letters, Roxanne had claimed the journal as her own. Audrey clutched it to her chest in gratitude, then flipped through the pages. Excepting the last few leaves, all were covered with writing. The urge to read at least a few entries nearly overwhelmed her, but incessant scrabbling noises had accompanied her entire search; and if she was not wrong, the scratchings were growing louder. Loathe to have company even of the small, four-legged kind as she made her discoveries, she slipped the journal in her pocket and closed the trunk.

She took her leave of the nursemaid as quickly as decency allowed. The path to Far Winds, so short a trek before, seemed to stretch into infinity. She could not wait until she achieved the privacy of Roxanne's bedroom to begin. Looking guiltily around, she saw no one on the lane and pulled out the diary. With frequent glances at the road to avoid puddles, she started to read:

My name is Roxanne Hastings and this is my first diary which my mother has given me to record my thoughts. I have to write in this for a half hour every day. I am eight years old. I don't think my mother cares about my thoughts. She makes me do this to keep me out of the way because she has a new son to take my brother's place. That's not what she says, but it's true. Everybody talks about Lord Harry, Lord Harry, Lord Harry, even my papa. We didn't need another boy. We have Thorn.

*Thorn is my very good friend, and Lucy is too. We don't
like Lord Harry. Lord Harry thinks he is a grown man.
He acts so proud and there is no reason because everybody knows he is a murderer.*

Audrey felt the blood drain from her skin. Suddenly she
didn't want to read any further, not here. She needed privacy and time to reflect, to separate fact from a little girl's
resentment of the—imagined, most certainly—usurpation
of her place in her parents' affection. She slammed the
journal shut and shoved it into her pocket.

By this time she had reached the main road. A hay
wagon passed by, its driver tipping his hat at Audrey, then
giving her an audacious wink when she nodded back.
Thinking it might have been best not to walk alone after
all, she increased her pace. Fortunately, the farmer showed
no further signs of impolite behavior, his wagon narrowing
against the horizon.

Still, her uneasiness persisted. Both sides of the road
were heavily forested. Anything, anyone could be watching
her. She *felt* as though she were being watched.

It's only my imagination, she told herself, and tried to
believe it. The hairs at the nape of her neck began to rise.
Something moved in the undergrowth. There was sudden
quiet.

No birds sang.

The air she breathed became thick with tension. She
could not take it in, could not breathe.

One part of her brain pled for her to bolt. Her body
stubbornly refused. She moved slowly now, as if wading
against a strong current.

Thwang. A brush of air sped past her nose, a blurring
line crossed her vision to pierce an oak on the far side of
the road. An arrow, still quivering. She could see it plainly.

It had passed within a foot of her head.

A hunter, a hapless poacher perhaps. No one had tried to shoot *her*, certainly.

"Look out!" she cried angrily, and was dismayed to hear how much her voice quavered. "Do you not see someone is on the road! You almost struck me!"

Silence. Of course there was silence, she thought, searching the thicket with frantic eyes. No trespasser would give himself away by screaming out an apology.

She tried to move forward but could not. Her bones were paralyzed. She had never felt so vulnerable and afraid in her life.

When a second arrow whizzed by and landed in the oak an inch lower than the first, her paralysis ended. She dived for the ditch opposite the archer and lay as flat as she could. But this was no good. Her attacker could simply cross the road and kill her. She had no defense. She must get away, lose herself in the forest. Perhaps she could make it back to Naddie's cottage and send for help.

Shivering in fear, she crawled upward from her hiding place, staying as close to the ground as she could, her eyes transfixed by the two arrows piercing the tree above her.

A piece of cloth hung from the second arrow. A puff of wind turned the scrap slightly. She saw letters. Something was printed there.

A message.

She eyed the symmetry of the arrows. This was not the work of a poacher. Only an expert marksman could align the arrows so precisely. Someone had drawn her attention with a warning shot—which only missed her by inches—and then sent her a message—which also only missed her by inches.

If the archer thought she would now stand up and read that message, he or she was quite mistaken. She would not willingly make herself a target again. The marksman might not miss her the next time.

She did not want to think about who would do such a thing.

But who was she deluding? The archer could only be Lucy. Or Thorn; his sister had accounted him with an accurate eye. Or even Harry, who was at this moment riding toward her at breakneck speed.

It could not be the baron who had launched arrows at her, she told herself. There hadn't been enough time for him to flee through the woods and mount his horse and ride toward her. Had there?

Everybody knows he is a murderer. Roxanne's words rolled painfully through her mind, as if they had been etched there for all time.

But she needed help, and he looked to be intent on riding past her. If he had shot at her, he'd certainly know she was cowering beside the road. That in itself must be proof of something. Timidly, supporting herself against the oak, she rose and called his name.

He pulled up his fine black, who snorted and pawed the air at the indignity of such an abrupt stop. Looking shocked, the baron took in her soiled gown and mussed hair.

"What happened?" he demanded, climbing down and approaching with fire in his eyes. "I thought you were visiting the nursemaid. Has someone harmed you? Did you fall?"

So he had been searching for her. Someone from the kitchen must have told him. Or Lyddie, traitorous maid. *Wonderful* maid.

"Someone shot arrows at me," she said, her teeth chattering. Reaction was setting in, embarrassing her. She wanted to appear brave for him.

"What!" He grabbed both of her shoulders and peered into her eyes as if he did not, or could not, believe her. Wordlessly she pointed to the tree.

He released her. She watched him closely as he eyed the arrows, then tried to pry the uppermost one. It did not give easily. He didn't bother with the second, but snatched the piece of cloth from its shaft, glanced at it and stuffed the scrap into his breast pocket.

He turned to her, his eyes ravaged, his cheeks suffused with color. "Stay here. I'm going to search the wood."

"No, don't! It's too dangerous."

But he was already on the opposite side of the road, peering into the undergrowth. After a few moments he returned.

"No one's there now. I'll take a better look later. I wish you had told me you were leaving and I would have accompanied you. Don't go out alone again. Promise me."

"What did the note say?" she asked, thinking: *Either he is the greatest actor in the world, or he could not have done this to me.*

Abruptly he swept her into his arms. She sank against him in dizzy relief, feeling protected beyond reason. Surely nothing bad could happen to her now. She turned her cheek against his coat, relishing the gentle roughness of the material, the clean masculinity of his scent. She fancied she could hear his heart beating beneath her ear.

"It doesn't matter," he said.

She pulled back a hand's span to gaze into his eyes. He was staring into the wood across the road with a fierce expression.

"Someone nearly killed me. It matters to me."

He pulled her close again and murmured into her hair, "Whoever shot those arrows didn't intend to kill you or he would have. The message is a piece of nonsense. Let's get you home, then I'll come back to search the wood." With his arm circling her waist, he pressed her toward his horse. Once they reached the road, she slipped from his embrace and planted her feet defiantly.

"I am not moving until you show me that piece of cloth," she said.

He pulled at her hand. "Our enemy could still be hidden, watching us. We need to get to safety."

"As far as I can judge, he—or she—is not *our* enemy but *mine*," she said rapidly, irritated beyond measure. Was he trying to protect her or drive her mad? "And that message was intended for me. If you wish to hurry, you'd best give it to me now."

"Must you be so stubborn?" he cried.

"Must *you?*" she returned.

Rolling his eyes heavenward, he jerked a hand into his pocket and handed her the ragged cloth. She stretched it between trembling hands. The words were printed with jagged, bleeding strokes where the ink had run. The handwriting looked purposefully childish. It could be anyone's.

Imposter, go away, she read. *No one wants you here. Leave or Die.*

She looked up. The baron regarded her with solemn eyes. Without speaking a word, she handed the hateful message back to him. He replaced it in his coat pocket and lifted her sideways onto his saddle. Swinging up behind her, he pulled taut the reins, his arms encircling her to do so. Before clicking the horse into motion, he leaned forward, his cheek brushing hers. She felt the contact all the way down to her toes.

"Pay it no mind," he said quietly. "Whoever sent that is the lowest kind of coward."

Audrey silently agreed that the hidden archer must lack bravery. But weren't many murderers cowards? She did not argue but leaned back against him, enjoying his strength and wishing she could believe the words of a man who had every reason to want her gone.

Nine

When they reached Far Winds and Harry assisted the girl to the ground, he knew her dishevelment and shocked eyes would cause instant alarm within the house. He steadied her a moment before leading her beneath the portico. Brushing a leaf from her hair, he felt a tremor run through his body at what might have happened. He could not imagine a happy end for her treacherous charade, but the last thing he wanted was to see her come to harm.

Obviously someone within the walls of Far Winds did not share his sentiments.

"I wish we needn't tell anyone what occurred, but there's no avoiding it, I'm afraid. If we don't give an explanation for your appearance and our arrival together, the servants will imagine even worse things."

She looked instantly doubtful and measuring, as if his statement had made her suspicious of *him*. She didn't trust him, not entirely; he'd sensed that before today. How it disturbed that he must return the feeling. There was a deep wrongness in their relationship, if relationship it could be called, and it rankled. The only woman for whom he had felt anything since Carradice, and she was as conniving as the first.

He brushed away his anger. This deceitful angel had

nearly been killed on his own property. His aunt had been correct, as always; she needed his protection. The little fool. Didn't she realize she was endangering her life with her act?

"I think it best we downplay what happened," he continued. "We could call it an accident and demand to know who was so careless."

"But what is the point of that?" she asked. "We could tell the truth and still ask questions."

"If we seem annoyed rather than desperate, the servants will be more forthcoming. It will give us free rein to question everyone as to their whereabouts during the crucial time. Almost everyone on the estate has taken a turn at the bow. We even hold competitions at our harvest time celebration."

"You don't really believe a servant is at fault, do you?"

So she suspected Thorn or Lucy, as he did. And she suspected him as well. "Who knows what goes through anyone's mind? There are several servants who anticipate sizable bequests when my aunt passes. One of them could be worried she might change her will exclusively to you."

"The message," she whispered. "Whoever did this will know there was a message."

"We'll say nothing of that. And then if the archer doesn't confess, and if our questions don't reveal the villain, then perhaps curiosity at our silence will force him to make a mistake."

"What kind of mistake?" she asked numbly. "Shooting me, perhaps?"

He kissed her forehead gently. He hadn't meant to, but there it was. "Don't be afraid," he told her. "I'll be watching."

Her luminous, sober eyes tilted upward, and he saw his words offered her little comfort. Such beautiful eyes they were, reminding him of the achingly blue skies of spring and the innocent frolicking of lambs among clover. *You are lost, lost,* he chided himself. Swallowing an unwanted and inappropriate tide of emotion, he pointed an admonishing finger and tapped the end of her perfect nose.

"Don't you dare stir from this house without telling me first," he said, and would not permit her to break away until she agreed.

While Lord Harry went to question the servants, Audrey permitted herself to be cossetted by an exclaiming Lyddie, who, as soon as she heard the news, had rushed to bring hot water for a bath and scurried off to press a fresh gown. Audrey surreptitiously removed Roxanne's journal and hid it between her sheet and mattress before the maid returned. Later she would find a better hiding place. For now she was content to luxuriate in the warmth of the hip bath and the smooth glide of perfumed soap upon her skin. Eventually her legs stopped trembling, and when she rose from the bathwater and wrapped herself inside a thick white towel, she felt somewhat restored.

After she dressed and Lyddie finished her hair, Audrey sent the maid away. There remained an hour before she was due at luncheon, thank God. Let Harry question anyone he wished; she intended to devour as much of Roxanne's diary as she could.

She had no faith in the success of the baron's endeavor. No one would confess, not even a servant, for fear of losing his or her position. And she could not believe a servant was responsible anyway. Not unless he had been hired by Thorn or Lucy. Although Lucy was her favorite contender—she had been unreasonably disturbed on the day of the archery competition, had even acted humiliated at her defeat, and such a one as Lucy might think it clever to frighten her by the same means—she must not forget that Harry could have been responsible as well. The thought made her want to weep.

Propping pillows at her head and taking care not to wrinkle her gown, she lay upon the bed and began to read.

As the moments ticked by, she became increasingly perturbed. Some of the entries were simple catalogues of daily activities, often citing games Roxanne had played with Thorn and Lucy, or outings they had taken. But many bespoke an uneasy relationship with her mother, especially after the death of Sir Hastings, when the diary took on a darker tone. The little girl had loved her father deeply, that was plain, and her sorrowful childish phrases of grief wrung Audrey's heart.

After her father's death, Roxanne's hatred of Lord Harry became even more evident. She accused him of purposefully stealing her father's last days from her. That she had been spending a much-anticipated fortnight at Brighton with her governess and Lucy and Thorn at the time of her sire's death did not figure in her reasoning. But children were not often reasonable, Audrey excused. She knew the loss of a parent and how it disturbed the rightness of the world.

She thumbed the remaining pages impatiently. Almost halfway through, and nothing of usable information about the baron had been mentioned; nothing more about his being a murderer. By this time Roxanne had reached her ninth birthday, a gloomy-sounding celebration with her father gone. Audrey eyed the clock and saw she had only twenty minutes before the noon meal. She considered taking luncheon in her room, but that would signal weakness to whomever had used her as target practice this morning. Sighing, she returned to the diary, determined to read until the last moment.

When the gong reverberated through the house in what seemed mere seconds later, she tore her gaze from the page she had read and re-read and walked to the wardrobe. Moving woodenly, she stared at her gowns, selected a clean, plain one near the end, and secreted the journal into its far pocket. She must go downstairs, she must. She had to act normally.

Lord Harry could not know what she knew, or her life would not be worth a feather.

"Well, don't look at me, *I* had nothing to do with the accident," Lucy said over a plate of cold beef and fresh garden greens. "I was upstairs sleeping."

"No one has accused you," Harry said mildly.

"I see it in your eyes," she retorted.

"That's the first sign of guilt, I hear," Thorn said, apparently enjoying his sister's discomposure. "Seeing accusations in everyone's eyes but your own."

"Oh, stop it, Thorn," she said crossly. "You know I'm not capable of such a thing."

He shrugged and opened his hands outward. "I know nothing about anyone. Life has taught me that."

"It's good you've learned something," Lucy said.

Audrey nibbled at a morsel of spinach which seemed to expand and splinter within her mouth. Neither brother or sister seemed unduly surprised at her morning's incident, nor did they appear overly upset.

She hardly cared. All she could think about was finishing the journal. Roxanne had at last recounted what happened to make Harry leave his own estate and live at Far Winds. The account was so horrific that it stretched belief. She must ask someone of its truthfulness, perhaps Lady Marianne. Audrey did not want to disturb a sick woman with such unpleasantries, but she had to know. Her own safety depended upon it.

Once one murder had been committed, surely others would come easier to the murderer.

She dabbed her eyes with her napkin, then saw Lord Harry watching her with compassion. Quickly she dropped her gaze to her plate and traced lines in her beef with the fork.

"Did anyone see you sleeping, sister?" Thorn was saying with a teasing light in his eyes. "Harry wants proof, I daresay."

"Of course no one saw me sleeping, imbecile. What were *you* doing?"

"Shooting." Meeting Audrey's startled look, he chuckled. "Guns, not arrows, my dear. The dogs are frothy with the sweat of our journey to the back meadow, and I have a brace of quail for our dinner to prove it." Around a mouthful of bread, he added, "Nothing could make me want to hurt you."

Lucy said, "There you are, Harry. Whatever happened was an accident. *If* it happened at all, that is." She slid a meaningful glance at Audrey.

The faint lines bracketing the baron's mouth deepened. "I saw the arrows with my own eyes."

"Yes, but who shot them?"

"That is the question. I hope you're not suggesting she did so herself."

"It would be a means of gaining attention," Lucy suggested.

Audrey had had enough. "Only you would think of such a way."

"Ho!" shouted Thorn. "She has you there, Lucy!"

Sick to death of their bickering, Audrey excused herself and walked from the room. Before she could mount the stairs, she heard the baron's voice behind her. With one hand on the newel post, she turned slowly. When he drew near to her, it was all she could do not to shrink away.

"Don't let them disturb you," he said quietly, his gaze moving across her face. "I try to ignore them as much as possible. Of course I know you're afraid now, but as long as you're not alone, you should be all right."

Struggling to keep her expression blank, she thought, *As long as I am not alone with* you. "I'll try to remember," she said, turning to ascend.

His hand on her arm stayed her. "I'm sorry I haven't been able to find out anything useful from the servants, other than weeding out those who vouch for one another."

"I confess I'm not surprised."

"Take heart," he encouraged, misunderstanding the source of her doleful tone. "I haven't done with the servants yet, and I'm planning to search the wood this afternoon. Maybe the archer was careless and left evidence."

"May fortune go with you then," she said, and, jerking her arm from his fingers, rushed up the stairs.

I've begun to call him Lord Murder every time I see him. He hates it. I am glad, because he deserves such words. Yesterday he caught me and said he wouldn't let me go until I stopped calling him that. I was afraid but I laughed and said I would tell Mother. That stopped him. But he means to hurt me, I know he does. I said as much to Mother, but she would not hear of it. Her precious Lord Murder can do no wrong. So I shall just have to take care of myself. He is so strong.
I am afraid.

It was the final entry. Audrey closed the journal, laid it aside, and covered her face with her hands. After a moment she crept from bed as slowly as an old woman might, then splashed her face with water and patted dry with a monogrammed linen towel. Everywhere she looked were remind-

ers of him. She could not even wipe her hands without
seeing the Hastings stamp of ownership.

Surely he had not done away with the child. Please, God.

Lifting her gaze to the mirror, she saw a young woman
she hardly recognized. The change was all in her eyes, she
thought; her shocked, disillusioned, desolate eyes. Papa and
Rebecca would not know her when she returned.

If she lived to return.

But Roxanne was an embittered and unforgiving girl,
pled a small voice of reason. Before condemning the baron
as a murderer twice over, she must have confirmation that
Marianne's daughter could be trusted. If so, Audrey had no
choice. She would have to show the lady her daughter's
journal and let her draw her own conclusions.

Too late, she reflected now that she probably should have
given the diary to Lady Marianne at once, before greedily
reading it herself. That would have been Papa's advice, certainly, even though it meant the end of her pretense and
the loss of the money. If her own dear mother had lost one
of her daughters, she would have wanted any information
pertaining to them.

But she had her own reasons to seek understanding, and
no one would tell her anything. And now that the deed was
done, she hesitated to betray the baron without further
proof. Despite everything, she wanted him to be innocent.
He had shown her kindness in spite of disbelieving her
impersonation—although that conviction took on more sin-
ister overtones now—and she could not forget the warm
regard of his eyes or the touch of his hands. And his kisses,
she could never, *ever* forget those.

Oh, she may as well admit it; her heart leapt gladly at
the very sight of him. Could her spirit be so terribly, hor-
ribly wrong?

One further thought soothed her indecision. If Roxanne
had wanted her mother to possess her diary, she would

have given it to her. There were a number of entries that would hurt Marianne deeply. Audrey saw no reason to fracture her pleasant memories so cruelly, not unless absolutely necessary.

For now, she believed her best course lay in discovering if Roxanne's diary was fact or fiction. Taking a deep breath, she crossed the hall to Lady Marianne's room. Bertha greeted her sweetly and led her through the sitting room to milady's chamber. To her surprise, Audrey found Lady Marianne sitting in a bedside armchair and reading, her feet propped upon a plump cushion.

"There you are," Lady Marianne said, putting aside her book and smiling while extending her arms. "I'd begun to wonder if you intended to see me today."

"I'm sorry I'm later than usual this afternoon," Audrey said, pressing her hands but not moving nearer for an embrace or a kiss. During her first few days she had been chagrined to discover that the lady disliked closer contact. "I was resting."

"I'm not surprised after what you went through this morning. Truth, I wouldn't have been offended if you'd slept all day. What a horrible accident!"

"So they told you. I wish no one had." Audrey glanced at Bertha, who blushed and bustled from the room. "I don't want you to worry."

"Oh, I miss very little in this house," Marianne said. "But I'm sensible enough to know how easily a hunter can miss his mark. What *does* worry me is your walking unaccompanied. Now you must promise me that you won't do so again, do you understand? Walk or ride anywhere you wish, but have Harry go with you. Tell me you will, child."

Audrey forced a smile and murmured, hoping the lady would take that for agreement and not press the issue. Hurriedly she added, "Speaking of Lord Harry . . . I've been wondering about him. About how and why he came to live here, I mean."

The lady fixed her gaze upon Audrey, her expression growing austere. "I thought you understood that he is my husband's heir, and that he came to Far Winds shortly before Sir Hastings's death to help with the estate."

"Yes, I did know that." Swallowing her discomfort, Audrey told herself she could not allow Marianne's disapproval to halt her questions, not this time. "But I would assume he is his own father's heir as well? I'm guessing his father is deceased, since Harry has the title, but no one ever talks of him."

"And no one ever will, for I forbid it."

"But he *is* deceased," Audrey pressed.

"Of course he is. He died before Harry came to us."

"But what of the late baron's estate? Who manages it?"

Marianne made a noise in the back of her throat. "What estate? There was nothing left to inherit, thanks to Edward's gambling and bad investments."

So Far Winds was all Harry owned after all, not one of many estates as she had once imagined. All the more reason to defend its loss any way he could, she thought sadly. Summoning all her courage, for this was the heart of her query and the crucial part of Roxanne's jottings, she asked, "And how did Lord Harry's father die?"

The lady's eyes narrowed. "You are very inquisitive today. Why such curiosity about Harry?"

"It's his father I want to know about," she said carefully.

"Don't be impudent. I refuse to discuss anything about my husband's notorious brother."

"Please, Mother—"

"Have the servants been gossiping?" she interrupted loudly, sounding stronger than Audrey had heard her, sounding healthy in her anger, healthy and *well*. "Tell me

who has spoken to you, I demand it! They have known for
years to keep quiet!"

"No one has said anything—"

Sudden voices in the sitting room drew their attention,
and, squeaking with pleasure and flapping her apron, Bertha ushered Nathan Turner into the bedchamber. Audrey
felt a surge of joy at the sight of him. Surely now she
would find answers.

"I knew you'd want to see him as soon as he arrived,
milady!" the maid exclaimed.

"Nathan, at last!" cried the lady, her anger forgotten.
"You are welcome indeed. I had not expected you to be
gone this long!"

"Mr. Turner," Audrey breathed, her gaze locking with his
for an instant.

The steward, hat in hand, bowed to both ladies. He
looked younger than Audrey remembered, and his eyes
were bright. She could not read his expression, though.

Lady Marianne said, "Now, Nathan, I want a full report.
But before you begin, I think it best that Audrey leave us
so that you may speak freely."

Having expected no better, trying but failing to capture
Mr. Turner's glance once more, Audrey left the room and
entered Roxanne's bedroom feeling strangely anxious.
Leaving the door open wide, she scooted a wing chair to
the foot of the bed in order to watch the corridor. The
moment Mr. Turner left Lady Marianne's room, she would
pounce.

She tried not to think about why he had avoided her
gaze, or why he had looked so . . . troubled, was it? Maybe
he only hated lying to his employer about Audrey's "past."
Perhaps Lady Marianne's recovery had surprised him into
considering how they could decently end her role.

He might be dreading telling Audrey that he could not
pay her after all.

Surely he was not considering exposing the truth about her. He wouldn't do that without a warning. Would he? She knew very little about him.

Once again she labeled herself a goose for accepting this hare-brained scheme. Nothing good was coming from it. She hardly minded that she would not be paid. She simply wanted to go home, to hear Papa's soothing voice and Rebecca's scolding one, which now seemed endearing. Even the marketplace and their austere cottage were preferable to the intrigue and innuendos and criminal behavior found at Far Winds. She could not wait to put this chapter of her life behind her.

You lie, a voice told her as she recalled the feeling of the baron's arms around her, the angle of his jaw and beauty of his lips as he touched his mouth to hers. *Liar, liar, liar.*

After what seemed hours, Mr. Turner emerged from Lady Marianne's sitting room and closed the door softly behind him. Audrey flew to his side. Whispering, she urged him toward her bedroom, but he would not hear of it. "What would people think if they saw me there, Miss Lassiter?" he whispered back, his eyes scanning the corridor. "I'll come to you tonight when everyone's asleep."

Her fingers clenched into fists at her sides. "I cannot wait until tonight, I've waited too long already! I need to know how Lord Harry's father died, and I need to know now!"

"I can't say, miss, it's forbidden."

She grabbed the lapels of his coat. "Tell me!"

Looking considerably taken aback, he said, "Very well, but the story's not quickly told. I'll give you the history tonight. I've left my horse untended in front, and I—"

"I don't care about your horse! If you don't—"

The sound of footsteps charging up the stairs brought her to a halt. She discerned Lucy and Thorn talking excitedly, their voices growing nearer. Reluctantly she released the steward and stepped back. An instant later, the siblings appeared at the end of the corridor.

"Nathan! We heard you were back!" Thorn called.

"What news have you brought?" Lucy chimed, giving Audrey a dismissive glance.

Smiling showily, Mr. Turner whispered from the side of his mouth, "Your family is well, by the way," then raised his voice to answer the Browns, "You must ask Lady Marianne. The news is not mine to give." In another aside, he said quietly, "Except for a minor incident with Mr. Ingerstand, but all is fine now."

She had almost forgotten that he had promised to visit her family. "What minor incident?" she hissed.

But he could not answer; Thorn and Lucy were too near. Audrey thought she might scream with frustration. And guilt. She should have asked about her loved ones before anything else. Her present worries were throwing off her priorities.

At that moment, Bertha opened the door. "Milady heard you, Master Thorn and Miss Lucy," she said, while looking only at Audrey, as if mesmerized by her. "She wants you to come inside. I was to fetch you, miss. Lord Harry, too."

"He's out in the wood somewhere, I think," Thorn said. "Searching for arrowheads, no doubt."

The maid nodded and signaled them to enter. Thinking only black thoughts, Audrey allowed herself to be shepherded into the lady's presence again. With pain she watched Mr. Turner hang back and turn down the hall. If he had betrayed her, he was not going to be present for the unmasking, the coward.

Her heart drummed against her chest as if it wanted out.

But Lady Marianne's face was wreathed in smiles; surely that was a good sign. "Come in, children. Come in. Lucy and Thorn, it looks as though you shall be the first to know, and I expect you to spread the word. Although I never doubted this young lady was my daughter, our Nathan has brought the final proof of an entire neighborhood in Bournemouth. Now let there be an end to speculations and conjectures. Welcome with open arms my daughter, Roxanne!"

"That's impossible!" Lucy screeched. "No!"

"How very interesting," Thorn said, his face paling. He turned to Audrey, his eyes flat with suppressed emotion. "Didn't I say I was coming to believe you? To have my suspicions confirmed by an impeccable source is . . . gratifying. Allow me to be the first to welcome you home, Roxanne."

"Thank you," Audrey said perfunctorily over Lucy's moans. "Thank you all. Would you excuse me, please? There's something I must do."

Without waiting for permission, she fled the suite, raced down the corridor and stairs and out the front door. Mr. Turner, thankfully on foot, was leading his horse toward the stable. Audrey plucked her skirts higher and ran as fast as she could. By the time she reached him, she was out of breath and had to endure his exasperated look as she propped one hand against the horse's saddle and recovered.

"Now, what's this about Burl Ingerstand?" she gasped. "Is Rebecca all right?"

"Yes, Miss Lassiter, she's well; as is your da. I already told you." Seeing storm clouds gathering in her face, he hastened on, "The smithy was making a nuisance of himself, going on about how Miss Rebecca had said he could court her. When she let him know she wasn't interested, he still persisted, bringing her flowers that paled beside the ones she grows herself—she's quite a hand at the garden, isn't she?" Audrey opened her mouth to agree, but he didn't give her time. "And her vegetables are better than any I've ever tasted, bursting with flavor they are, and crunchy to the teeth. She's a fine cook, your sister, and doesn't boil her produce 'til it dies like most do."

"Burl Ingerstand," she reminded.

"Oh yes. Anyway, he started bringing her little trinkets from his shop, strange metal concoctions which he designed for her and expected to see mounted on the walls. He has little talent, I fear. The last he brought was a set of horse shoes with Miss Rebecca's name scratched in them—Rebecca Ingerstand."

"My goodness!"

"That's what she said. So, seeing that his attentions were unwanted, and as I was having dinner there at the time—I'd brought a fine slab of ham to go with her potatoes and vinegared spinach—I stood up and claimed she was to be my bride and to leave her alone."

She clasped her hands together. "How magnificent of you! I know Rebecca is grateful for your pretense, as I am. . . ."

"Well," he said, turning pink.

She didn't hear. Something had been troubling her during their conversation, and now, as Mr. Turner's horse stamped and snorted with impatience, her eyes focused on the cause of it.

A bow was slung over the pommel of his saddle.

A bow and a quiver of arrows.

Ten

Lord Harry returned to the stables in time to dress for dinner. He was tired and discouraged from an afternoon spent searching the wood and questioning servants without much to show for his trouble. Although he had discovered a well-foliated hollow bordering the road that could provide a likely hiding place, no tell-tale lost buttons littered the ground, nor did strands of hair glimmer Absolom-like from branches. And though the earth was disturbed by footprints, the forest's carpet of pine needles and dead leaves made identifying the size and type of shoe impossible.

An interview with the groundskeeper produced nothing more than the shamefaced acknowledgment that the out-building which housed their gaming equipment had been unlocked all day and was accessible to anyone on the estate. All of the bows were in place, the servant had offered in a humble voice, but that meant nothing, either; the culprit could have replaced the bow as easily as he took it, as no one had seen anyone enter or leave at any time. Suspecting the groundskeeper of spending his morning smoking in the stable with the stableboys, Harry had given him a stern dressing-down and ordered him to keep the building locked in the future.

Handing over Fortune, his black, to James, the head

groom, Lord Harry loosened his cravat and spied a familiar bay in the third stall. "Is Nathan back?" he asked, his stomach knotting. Until this moment he hadn't realized how anxiously he'd awaited the steward's return and the news he would bring.

"Yes, milord, he's checking the roof at Tober's cottage like the lady asked him to. That last rain busted a hole right through it and their bed's sittin' open to the sky. No rest for Turner, eh?" The old fellow wrinkled his hooked nose, gave a coughing laugh, then signaled regally for a stable boy to remove Fortune's saddle. "I guess you don't know then, what he's said. That 'un up there? That girl? She's our Roxanne a'ter all. The lady is beside herself with joy. Now what think ye o' that, milord?"

Harry felt as if the world had tipped too far on its axis. He made some sort of reply and turned toward the house, his steps slow and labored.

It couldn't be.

But Nathan wouldn't lie, nor was he incompetent. So it must be true.

He had been so certain she was not Roxanne. But he could be wrong. He'd been wrong before, hadn't he?

Remembering, his mouth twisted in self-disgust. No point in going over that again; the nightmare was well in the past.

That nightmare was, but now he had a fresh one—one more painful than the last, if such was possible.

Roxanne . . . his cousin.

He was in love with her, God help him. In love with a cousin of the first degree.

Of course cousins had fallen in love before, had even married. But such was frowned upon. Marianne would disapprove; she had already made that plain. And didn't such marriages spawn more than the usual number of sickly, weak-minded children? One had only to look at certain monarchies.

What a fool he had been.

A flush spread upward from his collar as a succession of scenes played through his mind: him chasing and catching Roxanne as though she were an escaped prisoner during her first moments at Far Winds; throwing his doubts in her face like blows; grabbing and kissing her as freely as he would a wanton.

And all along, she was right and he was wrong. How was it she even deigned to speak with him? He saw his actions over the past week as those of a self-righteous, overpassionate madman. Thornton had behaved better toward her than he.

Tidwell opened the door for him at the house, his eyes meeting the baron's with something like sympathy. Harry could not respond; his face felt as immovable as rock. Lucy heard him enter and rushed from the salon to embrace him tearfully.

"Have you heard, Harry? Oh, have you heard? They're saying she truly is Roxanne! I still can't believe it! Roxanne and I were so close, surely I would recognize her? Oh, what are we to do?"

Patting her back absently, he murmured soothing nonsense while Thornton emerged and leaned against the doorway, his features grave. He lifted his shoulders and shook his head. Harry found himself shaking his head in response. Sharing sentiments with Thornton was enough to stir him back to reality. He set Lucy aside and headed for the stairs.

"What are you going to do?" she wailed, trailing him.

"I'm going to change and visit Aunt, and then I'm coming down for dinner."

"But what are we going to do about *her?*"

"The moment I set eyes on Roxanne again, I intend to

apologize for my appalling behavior. I suggest you do the same."

This was clearly not what Lucy wanted to hear, but he had no time for her hysterics. After washing up and dressing in his favorite tan jacket, he visited awhile with his aunt, who, as expected, was brimming over with details about how many families Nathan had visited and how glorious was their praise of the girl they had known as Mary Hill.

"But why so glum, my dear?" she asked, finally winding down. "Surely this news brings you joy, to have your cousin restored to you."

"I haven't been as kind to her as I should."

She waved that away, as if it were a trivial thing. "Roxanne will forgive you for that. There's no need for you to feel low. After all this time, doubts were to be expected."

He hoped she was correct. He was of two minds on the matter. A part of him could not wait to set things right with her, to make amends and at the same time see if he could adjust his feelings to a more cousinly nature. Because he seriously doubted he would ever be able to feel toward her as a blood relation should, another part of him wanted to settle behind the woodwork like a particle of dust and remain there.

But at dinner he was unable to find out either way, for Roxanne took the meal in her room. When he scribbled a note asking her to meet him for a stroll that evening, she sent a polite refusal via Lyddie. Discouraged, he established himself in the salon with a bottle of claret and outlasted both Lucy and Thornton, who gave up trying to engage him in conversation or cards and eventually went up to their beds.

Although it was temperate in the house, he built a fire to keep him company and stared into the flames, one leg on the settee, the other braced against the floor. He had no desire to toss and turn in his own bed. Eventually the warmth and alcohol dulled his misery, and he dozed.

Sometime during the night, fitful with broken dreams, he snapped awake and peered at the clock on the mantel. It was a few minutes past midnight. He ran his fingers through his hair and felt despair returning with brute force. Longing for oblivion, he eyed the half-empty claret bottle. As he reached for it, a muffled noise, unexpected in its stealthiness, stayed his hand. His senses fired to alertness. That was not the sound of a house settling. Someone was walking on the stairs. He was glad to see the fire had collapsed to embers and would not illuminate him to the thief. Moving silently, he slipped into the hall and could not believe his eyes.

"Nathan?" he wondered aloud in a heavy whisper.

Halfway up the stairs, the shadowed figure froze, then turned slowly. "Why, my lord," Nathan whispered hoarsely. "You're—you're up late this evening."

"As are you." As the baron moved forward, the steward descended with obvious reluctance. "What are you doing here?" Their most trusted servant, Nathan had been given his own tenant farm and lived on the outermost edge of the estate.

Moonlight slanted through the windows on either side of the door and emphasized the steward's pallor. "I—I forgot my hat upstairs."

"And you were coming to retrieve it at midnight?" he asked incredulously.

"I don't know what I was thinking, my lord."

"Wait a moment," the baron said, understanding coming to him all at once. "I've interrupted an assignation, haven't I?"

If possible, the steward turned even more pale. "No, my lord. No, nothing like that, I assure you."

"Relax, Nathan, I won't condemn you. Who's the lucky girl? The new downstairs maid?"

His lips grimaced into a ghoulish smile. "A gentleman never tells."

"Indeed he doesn't. Well, I won't plague you further, but I have to say I can't approve since the servants are under my protection when beneath this roof."

"No, of course not," Nathan said, shaking his head vigorously. "I've been wrong in coming, but I'll be going now."

Harry gave him a companionable slap on the shoulder. "Too bad you didn't use the servants' stair. I wouldn't have known the difference."

"I was going to, but the scullery maid fell asleep on them. She'd been into the port, I think. The bottle was empty beside her."

"I'll have Tidwell speak with her. Come, don't look so ashamed, Nathan. I don't think any less of you." He felt awkward framing his next words, for he did not want to scold a man over five years his senior about such matters. Still, it must be said, though he softened his message with a smile. "Now, what you do on your own property is your own business. Just be careful you don't get one of ours with child and find yourself walking down the aisle for your trouble."

"No, sir," the steward said miserably. Head down, brushing past the baron, Nathan mumbled farewell.

"Good night, Nathan," Harry said pleasantly, and wandered back to the salon feeling much lighter. People would never stop surprising him. Then it occurred that he had been so startled he hadn't asked a question about Roxanne. His spirits plummeting again, he poured another glass and stared into the darkness of the room.

But after a sip, he found he had no taste for the wine anymore and set it aside. Sighing, he walked to the window and stared out, bracing his hands on the sill. The moonlight and a soft wind played light-and-shadow games with the hedge and shrubbery. As he watched, a rabbit loped across the garden then stopped to sniff the air, loped and stopped again, continuing the pattern until it disappeared from sight. "The vegetable garden is in back, foolish," he whispered, then wondered why he should be so concerned with one of the creatures who plagued his gardener's existence. Well, it provided a diversion, and he couldn't sleep. He turned a side chair to face outward and prepared to observe more moonlit dramas.

Thus he was awake when he heard the stairs creak again nearly an hour later. His back stiffening in outrage—was this subterfuge at work every night at Far Winds, and he had missed it sleeping like a child all these years?—he stood and approached the hall, half expecting to find the maid Nathan had intended to visit, going in search of him. When he cornered the doorway, he did spy a feminine figure on the stairs, but she was the last person in the universe he would have expected.

"Roxanne?" he hissed.

She was so startled that she visibly jumped and nearly lost her balance, a valise falling from her hand and tumbling softly to the bottom stair. He was not too stunned to recognize the satchel as the pitiful one she had arrived with, as was her attire, a simple muslin gown and a frayed bonnet.

But her beauty shone undimmed by the lack of finery, he also noted as the slow, silent seconds ticked by, for nothing could hide the golden gleam of her curls or the luminosity of her eyes, which were now fixed upon his in terror.

"Were you going somewhere?" he asked, when it appeared she would not, or could not, speak. A sudden, sickening thought occurred. "Did you plan a tryst with

Nathan?" He would kill the steward before he allowed him to touch her. Surely the man had not already—

Instead of answering, she whirled and began to run up the stairs. He caught her in a trice, and when she squeaked the beginnings of a scream he drew her backward into his arms and whispered against her cheek, "Please speak to me, Roxanne, don't run from me. Don't scream. Surely you realize I wouldn't hurt you. I know I've been harsh with you. I've been unfair in not believing you, but that was because"—here he drew his lips more closely to her ear, for he felt the tension slowly leaving her body—"I never believed I could feel toward Roxanne the way I feel about you."

She shifted in his arms, turning to face him, her eyes intent on his. "How—how *do* you feel about me?"

"Don't tease, Roxanne," he said gently, releasing her by degrees, his hands traveling down her shoulders and arms and linking with her fingers. "You know my feelings are inappropriate for cousins."

"You have believed all this time that I'm not your relative," she whispered solemnly. "Could you not pretend for one more moment that nothing has changed?"

Standing on the step above his, she stood almost as tall as he, and her gaze burned with a brilliance that melted his resistance. The words came from him slowly, for he knew they were wrong, but he couldn't stop himself. "If that were the case, then I would say I love you, beautiful stranger."

She closed her eyes and inhaled deeply, as if breathing in his words. "Say it once more."

"Roxanne—"

"Please. Just once more, and then we won't mention it again, ever."

He waited until her lashes lifted. "I love you," he whispered.

Her lips turned upward in the sweetest smile he had ever seen, but her expression was sad. His heart tumbled over as a look of determination stole across her face.

"If you truly think I am Roxanne, then you could not have killed her," she said incomprehensibly, and placed her hands on his cheeks and pulled him to her lips. All logic and questions fled. Blood pounding at his temples, he surrounded her with his arms and drew her to him, the kiss deepening until he broke away to pepper little kisses at her forehead, her cheeks, her eyelids, then back to her lips, desire raging through him like a flood.

Hardly aware of what he did, he led her down the stairs and into the salon, the tip of his boot nudging the abandoned valise as he passed it by. He was too drunk with her intoxicating presence to wonder about anything. Within the privacy of the salon, he needn't whisper his words of love but could speak quietly, his voice deep with passion as he embraced her. He thought of the settee with longing but dared not put her at such risk; he did not trust himself.

"I love you, Harry," she breathed as he nibbled at her earlobe and traced kisses down the line of her neck. "I do love you. No matter what you've done."

"Then you forgive me?" he asked between kisses. "You're not angry that I didn't believe you were Roxanne?"

"No, it's not that . . . I mean . . ."

"What are we going to do? I can't live without you, certainly not beneath the same roof." He untied her bonnet and threw it on the floor. Her hair, unpinned, tumbled across her shoulders, wild waves of gold. He stroked it, clutched handfuls and drew her closer. "Marianne will have to understand that we must be together, cousins or not."

"Harry," she said, leaning back weakly in his arms. "Harry—"

"I don't care if we have to leave Far Winds. Italy! No

one would know us there. We could start fresh beneath a Mediterranean sun. How does that sound?"

"Heavenly. But Harry, I must tell you something, and I can't if you keep . . . Harry, wait . . . I—I'm not your cousin."

Two kisses later, her words penetrated his brain. He looked at her questioningly, his grip loosening.

"I'm not Roxanne," she said with a sob, and winced as if expecting a blow.

His arms dropped to his sides. He stepped back a pace. "Do I understand you correctly? For over a week you've claimed to be my cousin despite everyone's objections, and now that we have the proof you are Roxanne, you say you're not?"

She nodded silently, her head downturned. A tear trickled from each eye. He hardened his bewildered heart, thinking now of the satchel lying in the hall and her unexplained midnight journey.

Once again, he had acted the fool over a woman. He had promised himself it would never happen twice. He would sooner slit his throat than let tears soften him for a third time.

"Then you *were* going to see Nathan," he raged. "The two of you have schemed together to defraud my aunt, and that's why he came back with his so-called proof that you're Roxanne. Wasn't the bequest he was to receive enough for the man? I'd never have believed it of him. Never."

"You wouldn't believe it of *him,* but you suspected me of everything."

"With good cause, apparently."

"That was deserved," she said, swallowing and blinking and appearing meek. She sat on the settee, hands in lap and looking very small and vulnerable. Her pretended emotions failed to move him a whit. "I wasn't going to see Mr. Turner. I was going home."

"Am I supposed to believe that? How can I believe anything you say?"

She cast a defiant look at him. "Then there's no use of my explaining anything, is there? I may as well leave."

She moved as if to rise, and he pushed her back against the cushions. "No, you don't. You're not destroying my aunt's happiness without an explanation."

"I did leave a note on my pillow," she said, having grace enough to look ashamed.

"How generous of you to think of it. But I believe she deserves more. First thing tomorrow morning, you're going upstairs and telling her the truth."

"Oh, no," she said, distress lengthening her face. "Please don't make me do that."

"You're going to explain everything to her," he said. "But first you will tell me." And because he could not hold it in any longer, he blurted, "Are you romantically involved with my steward?"

"Good heavens, no!" she cried, and he knew a moment's easing of his hurt. Surely such vehemence could not be summoned at will. "I'll tell you how and why I came to impersonate Roxanne, Harry, if you will promise to listen fairly. A moment ago you told me you loved me. No, don't say anything—I know that has changed now, because you view me only as a liar and a fraud. I knew that would happen when the truth came out. But please keep one thing in mind that was never fabricated. When I said I loved you, I meant it. And now I expect nothing from you except a fair hearing. I will make no excuses, Harry, but will let you be the judge. Just understand that every word I tell you is true."

He could not keep disdain from his expression as he settled in a chair across from the settee and angled one leg over the other. "I await your story with as much credence as I can muster."

"Very well, then." She took a deep breath. "My true name is Audrey Lassiter, and I live with my father and sister in Saint Duxbury. . . ."

By the time Audrey finished speaking, her mouth felt dry as dust. But that was appropriate; her heart had turned to a lump of clay. She told Harry everything concerning the conditions of her impersonation, not sparing Mr. Turner, for his complicity had to be assumed since he brought a false report about her identity. She did not wish to excuse him anyway, not since he became her most likely candidate as mad archer.

Or not so mad. It made an evil kind of logic that he would warn her away. He couldn't pay her a groat since Lady Marianne seemed determined to live.

Lord Harry was silent for some time following her speech. She felt his eyes, his cold green eyes, watching her, though she kept her own gaze centered on her fingers, which were creasing wrinkles into her muslin.

"That is the most ridiculous plan I've ever heard."

"I'll not argue with you." She had said as much to her family and herself a hundred times. "I suppose Mr. Turner's intentions were good." This she felt she must say, since he had helped Rebecca in her time of need. He would undoubtedly be sacked, but perhaps the lady would be willing to give him a reference.

The baron huffed. "Good? If you've told me the truth, Miss Lassiter, he has played you false as well."

"Then you also think he was the archer?"

"What?"

She had not told him of her suspicions about the steward nor about the baron himself; neither had she disclosed anything about Roxanne's diary. She could not yet decide if she should. As for the journal itself, that she had placed beneath her letter on the counterpane. Within her confession lay a warning to Lady Marianne that she might prefer not to read her daughter's writings, as it contained hurtful things. Putting the choice in the lady's hands seemed the only fair way to handle the dilemma.

"I saw a bow and arrows on his saddle this afternoon," she explained further.

"Nathan always carries a bow when he travels long distances," he said. "He claims it's a faster weapon than loading a blunderbuss, although I disagree."

"Oh." The room swam dizzily as she adjusted to this knowledge. "Then what did you mean, he's played me false?"

"He said he would give you half his inheritance—ten thousand?" She nodded. "Which would indicate he was getting twenty thousand. His portion is not near that, and he knows it well. Five thousand and a life tenancy at his farm, that's what he expects."

Audrey could not breathe. "Then . . . I have been tricked as much as anyone."

"You'll forgive me if I don't offer my sympathy."

She gave him a direct, hurt look, but he avoided her eyes. "Then Mr. Turner still might have been the one to shoot those arrows," she mused. "Maybe he heard about Lady Marianne's recovery and arrived earlier. Perhaps someone in the house told him where I had gone." Seeing the skepticism in the baron's face, she said, "Well, someone certainly told *you*. It would be a simple matter for him to lay in wait for me. How much easier to frighten and warn me off than admit he had lied."

"Your theory is rife with *maybes*. And stop being so formal by calling him 'Mr. Turner' when no one else does. If you hope to make me think you hardly know the man by such devices, you're wasting your time."

"I don't know him well at all!"

"No? Then why was he creeping up the stairs to see you tonight like a lovesick swain in a farcical play?"

Audrey felt secret pleasure at the intensity of the baron's rage. Surely he had not stopped caring, not altogether. "Oh, has he already been here? I intended to leave before he came."

"Then you admit you knew about his visit?"

"I had asked him to see me before I suspected him of this morning's incident."

"You demanded he visit you during the small hours of the night," Harry echoed, the *why* implicit in his tone.

She was silent a moment, considering. What could it matter now if she told him of her suspicions and of Roxanne's part in them? Her fear of this beloved man had dissolved during the past half-hour. Her physical fear, that was. She could not have admitted she loved him were it otherwise.

No, whatever the young Roxanne had believed, he could not have murdered her or anyone. Not a man who cared deeply and protectively for his aunt. Not a man who tolerated the intrusions on his life of Thornton and Lucy, when it was plain they annoyed him. Not a man who devoted his life to building an estate capable of housing its least members in comfort and safety.

Most especially, a man who could, in one moment, be willing to leave his world and wealth behind to love her. . . . This was not the character of a murderer. She wanted to weep over what she had almost grasped but now had lost. And weep she would, for a thousand days. For the rest of her life.

In spite of this, she knew he retained the power to hurt her, and hurt her deeply. On the mundane level, he—or Lady Marianne—could press legal charges against her. On the personal front, he might make a difficult parting intolerable.

Audrey felt something within her shift and crack. How many times had she argued with Rebecca when refusing suitors; how many times had she demanded that love be a part of the equation? She had not known what she sought. For the first time, on this strangest and most uncomfortable of nights, she understood the power of love.

The power over determining her own happiness had now become his.

"I asked Mr. Turner to tell me about your past."

A line grew between his brows. "*My* past?"

"Well, you would not. Lady Marianne wouldn't. No one would, and I had to know."

He studied her unfavorably. "Why was my history so important to you?"

"At first it was because I wanted to know more about you." When he made a grunt of disbelief, she stared at him defiantly. "That *was* the reason, Harry. And then . . . I found Roxanne's old journal. She said things that frightened me. She said you had murdered someone before coming to Far Winds. On the last page in the diary, she wrote of calling you 'Lord Murder' and how angry it made you. She said she was afraid of you."

A great stillness came over his body as she spoke, and for a moment Audrey felt the vague stirrings of an old fear. When he replied, his lips scarcely moved. "Lord Murder. I had almost forgotten. No, I'm not being truthful. I could never forget that."

His words were uttered so softly, Audrey leaned forward to hear. His attention returning to her, he said, "Where did you find her journal?"

"The nursemaid."

"Of course. She was the only servant who tolerated the girl. I'm surprised Nurse Spencer kept it to herself all these years, though."

While Audrey explained about Roxanne's demand for secrecy, the baron watched her closely. "You've read all of the document today, then?"

"Her entries were short. She was only a child, after all."

"And did you believe her? About my being a murderer?"

"I was afraid it might be true," Audrey admitted. "I felt I could no longer trust anyone. Not you, not Mr. Turner. After I was nearly hurt this morning, I was frightened. That's why I decided to run away." She turned her head and looked at the embers sputtering in the grate. She knew he wouldn't believe her next words, but they must be said. "I didn't know then what I know now, that you are not the kind of man who would harm anyone."

"Do you think not?" he asked, his expression like someone dead. "What changed your mind?"

"Well, first of all, when you heard Mr. Turner's report, you were willing to believe I was Roxanne, which would be impossible if you'd harmed her. And then"—her voice began to weaken as tears thickened her throat—"then I began to think of all the wonderful things I know about you, such as how tender you are with your aunt, and how kind you have been to me, or most of the time, I should say, and when you said"—she pulled a handkerchief from her sleeve and wiped her tears, then waved it. "See, I have learned to carry my own now. Anyway, when you said you lo-loved me, which I know you don't, not anymore, because you can't trust me and all your worst imaginings of me have come true, but when you said it, and were willing to run away with me to Italy, I just . . . knew. You could never murder someone, not unless there was a very good reason. By that I mean, if it were in war, or in self-defense, or . . ."

She trailed away, not knowing how to end. There was still much she didn't understand about him, she realized. And may never, to judge by how unmoved he appeared at her tears.

For a long interval of time, he remained silent. When he moved suddenly to walk behind his chair and lean his forearms across its back, it was as if he intended to place a barrier between them. Whether he meant it or not, she could not fail to notice the symbolism.

"I don't like to talk about my life before coming to Far Winds," he said. "But since you will be going away tomorrow—if my aunt allows—"

"Do you think she will send me off to gaol?" Audrey interrupted in trembling tones, unable to think of anything else now that he had mentioned it.

"I don't know, Miss Lassiter. I truly don't know how she will react."

"Is that what you want?" she whispered. "Do you think I should be imprisoned?"

His eyes melted her heart with their sadness. "No."

"Oh, Harry," she said, nearly singing with hope. "Do you believe you can find it in your heart to forgive me?"

"Do you think I'm a saint?" he lashed. When she recoiled, he looked down at his hands and waited a beat, then said more calmly, "If what you have told me *this* time is true, I can almost understand why you took the assignment from our traitorous steward. You hoped to provide for your family, and I find it difficult to fault anyone for that. The facts are easily looked into, and I plan to discover the truth myself. If I find you have been truthful and my aunt wants you charged, I'll do my best to persuade her otherwise."

"Thank you," she said humbly.

"But as to forgiveness . . . you had best look to yourself and your Maker for that. As far as I'm concerned, the important thing is for you to leave here as soon as possible. Your continued presence will be hurtful for everyone involved."

Audrey met his gaze and strived to keep her feelings

hidden. He was tearing her to shreds inside and all she could think was, *I deserve every word.*

"I believe you started to say something about your life before Far Winds." She was pleased to hear how controlled her voice sounded, as if she were asking about the weather outside.

"Yes. Since you'll be gone after tomorrow, I want to clarify any misconceptions you might have about my history. We can't have you spreading Roxanne's ramblings as fact. I shall be mercifully brief.

"A young man of eighteen meets a fetching young woman and falls desperately in love with her. He offers for her hand in marriage, and she accepts. In his joy he invites his betrothed and her family for a week's stay at his home. She meets his widower father for the first time, and it soon becomes apparent the sire and his fortune have been her objective all along."

"Oh no, Harry." *He had fallen desperately in love with her.* More than he'd loved *her?* she wondered. He certainly must have loved his betrothed longer than the two minutes Audrey had enjoyed.

"I didn't suspect she planned it, not at first," he admitted. "I believed her when she told me she had fallen in love with him, that what she'd felt for me was only a shadow of what was to come. It was devastating, of course, but the only person I blamed was my father and his well-used charm. I thought he had stolen her from me. We had never got on well together, you see, and she gloried in the friction between us. She knew how to fan the flames and keep them high."

Audrey pressed her fingertips over her eyes. "Did she break your engagement?"

"She pretended it had never taken place. Said it was all a misunderstanding. One month later, she and my father were wed."

"I don't know how you stood it. Did you leave home?"

"No, because almost immediately my father began to suffer bouts of illness. She pretended distress, but by this time I understood her better. She was most disturbed about his lack of fortune. My father had misled her, just as she had misled him. At this juncture in his life, his gambling fever and expensive taste in wines and horseflesh had virtually decimated the estate.

"As she began to realize that she had made a mistake in her calculations, Father's illness increased. Each time he took to his bed groaning with stomach and joint pain and not being able to eat, she took advantage of his absence by ordering expensive clothing and jewelry and enjoying other men."

Something about how he delivered this last statement triggered a primal alarm within Audrey. "You don't mean . . . she didn't . . ."

He smiled grimly. "Try her seduction techniques on her husband's son? Yes, Miss Lassiter, she did, but by now I hated Carradice. When I spurned her, she became very angry. I suppose that's the reason why, when my father died and the physician determined that poison had done him in, she blamed me, citing the very true fact that we argued constantly. Perhaps I would have been a convenient scapegoat in either case.

"At any rate, her accusation was enough to have me carted to gaol. For weeks I was known as the 'Father Killer.' How it infuriated me to be accused unjustly. Had it not been for the testimony of our cook, who had on several occasions seen Carradice dusting my father's evening port with something she had called 'healing powders,' I might have been in the ground long ago."

"I have never heard anything so terrible," Audrey cried. She moved forward only the slightest degree, wishing she had the right to give him comfort, but his swift frown stayed her. "What happened to that—woman?"

"She was sent to a penal colony in Australia where she will remain for the rest of her days. Or so one hopes."

"I can understand now why you would become angry when Roxanne called you . . . what she did."

"Lord Murder. She knew I detested being reminded. Though it pains me to speak ill of the dead, she seized every opportunity to make me look small in her mother's eyes."

"In her childish way, she was afraid you would steal her place in Lady Marianne's heart. I feel I must tell you that, since I've read the diary and have grown to understand the girl better. But you were justified in your anger. She should have known better than to tease you so."

"I was immature myself. That's why I overreacted. I had not yet grown enough to realize that no woman can be trusted to tell the truth. But I know it well now."

That was why he couldn't forgive her. He had believed she was different from that terrible woman he'd known before—Carradice, was it?—and she had failed him.

"Well, enough speeches," he continued. "Stretch out and sleep, Miss Lassiter, and I'll guard you. At first light I'll send a message for Nathan Turner to come to the house, then we'll all visit my aunt."

"You expect me to sleep here? With you sitting there?"

"Are you worried about propriety, Miss Lassiter? You surprise me. But don't be concerned; we'll be upstairs tomorrow before anyone spies our little love nest. You didn't truly think I'd allow you to return to Roxanne's room, where you might escape down the back stairs, did you?"

This did not deserve an answer. He sounded so aggrieved. Giving him a baleful stare, she lifted her legs onto the settee and settled her gown primly, then watched as he circled the chair and slouched into it, his long, muscular legs extended. She shivered at the sight.

"Are you cold?"

"Yes," she said immediately, hoping he would stir the fire to a blaze which might help melt his feelings toward her.

A bundle of lacy threads flew across the space between them and landed in her lap. "Lucy's shawl. She left it downstairs earlier this evening."

Feeling wounded, Audrey spread the covering across her shoulders and turned on her side, facing him. She determined to watch him until her eyes closed, but he leaned his head the other way.

It was, she thought, very obstinate of him.

If only she had more time, she could prove to him she wasn't like Carradice or Roxanne, that she was a trustworthy person. But her time at Far Winds had suddenly run out. For the first moment in her life, she had glimpsed a vision of heaven; but the gates were slowly closing, and she was left outside.

Eleven

A shaft of sunlight speared Lord Harry back to consciousness on the following morning. His muscles felt strained from holding an unfamiliar posture too long, and he wondered fuzzily why that should be. Someone was padding around his room. Reluctantly, he opened his eyes to see Tidwell stealthily collecting last night's glasses and wiping the rings from the tables in the salon.

Memory returned in full force. Harry jerked upright, took in the empty settee, and cried, "Where is she?"

Tidwell started in alarm, fumbled and nearly lost one of the glasses but managed to capture it in time. "Where is whom, my lord?"

"Was no one asleep here when you arrived?"

"Only your lordship," he answered in bewildered tones. And then, as if he feared Harry was being sarcastic, said meekly, "I'm sorry I awakened you."

"Did you see—has anyone left the estate this morning?"

"Not to my knowledge." Curiosity had now replaced diffidence in the servant's demeanor. "Has someone run off, my lord?"

Harry set his jaw. The last thing he wanted was to start a round of gossip. How could he have been such a clod as to fall asleep? "Don't worry your head, Tidwell. I had a bad dream, that's all." Grimly he added, "But now I'm fully awake. Send a footman to fetch Nathan Turner immediately."

He strode from the room, flung wide the front door, and thundered to the stable. A boy with sleep in his eyes struggled to saddle Fortune for him. Harry pushed him away and finished the job himself, then rode like the wind in the most likely direction, the road leading to Saint Duxbury.

But she had probably lied about that as she had everything else, he thought, his conviction growing as he crossed the miles and found no sign of her. She could not have walked so far unless someone had given her a ride. After nearly a half hour had passed, he turned Fortune homeward, determined to cover as much ground in the opposite direction before giving up.

But when Harry reached Far Winds, Nathan Turner was dismounting in the drive. The baron decided to use the traitor in hand while he had the chance. It was unfair to his aunt to keep her in ignorance a moment longer. Beneath the portico, the steward turned to watch him, his gaze wandering from the steaming black to his slept-in clothes, then landing curiously on his face. Whatever he saw there, the servant blanched, but he offered a tentative greeting.

Dismounting and tying Fortune's reins to the post beside the steward's bay, Harry could scarcely prevent himself from violence. "Don't waste your good mornings with me, Turner. I know everything."

"Everything, my lord? I'm sorry, I—"

"Don't try my patience with your excuses." He clutched the servant's upper arm, his fingers digging in like talons. "I caught Roxanne—excuse me, I mean *Miss Lassiter*—trying to run away last night. We had a long talk, as I insisted upon it, and now you and I are going to have a similar discussion with Lady Marianne."

"Oh, my dear Lord," Turner said.

"Yes, you had best pray. How could you have done this to us? And especially to my aunt, after all the good things she has provided for you?"

"Well, I thought it was for the best—"

"And lying to Miss Lassiter as well. If she spoke truth, that is. You can put us in the straight about that." An unwanted flare at the injustice of raising a penniless young woman's hopes suddenly blazed within. How destroyed she had looked last night when told of Turner's true expectations of inheritance. She'd reminded him of his own feelings of disappointment in certain women. "One would think you'd be honest with your cohort in crime, at least."

"Keep your voice down, my lord," pled Turner.

"Keep my—! You're a nervy one, aren't you?"

"But you don't—all right, Lord Harry, all right. We'll go see my lady, just don't push at me, please."

Harry released him with a flourish, then shadowed him up the stairs and down the bedroom corridor. He rapped loudly on his aunt's door. Hearing Bertha call that she would be there in a moment, he stood toe to toe with Turner, his gaze furious upon the steward, who looked everywhere but at him.

And then the door across the hall opened, and Miss Lassiter stepped out. He could not hide his surprise, but he hoped the surge of joy he felt was not evident. He would have a strong quarrel with his traitorous feelings later.

"I thought that would be you; your knock is loud as a drum heralding war," she said. After a dismissive glance for the steward, she locked her eyes on his. "When you fell asleep in the salon, I went upstairs to bed," she explained. "You may not have been afraid of scandal, but I was."

"*You* were afraid of scandal," he said. He noted that she still wore her muslin from last night but had restored her hair beneath its bonnet. "In a few moments, gossip will be the least of your concerns."

Instead of answering, she narrowed her gaze on Turner. "You lied to me," she said.

The servant's head drooped. "I had to, miss."

"No, you did not." Blue brilliance flashed. "When do lies ever help?"

"Yes, when?" the baron contributed, staring at her.

Lady Marianne's sitting room door opened. "You may come in," Bertha said, smiling. "Milady's finished with her breakfast now."

One by one they filed into her chamber, Miss Lassiter going first. Marianne looked elegant in a pink satin dressing gown, her nightwear beneath frothing ruffles at the neckline. She appeared startled to see the three of them together, and a frown developed as she scanned Lord Harry's clothing and Miss Lassiter's.

"Why are you wearing that odious old thing, Roxanne? I thought I told you to burn it."

"It's what I wore when I came here," Miss Lassiter said, "and I won't take away anything you have giv—"

"I'm afraid I have some bad news," Harry interrupted, thinking the girl would confuse Marianne if she continued in this vein. "There has been a deception played upon us, and it pains me to say that Nathan Turner is at the heart—"

"My lady, he has guessed—" Nathan began, surprising the baron into an outraged pause.

"Stop!" cried Marianne, holding up a restraining hand. "Just be quiet for a moment, all of you!"

For the space of five seconds, all that could be heard in the chamber was the ticking of the clock. Finally, her lips pressed into a straight line, Marianne drew in a deep breath. "Bertha!"

The maid responded at once, looking eager. Harry wondered fleetingly of her devotion all these years. Older than his aunt, surely Bertha had her own aches and pains and troubles, yet they never heard a complaint.

"Bertha, I want you to go downstairs and have a cup of tea in the kitchen. Then tell the gardener to snip a dozen roses, and I'd like you to arrange them in my mother's silver vase. The one that's kept in the attic."

Looking disappointed, the maid curtseyed and backed from the room. Harry heard the hall door open and close softly, then turned to his aunt.

"You might as well have allowed her to stay," he told her. "Everyone will know what I'm about to tell you soon enough."

Instead of exhibiting curiosity as he expected, Marianne turned a flat look on the steward. "Did you betray our plan, Nathan?"

"No, milady—"

"Betray *your* plan—!" Harry said at the same instant.

"What exactly is it you think you know?" Lady Marianne said.

Harry told her, his words faltering now in confusion. When he spoke of Miss Lassiter's attempt to run away, Marianne looked annoyed, not angry or sorrowful as he'd imagined. He concluded with dying venom, "According to the imposter, our steward offered her ten thousand pounds that he didn't own to impersonate Roxanne. She claimed his intention was to make your dying days happy."

His gaze fell on Turner, who, instead of looking ashamed or repudiating the story, was watching Marianne with a resigned expression.

"He only said what I told him to say," the lady remarked.

"Do you mean to tell me *you* planned this?" Harry demanded.

"She devised the whole thing!" Miss Lassiter cried simultaneously. And then, her voice a trembling solo, she added plaintively, "Why?"

"Because I believe my daughter lives, and that someone from this house has been hiding her all these years," Marianne said, her chin lifting stubbornly as she looked at her nephew. "The only way I knew to force him or her to speak the truth was to threaten their inheritance with an imposter."

"Oh, Aunt," groaned Harry. She had spoken of her fears before, but that she would go to such lengths to prove them amazed him. All of his pain had been caused by a mother's wounded heart. She would never give up hope that Roxanne lived. Her conniving grieved, then shook him with wrath. "Do you know what you've done?"

Marianne swept back her covers and stood strongly to her feet, surprising him. "What, Harry? What have I done?" She gestured toward Miss Lassiter. "At worst, I've given this household and neighborhood a drama to talk about for years. At the same time I've provided a young woman with the opportunity to deliver herself from poverty, all for a few weeks' playacting."

"A false opportunity, for Mr. Turner lied to me about his inheritance," Miss Lassiter said. Harry's spirits sank at her wounded appearance. In a way, they were both victims of his aunt's machinations, although that did not excuse her own participation. Yet, he must admit that she had the most to lose in this sham, at least in a material sense.

"Not false, child. It was I who intended to award you the ten thousand pounds. I told Nathan to inflate his portion to entice you."

Miss Lassiter brightened a little at this news, but Harry sensed her continued frustration. "But why keep *me* ignorant?" she asked.

Marianne looked distant for a moment. It was an expression the baron knew well. She was weighing her next words, and he anticipated a carefully thought answer. His hackles rose.

Experience had taught him over the years never to trust a woman, but his aunt had been the one sterling exception. Now even that was gone.

"Sit, won't you?" the lady said, taking the chair beside the one she indicated for Miss Lassiter. "Harry, Nathan, bring chairs and be comfortable." While the steward hurried to comply, Harry continued to stand with his arms crossed over his chest.

After an irritated glance at him, she returned her attention to the girl. "My dear. The night you arrived, you were so involved in your role as my daughter, you wept genuine tears. You were very convincing in telling the story I'd devised for you. I felt like a playwright! Shakespeare, even!" She gave a lilting laugh, which no one joined. "All right, perhaps not quite so good as that. But do you think you could have produced such genuine feeling if you weren't trying to convince a dying woman that her daughter had returned?"

"I don't know why you didn't hire an actress," Miss Lassiter said.

"One of those scandalous people? No, no, no. I didn't want to have to check the silverware afterward. No, you were carefully selected by my faithful steward, who interviewed a number of likely prospects for weeks before finding you. The requirements weren't easy, were they, Nathan?"

When the servant shook his head vigorously, Harry sent him a contemptuous look that stopped him cold.

Marianne continued, "The physical aspects were easier than the other, we found. There were several young women who were lovely, fair, and petite, all qualities which Roxanne promised to fulfill. But to find one who exhibited good character, breeding, and education and who was also impoverished enough to be tempted by such an offer—that was much harder. You were the only one, Miss Lassiter.

The people Nathan questioned in Saint Duxbury sang your virtues to the heavens, speaking of how you consistently put your family's needs before your own. Very admirable, and precisely how I would expect Roxanne to act."

Harry's gaze drifted to Miss Lassiter, who appeared underwhelmed by this praise.

He was stunned by it.

His lids lowered as he struggled to keep his conflicting emotions from his expression. Marianne delivered compliments sparingly. Evidently Miss Lassiter had been speaking the truth when she told him about her wretched life in Saint Duxbury. Of course, she had not described it as *wretched,* but he knew no more fitting description.

Now a nagging voice whispered, *What would you have done if offered such a windfall?* Anything else, he argued back. *But a penniless lady's options are limited, especially when she has a disabled father and a sister to support,* the voice badgered again.

Marianne continued to speak.

"Yes, it was a long struggle, but Nathan's search provided me an interval to fall into a believable decline, which I knew would hasten the sense of time running out in the villain's heart. Promote immediate action, as it were."

"So you are *not* on your deathbed," Harry said.

"I continue to have problems with my heart, but my physician assures me I have many years left. I hope that doesn't disappoint you."

"Of course not. What does disappoint is that you saw fit not to tell me. Am I on your list of suspects? Is that why?"

Lady Marianne's eyes blazed. "As I've said to you before, Harry, *never!*" She undid the knot in her sash, then tied it again. "I knew you would disapprove my plan."

The baron made a noise of disbelief. "You have never been more correct."

"You see?" She turned to Miss Lassiter while gesturing toward him. "He would have spoiled all my hard work by telling everyone who you truly are."

"Would that he had," Miss Lassiter said. "On the very first evening."

Harry's gaze snagged hers and held. "I did my best," he said.

"I believe you did."

When the young woman's lips twitched briefly, his pulse raced, his memory pouncing upon the feeling of her in his arms as he had struggled to keep her from his aunt.

And then Miss Lassiter had bitten him, he reminded his pounding heart. Had made him bleed.

It was a foretaste of things to come.

His aunt and her *ridiculous* plan. She had caused this. His temper rose to full force, and he circled the bedpost to draw nearer.

"Whatever possessed you, Aunt Marianne? Do you realize the grief you've caused me and others in this household concerning your health? We were mourning you early and without cause, and it has accomplished nothing. And though I understand your sorrow, I cannot, *cannot* fathom why you believe someone has hidden Roxanne away for years. What could possibly be the point in that? There was no request for ransom!"

"We have spoken of this before, nephew. The inheritances."

"Yes, yes, but if that were the intent, why keep her alive when it would be simpler to—" He was not exasperated enough to finish the thought and was immediately sorry he'd begun it.

"Simpler to kill her," the lady stated, closing her eyes briefly. "I'm aware of that possibility, too. Listen to my reasoning. Roxanne's kidnapper *must* be someone on the estate. There were no visitors the day she went missing.

No one saw a stranger lurking about the house. Whatever happened, I cannot believe anyone would murder her. I simply refuse to think it. And what would the purpose of hiding the body if someone had? Indisputable evidence of her death would have made me increase everyone's portions sooner. There could be no purpose in making me wonder for seven years."

The baron raked a hand through his hair. His aunt was mad, and his head was splitting. Worst of all, her ravings were almost beginning to make sense to him.

"Oh, Harry, I know my belief staggers your sense of logic. But if I told you the truest and most strong reason I've clung to this hope through the years, you would laugh."

"I doubt it," he said wearily.

The strength of conviction fired into her eyes. "When I have spoken to you in the past about a mother's senses concerning her child, you've brushed my words aside as so much wishful thinking. But I tell you, I have always had a connection to my children that exceeds the normal one."

She reached for his hand, and reluctantly he allowed her to grasp it. "The day Joseph was killed, I was taking tea with a few ladies from the neighborhood. At the very instant my son fell from the saddle, I felt a sinking inside, an overwhelming darkness. I remember dropping my cup and watching it fall for long, long seconds, as if time itself had slowed." The lady paused, her expression a study in restrained grief. "I felt nothing of the sort when Roxanne went missing."

"Aunt," the baron murmured, moved in spite of himself. She was like one holding fast to a piece of wood while adrift in the ocean. She would grasp at anything, even mysticism, rather than admit her child was dead. How could he maintain indignation when faced with such devotion? A mother's love . . . He was out of his depth.

Across from him, Miss Lassiter met his gaze, her eyes luminous with unshed tears.

Marianne said, "If it had been only that, I might have accepted her loss. But for many years I have dreamed of her. Sometimes she is calling for me. At others she sits in shadow, as if veiled by a screen. In these dreams she does not speak, but I know the figure is Roxanne's.

"Recently my visions have grown more troubling. I see her fighting to come to me, but something or someone prevents her. Once she told me distinctly not to worry, that she was not dead."

"You've never spoken to me of your dreams," Harry said. She was breaking his heart.

The lady released his hand and seemed to withdraw into herself. "Because no one would understand. They would say, 'Poor Lady Marianne. She cannot let her daughter go.' Just as you are thinking now, Harry."

She was correct. The baron murmured sympathetically, not knowing what to say.

"I believe you," Miss Lassiter said abruptly, dabbing at her eyes. "I believe in the power of dreams."

"Do you, child?"

"Yes, my lady. Before my mother died, my sister Rebecca dreamed of two handkerchiefs made of fine linen and bordered with lace. Suddenly a wind arose, and the lace broke off and flew into the sky. Next she saw the two of us sitting in a garden and weeping. Clutched in our hands were the plain handkerchiefs."

Wonderful, Harry thought, though the soft sound of her voice had thrown its own spell over him. Now there were two mystics. All Marianne needed was support of this type.

"I'd take serious any dream Miss Rebecca had," Nathan contributed. "She's a truthful lass."

Three. Harry rolled his eyes and sat on the edge of the bed.

"Thank you for telling me that, Miss Lassiter," Marianne said, looking remarkably recovered. "Having lived through such an experience with your sister, it should be easy for you to see the rightness of continuing your impersonation until the ball."

"What?" both he and Miss Lassiter declared at once.

"Why end it now, simply because you know the entire story? I've laid such careful plans. Don't waste my efforts, I beg you."

She glanced eagerly from one to the other. "Miss Lassiter, you are accustomed to your role now; can't you pretend a little longer? The ten thousand will be yours in little more than a week, immediately after the ball, when I intend to announce publicly that I've changed my will entirely to Roxanne. It will be a lie, of course, but once the villain hears it, he will have to admit that he—or she—knows where the true Roxanne is.

"Harry, even though you don't believe me, won't you indulge my wishes this one time? What harm can it do?"

While he stared at his aunt and wondered if she could be serious, Miss Lassiter spoke.

"I won't deny that the prospects of so great a sum attract me. But now the additional reasons you have given compel me even more. If there is the slightest chance your plan might succeed, I cannot be the one to ruin it." She flicked the briefest of glances at Harry, who was watching her in disbelief. "I'm willing to continue, even though the pretension itself is repugnant to me."

"Oh, you delightful girl!" Marianne trilled, and clasped her hands together.

"Hold a moment," the baron said in commanding tones, taking to his feet. "Haven't you both forgotten something?" They regarded him mutely, waiting. "Someone tried to harm Miss Lassiter yesterday."

"Yes, and doesn't that confirm what I've been saying?" Lady Marianne cried.

"I've thought about that too," the younger lady said. "Such an expert marksman could easily have wounded me or worse. You said as much yourself, Lord Harry. The act was only meant as a warning."

Harry sent her a stern look. "And when you don't heed that warning, what then?"

The girl was not listening. She had an air of otherworldliness about her, as if hearkening to a heavenly call. Seeing such zeal, he half believed her when she said she was motivated by more than the money. This would make persuasion even more difficult.

"Am I the only one who can think reasonably?" he asked, his gaze resting finally on Nathan, who would not return his glance. Well, he was loyal to Marianne, and Harry would not fault him for that, though he still wished to throttle him until his teeth rattled.

"Naturally I considered there might be danger," his aunt said, finally. "Why do you think I asked you to guard her? Now you no longer need to do so, for Nathan has returned. All I ask is for your cooperation, Harry. You see that Miss Lassiter is willing. You simply cannot be the person who unravels everything just before the end. Surely you will grant me this one small request."

After all I have sacrificed for you, were her unspoken, concluding words.

His emotions warred within. He had not entirely forgiven his aunt for her deviousness, and he was certain Marianne had engaged Miss Lassiter by deception so that the girl would not realize the danger she faced. Even though she claimed otherwise.

Sincerity in acting, indeed. He had no doubt the young woman could trick anyone with those expressive, black-lashed eyes of hers.

Perhaps if his aunt saw her elaborate charade through to its conclusion, she would accept her daughter's death once and for all. It would be worth the inconvenience to accomplish that.

Inconvenience? He glanced at Miss Lassiter, who was regarding him with a hopeful expression, but one which held fright as well. This playacting could cost her a lot more than that. But if she were protected very closely, surely nothing would happen to her.

He could not entrust her safety entirely to the steward. Much as it pained him that her stay must now be extended—and pain him it would—he felt an unwanted responsibility for her.

It was the worst possible thing, but he could not let her out of his sight.

"If that is what you desire," he said, the words grinding from him as his aunt wept in happiness, "I won't stand in your way."

Moments later he took his leave, as did Miss Lassiter and Nathan. Preceding him into the hall, she said, "It appears we have both been duped, Lord Harry."

"Yes, my innocence is entirely gone now, Cousin Roxanne," he said. "I won't be tricked again."

He continued down the corridor with Nathan as she lingered outside Roxanne's door. He thought he heard her whisper, "I am not your enemy," but he did not look back to see.

Twelve

Her heart full with the morning's events, Audrey entered Roxanne's room and collected the missive she had written for Lady Marianne and the journal, then hid both in her gown's pocket to keep them from prying eyes. After removing her bonnet and dress, she hung the gown in the back of the wardrobe. She felt relieved that Lyddie had not already discovered the items and brought them to Lady Marianne. If the lady's scheme was successful, Marianne need never know the hurtful words Roxanne had written. If not, Audrey still intended to present her with the diary and a warning as to its contents.

Audrey gazed at the expensive apparel lining the wardrobe. She was not leaving Far Winds after all. Not yet. A wave of joy rushed through, making her tremble with excitement.

Perhaps, just perhaps, she would have a chance to win back Harry's trust. She dared not hope for his love.

Recalling the multitude of expressions crossing his face within Marianne's chamber, she ached with pity for him. After the things he had disclosed to her last night about Carradice, she had begun to understand his distrust in women. She did not blame him a whit for being disappointed when learning of her own deception. But now to find that his aunt, the one he esteemed above all others, had also betrayed him—how his heart must beat with outrage.

She wanted to renew his belief in womankind, if such were possible. And now it appeared she would have time to do so.

Pulling a blue-sprigged gown over her head, she experienced a flush of pleasure at the return of elegant fabric against her skin. Perhaps she need never wear her old muslin again. Thinking suddenly of Rebecca, she felt consumed with guilt. But soon she, too, would own well-cut gowns in flattering shades, and Papa would have new jackets of velvet and shirts made of the softest linens. Good fortune had returned.

Unless, of course, Lady Marianne had lied again and really intended to give her nothing.

She tossed away the thought. Although Marianne's halo had tarnished in her eyes, she was not so bad as that. Especially as she had stated her intentions before witnesses, including her beloved nephew.

People truly were complex. Yes, Marianne had hired her under false pretenses, but that was because she loved her child fiercely. It was not the correct thing to do, but Audrey could understand her actions now.

She had been an unwilling party to deception herself. Even though that deception had taken on the air of mission and purpose now that the truth was known, she had originally participated for reasons of personal gain for her family. The thought of making a dying woman happy had figured into her decision, but it had been a secondary consideration. In coming here, she had hurt the baron deeply, perhaps destroyed his faith in others forever. If she did not restore him, she would never forgive herself.

But as one hour followed another, she began to despair of making amends. It was not that she failed to have opportunity, for Harry continued his near-omnipresence. He shadowed her not because he wished to do so; he made that apparent by his polite but sparing, sometimes biting, comments. She suspected he felt a misguided obligation to guard her, but Nathan was already doing that. There was no need for both men to flank her like bookends everywhere she went.

Two afternoons after Marianne's revelation, Thorn and Lucy went to visit friends at a nearby estate, and Audrey, fitful with frustration, announced she intended to take a walk. As she expected, both men rose to accompany her, neither of them appearing willing.

Without voicing a destination, Audrey led the way across the flagstones toward the rose garden, her steps brisk. She purposely did not linger around Harry as if she longed to take his arm—which she did—or as if she expected him to enjoy the outing—which she knew he did not. She had only one plan in mind: to reach the most congenial spot on the estate and then to send Mr. Turner away. Whatever happened after that, she left to God.

The steward was not so easily lost, however. In fact, it was Harry who tarried at the garden gate while Mr. Turner followed her in like a lap dog. Something within her snapped. She could not endure another moment of this; she simply could not.

Turning on the servant, she said in commanding tones, "Mr. Turner, please return to the house and fetch my shawl."

"But it's so—" *warm,* he had almost said, then realized in time it was not the answer of a dutiful servant. Audrey helped him with this realization, her eyes communicating a desperation only a clod could fail to see. "Right away, miss."

"Don't hurry," she said, her gaze passing him to observe the baron, who was pacing beyond the iron bars, hands folded behind his back and head in profile. "You won't be shirking your duty; Lord Harry is here."

As the steward walked off at an accommodatingly slow gait, Audrey watched Harry view his departure with some surprise, then turn to her.

"Perhaps you should come into the garden, my lord," she said boldly, her heart hammering in fear that he would not. "Someone might be hiding behind a rosebush."

He did not respond to her feeble attempt at humor, but he moved toward her, his face impassive. When he stopped some five paces away, she stepped closer. To her dismay, he ambled further, halting at an even greater distance as if to admire a rose.

"Are you trying to avoid me?" she asked softly.

He appeared mildly shocked. "I should think it would be evident that I'm not."

"I had hoped to speak with you, Lord Harry, but you are making it difficult."

"Am I? My pardon." Without moving a muscle nearer, he said, "Please, go ahead."

Feeling anger stir, she swallowed it down and approached him. Again, he kept distance between them, this time becoming fascinated with a sculpture of a frog. It was the most cruel of dances, she thought.

"Are you afraid of me?" she flung, torn between hurt and irritation.

"I don't know what you mean." And then, seeing the emotions in her face, he came to sudden life. "Yes. Yes, I am afraid of you. Afraid of being near you. Why did you want to visit the rose garden alone with me, Miss Lassiter? You know what happened the last time we were here."

"Yes," she said, her eyes glimmering with the memory of the sweetness of his lips and the knowledge it could never happen again. *Camelot lost.* "A woman doesn't often forget her first kiss."

He held up a hand as if to stop her from going further. "Whether true or not, that's in the past now."

"Whether true or—Harry, it is true." She walked toward him, and this time he did not shrink away, though she saw a wariness in his eyes. "There are no lies between us now. That's what I wanted to tell you. I also wanted to apologize for deceiving you and everyone else, but mostly you, because you've been the one most hurt by my actions."

"You've already said as much. I've come to an understanding as to why you did it."

"You've come to an understanding, but you can't forgive me."

"My forgiveness is not the issue."

"I think it is. Had I known what happened to you in the past, had I an inkling of what Lady Marianne's plans were—I'd never have come."

"Wouldn't you?" He looked skeptical but cool, as if her declaration meant nothing to him. Was it possible he'd been so hurt that he didn't care anymore?

"Not if I had known how you'd be affected," she said earnestly. "You must think every woman is unworthy of your trust. Well, it's not true. My sister, Rebecca, for an example, has never deceived anyone." Sometimes she was too truthful, Audrey thought to herself.

He watched her for a moment. "You told me a story once about a girl named Rebecca who fell from a wagon and injured her face. You felt responsible. I have only now made the connection that she and your sister must be the same person."

"Yes." Audrey could say no more, the subject would never stop being tender to her.

"I have a friend who lost an arm at Leipzig," he offered. "Unlike our wounded neighbor, Captain Berkbile, who takes his disfigurement as a badge of honor, Tom refuses to go about in public for fear people will feel sorry for him."

"My sister is also shy of prying eyes," she said, unable to meet his gaze. Rebecca's reclusiveness had not always been a part of her personality. Had Audrey been more vigilant, it would not be so now.

Several seconds passed in silence. "Since I came to know the truth about you, I've often wondered why you didn't take a position somewhere to help support your family. Now it makes more sense that you did not." At his words, Audrey looked at him hopefully. "Still, I can't help wondering why you had one opportunity after another to tell me the truth and failed to do so. I asked you many times."

"But Harry, if I had said to you, *Yes, I am an imposter hired by your steward,* what would you have done? You would have taken me directly to your aunt, just as you did when I tried to run away."

"Would I? Had I known all of your reasons and background? We'll never know, will we?"

"You would have done your duty," she said in strident tones. "There is something in your character which will not allow for human frailty, understandable failings, no matter what the circumstances. You are—you are puffed up with your own opinions, Harry, and no matter what I've ever thought of you, I never expected you to be so—so vicious!"

She turned away from him, biting her lip to keep tears from falling. This time he would not make her weep. When his hands came to rest upon her arms, she stiffened. But no matter what her efforts, her resistance melted as he leaned toward her ear.

"I don't mean to be vicious, but it seems we have grave issues of mistrust between us. I believe you now, but how easily your stories came to your lips in the past. What's to stop you in the future from fooling me as easily?" She started to protest, but he hushed her. "And while we are on the subject of truth, let me remind you how little you've trusted me. You even believed for a while that I could have murdered someone."

"You know how much I regret that. Had you been more truthful with me, I never would have."

"That's precisely it. I believe that two people who cannot believe in each other have no hope of a deeper relationship, no matter how they feel about each other, no matter what words of love they may have professed. In short, Miss Lassiter, I don't know what you expect from me."

She turned in his arms, the sweet shock of the nearness of his face almost stealing her breath. "That's what I wanted to say, Harry. I expect nothing from you." She spoke intently and rapidly, hopeful of saying what must be said before losing all control. "Nothing except your goodwill, and if possible, your friendship. Even though we have spoken of lo-love, I understand that's gone from your heart now. All I ask is that you refuse to allow what has happened to make you bitter. Don't judge the entire world on what has occurred in the past, or your future will be forever unhappy."

For what seemed a long space of time, he didn't answer, though he studied her features solemnly. When he straightened an errant curl from her forehead, then smiled as it bounced back, she had to lower her lids to shutter her raw longing.

"Of course we are friends, Miss Lassiter," he said at last, and offered his arm, which she took immediately. "You're right about me. I have been judgmental. I won't have you thinking I blame you for anything, because I don't. Not now. If anyone is at fault, it's my aunt. But truth, I find I'm unable to hold my wrath against even her, for it was grief that caused this charade from its inception."

He squeezed her hand briefly as he led her toward the house. "I'm glad we had this little talk. It was foolish and limited of me to think that we must be enemies or strangers, simply because we couldn't be more to each other. Thank you, Miss Lassiter, for your candor."

And with this I must be content. Audrey forced a bright smile. Their discussion had gone even better than she expected.

She could not think why she felt so disappointed.

When he returned Miss Lassiter to the salon, Lord Hastings found Tidwell waiting with a message. Lady Marianne wished to see him. Reluctantly he took his leave of the young lady. Thornton and Lucy had arrived during their absence and were lively with gossip from their visit. Miss Lassiter threw him a look of appeal as he left, and had not Nathan been with her, he would have flown to her side no matter what his aunt wanted.

After Bertha ushered him into his aunt's bedchamber, Marianne waved him to the chair flanking hers. "Sit down, Harry," she said quietly. "The walls have ears, as you know."

He complied, noticing how rosy her cheeks were, how vital her eyes. How had he ever believed she was fading away? "Good afternoon, Aunt. You're looking exceptionally well today."

"Oh, give peace, Harry. I can't wear rice powder every day or my skin will dry like old, dead leaves. I will be glad when my decline is over and I can be myself again. I never thought to say it, but I long for exercise more than anything."

"You could end it now with a word."

She delivered him a sharp glance. "Do you think I'd consider such a thing with only a week to go?"

"No," he admitted tiredly. He could hope, but his effort would be wasted. He knew his aunt's determination. "Why did you ask to see me?"

"For the pleasure of your company first of all," she said in offended tones. "You haven't been to visit since the day I revealed my plan to you. If you're angry with me, I want you to stop."

Her demand almost, but not quite, made him smile. "I'm not angry with you."

"Good. Now, to business. I've decided to drop hints that I will be changing my will exclusively to Roxanne *before* the ball. I won't state it directly, you understand—only talk aloud about what I'm considering. It will give our villain more time to think."

"To think about what?" he asked, keeping his voice even with only the tightest control. "Ways in which he might murder Miss Lassiter?"

"Ways for him to confess," she said coldly. "And to see how hopeless his position has become. Harry, you know I don't wish for the girl to be endangered. That's why I've told Nathan to guard her."

"Nathan is a good man, but no one can guarantee she won't be hurt," he said, wrath uncoiling.

"You seem very concerned for someone who claims he doesn't believe I'm correct about my daughter's fate."

"Miss Lassiter may be in danger quite apart from Roxanne's fate, as you well know," Harry said. "Surely you haven't forgotten the warning she received."

"I haven't forgotten anything."

Staring into his aunt's irate eyes, the baron tasted sour disillusionment. Her willingness to sacrifice the safety of a defenseless young lady—a lady Marianne had been responsible for bringing to Far Winds—brought the final blow to his wavering belief in her. He had been as loyal to Marianne as he would his own mother, and now he could scarcely bear breathing the same air.

"Bringing forward your plans will increase her vulnerability," he said, reliving in an instant the moments he had spent with the beauty in the garden. She wanted to be his friend, she had said, though her eyes told a different story. How he had longed to crush her to him and never let go. But he would not forget the lessons he had learned and was still learning. No one was to be trusted entirely.

"She can help protect herself by keeping close to the house," Marianne said. "Don't think I'll start anything without informing her, but I know she'll be willing. It is, after all, what she is being paid to do—and paid well, I might add. You should remember that, my nephew. She's no more than a servant."

His stomach clenched. "She is a lady," he said. "Though a servant deserves more care than you're giving her."

Lady Marianne gripped the arms of her chair. "It's as I thought, then. You have an affection for this girl."

"I have an affection for all girls," he said lightly, turning his head to gaze at a bird landing on the balcony.

"Look at me, Harry," she said. With reluctance, he brought his eyes to hers. "She is not our kind."

"And what kind is that?"

"Don't pretend ignorance; it doesn't become you. She has no background, no fortune, and is willing to impersonate someone for money."

"You were willing to employ someone to impersonate for money."

Marianne's lips narrowed. "You know why I did it."

"Yes, and I know why *she* did it."

"Don't be impertinent with me, young man! I've seen the way you look at her, and the manner in which she entices you. You'd best remember that a girl willing to take on this sort of role for hire would be more than eager to snag a baron and his greater fortune!"

As though I've not thought of that myself, Harry fumed, his fury nearly blinding him. Not trusting himself to speak, he rose and stalked from the room.

"You remember what I've said!" his aunt cried after him.

True to his word, on the following days Harry did treat Audrey as he would a friend—a distant one—or perhaps a second or third cousin. Contrary to what she had thought, Audrey found his politeness almost as hurtful as his cynicism. Mr. Turner, continuing as her other faithful companion, acted as uncomfortable as a bashful suitor. She chafed under their watchful eyes.

Isolation began to seem more and more desirable. Thus whenever she wasn't required in Marianne's room, she frequently retreated to her chamber and its pleasant balcony. She would not allow herself to look for Lord Harry's bedroom across the way. Often she would lean against the railing and study the peaceful landscape. At such times she would remind herself to enjoy what she could of Far Winds, because she would not be present much longer. It never worked. She was only growing increasingly irritated with Harry, though she knew she was being irrational.

Adding to her discomfort, the servants had begun to notice the constancy of her companions. One morning Lyddie joined her on the balcony and remarked that Mr. Turner seemed to be spending an uncommon amount of time in the house. Sensing the sharpness of her curiosity, Audrey decided to put to death any rumors that might be circulating and at the same time reinforce how fond Lady Marianne was of her daughter. In doing so, she hoped to establish the validity of the lady's "announcement" on the night of the ball. During one of their visits, Lady Marianne had suggested Audrey seize such moments, and she believed it seemed a good idea. With her two protectors, she was not afraid.

"Since that day I was attacked, my mother wants to make sure I'm safe," she replied to the servant. "She's very fond of me, of course, and tends to overreact."

Lyddie paused in her task of dusting the outdoor chairs to look at her. "You do seem to spend more time with her these days."

"I treasure every moment with her I can, since I fear there won't be many more." Although her coming departure made this true in fact, Lady Marianne had asked her to put it about that she was declining rapidly, thereby exerting more pressure upon the villain.

"Bertha told me she has her good days and bad."

"Yes," Audrey said sadly, relishing her role now that she no longer had to fear imprisonment. "Mostly bad of late, I'm sorry to say. You and Bertha are great friends, aren't you?"

The maid smiled, a rare occurrence. "Yes, Miss Roxanne. She has been almost like a mother to me since I came to Far Winds." Her expression sobered. "I heard you and the lady didn't always enjoy getting on as a mother and child ought."

"It pains me to say you're right. My memory has been returning by degrees, enough so that I can recall how things once were between us. But any problems we may have had in the past have all been mended, and we are closer now than ever before."

"She asks for you more than anyone else, even Lord Harry, Bertha says."

"That's natural she would want her daughter, don't you think?" For good measure, Audrey added airily, "Sometimes I think she loves me *too* much. She's always giving me gifts. If I wanted the clothes on her back, I think she'd hand them over. Anything I ask for, she gives me. She has a way of bestowing far more than I expect. It's almost embarrassing."

Lyddie nodded and continued her task. Audrey felt a sense of satisfaction that she had planted seeds which would spread throughout the rank of servants.

Lucy and Thorn must have felt the hovering presence of both men strange as well, but nothing was said until a rainy evening three days before the ball. Since Lady Marianne's declaration that Audrey was the true Roxanne, the siblings had adopted a strained, though outwardly civilized, manner toward her. But now, sitting blessedly apart from everyone beside the window, Audrey sensed tension building.

As it was far too warm for a fire, Harry was restlessly poking at the ashes in the grate while Mr. Turner sat straight as a statue on the settee, a ledger propped over his knees. Across from him, Thorn paged through a book of poetry. Lucy, seated in the chair nearest Harry, worked on a needlepoint project, punctuating her endeavor with frequent heavy sighs.

"Give over, Lucy," Thorn said irritably. "If you hate it that much, why bother?"

"I have promised to make a pillow for Aunt Marianne," she said in aggrieved tones.

Unwilling to miss an opportunity, Audrey looked up from her book. "I would advise you to hurry, then." Putting a tremble into her tone, she added, "Mother was looking extremely unwell this morning, and the physician said he does not expect her to recover."

She dashed out her handkerchief and touched the corner of her eyes, only to glance up and meet Harry's emotionless gaze. She tried a secret smile behind her handkerchief, one that he alone could see, but he turned his head. Audrey felt his cut as sharply as she would a slap.

"I wouldn't know as she seldom asks to see *me* anymore," Lucy said, appearing more annoyed than saddened. "What is more, my task would be much easier if Nathan would stop staring at me over that accounting book he's always pretending to study."

Mr. Turner cleared his throat. "I'm not pretending, Miss Brown, and I'm not staring except when you sigh. I keep thinking something is the matter with you. I believe I told you that Lady Marianne has asked me to study the accounts over the past year."

"Yes, and you are taking an amazing long time with it, too," she said. "I've never seen you so slow before. It's requiring days and days, and I don't know why you must do it among *us*. Don't take this in the wrong way, but you send me into fits of the blackest melancholy."

"Lucy," Thorn said with a chuckle.

"Well, he does! He always wears those dark clothes, and he almost never smiles. One would think he was pining away for a lost love."

Without lifting his eyes, Thorn said mildly, "Perhaps he has other reasons to remain in our presence. Or in Roxanne's presence."

"Are you suggesting that she has won him over, too?" Lucy cried, focusing on Audrey. "Has every man in this household gone mad?"

As Audrey was opening her mouth in dispute, Mr. Turner closed the ledger and rose with great dignity to stand beside the fireplace, bringing everyone in the room into his line of vision.

"If I may, I'd like to correct any wrong thinking among you. It may be that I am pining away, as Miss Brown says, but it's not for a lost love. It's for a real one. My betrothed."

Audrey stared at him in surprise. All those days away with her family, even pretending to be Rebecca's affianced, and his unwavering presence with her since. When had he time to meet anyone? But perhaps the fortunate woman was someone he'd known before.

Nevertheless, her heart began to fly on wild wings of hope.

Harry replaced the poker and turned a smile on the steward. "You're betrothed, Nathan?"

"Yes, my lord." Mr. Turner's gaze fell upon Audrey. At that moment, she knew, and she felt she might explode with happiness. "That is, almost. What worries me is that I haven't been able to steal a moment alone with the most important member of her family about my suit, and my beloved Rebecca wants to know what that person thinks first before she gives her final assent."

Appearing mildly interested, Lucy said, "You needn't worry, Nathan. You would be a matrimonial prize to anyone of a certain class. What is she, a maid? A cook? Does she live on one of the farms nearby?"

"She is a lady," Mr. Turner said, his eyes remaining on Audrey. "A young lady who has fallen on hard times. I don't have a great deal to offer to make myself worthy. I'm not much to look at, and I don't spout a lot of pretty words every few minutes. I'm not wealthy, either, though I live comfortably enough. All I can say is that I will treasure her as long as I live, and that she is the most beautiful woman, inside and out, that I have ever met."

Audrey, tears raining down her cheeks, glided to Mr. Turner's side. "Those are the *prettiest* words I've ever heard. I know that this family member, whoever he or she may be, will wish you their very best blessings. In fact I'm quite sure they will find your suit thrilling beyond measure. May God bless you, your Rebecca, and your children to come, forever and always. May I kiss your cheek in congratulations, Mr. Turn—Nathan?"

Blushing a fiery red, the steward bent for his kiss, then beamed at everyone. When Audrey spied the first approval she had seen in Harry's eyes in days, she felt overcome and excused herself from the room.

"Some people are far too emotional," Lucy grumbled in her wake.

Audrey ran to Roxanne's balcony as she would to her mother's arms, if only that were possible. Rain sprinkled around her and dampened her hair, but she didn't care. She could not prevent the sobs which tore through her body. Oh, the joy, the exquisite joy that Rebecca would find happiness!

That her sister must at least be fond of Nathan Turner she did not doubt a moment; Audrey was, in spite of her frequent annoyance with him, and the sisters often shared opinions about people. Besides, her occasional irritation with the steward was brought on by his role in her own personal tragedy, not because of a flaw in his character or personality. He was more than acceptable.

As she lifted her face to the mist, her tears intermingling with the rain, she thought, *It's good that I dared come to Far Winds after all. Rebecca never would have had time to know Nathan otherwise.* Yet the irony did not escape her, that her sister would wed before she. All of these years she had felt the responsibility of her family like lead upon her shoulders, and it was Rebecca who won the solution.

If she weren't obligated to Lady Marianne, Audrey could stop her impersonation immediately if she wanted. Nathan had sufficient to support all of them in far better style than if she had wed Burl Ingerstand. He was the type to accept responsibility for his wife's family, she knew.

She considered the prospect. Rebecca, her father and herself, living on the edge of Far Winds. She could imagine peering out Nathan's window, hoping for a glimpse of the baron as he rode past on his handsome black. At harvest time and Christmas, she might even be allowed to visit the manor and stand in line to receive a handkerchief or an embroidered tea towel from my lady, with Harry looking on, probably his wife and children, too. Lucy and Thorn would be smirking somewhere nearby.

She had sooner die.

Audrey leaned against the railing, her mind a confusion of joy and regret. Surely she was not so petty as to envy her sister's bliss. No, never that. Rebecca deserved every ounce of happiness she could find in this world. Audrey did not begrudge her. It was merely . . . well, of course she wanted her own husband to love and cherish. And when she thought of *husband,* she could visualize only Lord Harry.

Her lips twisted wryly. How very droll her life had become. She had dared Far Winds for the simplest of reasons, reasons which became increasingly complex and complicated by her own pathetic dreams. And all of it for one end, apparently—to see her sister married. She could appreciate the humor, in a distant sort of way.

To live with Nathan and Rebecca within hopeless proximity of the baron would shrivel her soul.

But of course that wouldn't be necessary, would it? she thought, brightening. She would have a small fortune within a week's time and could dwell anywhere she chose. Perhaps Papa would want to remain with her. She could purchase a town house in London. Or a cottage near Oxford, where he could enjoy the companionship of learned professors.

No, he spoke often of appreciating the quiet life. He would be most secure with Rebecca and Nathan, for the time was coming when he might need the strength of a man to help take care of him. Of course, she would be able to hire a manservant. But knowing Papa, he would want to spend his last years leaving memories for his grandchildren to treasure.

For the first time in her life, she considered the prospect of freedom.

Her soul shivered, then grew stronger. It was almost . . . exhilarating. Or it would be, if such freedom did not mean a life without Harry.

The bonds and responsibilities of a family . . . how ensnaring they were. But how dear. She would be hopeless without someone to care for, without someone who needed her.

The vision of a life vacant of Harry's love yawned before her like the most lonely crevasse.

But there was no use mourning. If he could not love and accept her, she would have to go on. Her life had never been spent in idleness, and she had endured enough of that kind of existence pretending to be Roxanne. She must find work that would challenge and fulfill her.

Perhaps now she could become a governess, an idea which had appealed to her in the past but had been impossible because of her duty to her sister and father. Bringing knowledge and kindness to other people's children seemed a worthy substitute for her own dreams.

That was it. She would become a governess.

Audrey smiled bravely into the darkness and wiped her wet cheeks. She did not even need Lady Marianne's ten thousand pounds now. With the thought came the lifting of a heavy burden, as if ten thousand pounds of rock and stone had miraculously floated off her back.

She would finish this nauseating impersonation because she had committed to it. But when Lady Marianne drafted the cheque, she would politely return the paper to her. It was the only correct thing to do. She had not accepted the assignment for riches in the first place but to save her family. And now her family no longer needed saving.

Just as this worthy thought was resonating within her head, the railing snapped with a great crack, and Audrey, screaming, slid over the side.

Thirteen

Restlessly pacing in the salon, Harry could not dismiss the expression on Miss Lassiter's face when Nathan made his startling announcement that evening. Had he ever seen anyone look so sweetly happy for someone else's good tidings? No one came to memory. How well she loved her sister. Had it not been for that love and her feeling of responsibility for her family, Miss Lassiter would not be in the predicament she presently endured. He believed that completely now.

Miss Lassiter—*Audrey,* he amended, silently rolling the soft syllables across his tongue—was a good person, perhaps more good than anyone he had known before. That did not preclude her from finding him attractive for his fortune. He hadn't needed his aunt's unwelcome caution to understand that.

He scowled, remembering those taut moments with Marianne days ago. Since then he had visited her only once, and briefly. They had talked of trivialities, both of them skirting the more painful subjects. He could not discuss his innermost thoughts as he once had. Those days were gone forever. His childish faith in her was as broken as her pedestal. He still thought of her as a worthy woman, but he could not forgive her prejudice against Audrey.

The young woman's background did not concern him, as she was a lady more than fit for anyone's parlor; and a dowry was unnecessary, but he refused to tie himself to a woman who loved him for his possession of a title and a prosperous estate.

She had told him she loved him, that night she confessed her true identity. If only he could believe her fondness was not tempered by her desperation to escape poverty.

Harry stopped before the window and watched as beads of water glided downward on the opposite side of the glass. Rain was starting to fall heavily again. He hoped it would last all night and lull him into sleep, a sleep untroubled by thoughts and dreams of Audrey Lassiter.

He knew it would not happen. Enshrouded by ice, his heart had been entirely safe until she came. Like a warming sun, she threatened to melt his resistance.

Back and forth, his mind went. Back and forth.

Behind him, Thornton and Lucy were squabbling about something. Nathan Turner had gone home. With Audrey absent from the room, the scene was like every other evening before she came—tiresomely the same. He turned from the window and walked toward the hall.

"Oh, Harry, you aren't going off to bed already, are you?" Lucy asked.

"Yes. Good night."

Blinking fetchingly, Lucy extended one arm. "Please don't. We need you to settle an argument. Do you believe Amarinth Lovelace is gaining weight? Thorn declares she isn't, but I'm certain the gown she was wearing at Mercer's the other day had been let out, not to mention her face is round as a cooking pot."

"Haven't seen the girl in a twelvemonth," Harry said.

"That's because you aren't sociable enough." She threw down her embroidery, fluttered to the settee, and patted the seat beside her. "Won't you come and read poetry for us? You know how well I like the sound of your voice."

"Sorry, not tonight."

"I'll read for you, sister," Thornton volunteered.

"Oh, it's not the same," she replied shortly.

Lucy's elaborate pout would have been humorous if Harry weren't weary of her never-ending flirtations. She had to know he was a hopeless cause but never stopped trying.

After a brief foray into his small library for the most sleep-inducing book he could find, a heavy tome containing one hundred essays by eighteenth-century philosophers, Harry went upstairs to his bedroom. He tossed the volume on his mahogany four-poster, shrugged out of his jacket, threw it on the bench at the foot of the bed, and untied his cravat. Since attaining his majority, Harry had not employed a valet as he found such services intrusive. Tidwell looked after his clothes and would correct his shortcomings in the morning.

Idly unbuttoning his shirt, he wandered to the French doors which led to his balcony. He opened the doors just enough to allow the rhythm of rain to permeate the chamber, but not so much as to drench the carpet. Breathing in the fresh scents of wet earth and greenery, feeling a sweet breeze waft across his face, he sat with a measure of contentment and began to tug at his boots.

Instantly he paused as an unfamiliar noise struck his ears. It was a hopeless-sounding groan, very faint, a cry that might hint of ghosts sighing in the night, were he fanciful.

Harry walked to the doors and opened them wider. The keening came again, a desperate mewl for help that pierced the roots of his soul. He strode outside to the railing and looked across to the opposite wing of the house, the most likely source of the sound. Immediately he saw that a portion of Roxanne's balcony had given way and that Audrey was clinging with both hands to a single baluster, her legs thrashing the air as she tried to hoist herself upward.

Struck with horror, he yelled, "Audrey, hold on! I'm coming!"

"My fingers are slipping!" she cried. "The wood is about to snap!"

"I'll be there instantly!"

He tore through his bedroom and down the hall, his damp boots sliding as he turned at the landing, then slipping again at the east wing. Distantly he heard Thornton and Lucy enter the great hall downstairs, their questioning voices rising. Paying them no heed, he barreled down the final corridor, burst into Roxanne's room and through the open doors onto the balcony.

Audrey's terrified face turned up to his. For a fraction of a second, rage nearly rendered him useless. To see her in jeopardy and so helpless tore at his heart. Angrily, he crouched and clasped her arms.

"Take courage, my darling," he said. "You're safe."

He lifted her gently and steadily, her dead weight and soaked clothing making his task more difficult than he'd imagined, but an easy task nonetheless, a joyous one. When he had her securely on the surface of the platform, he pulled her into his lap and locked his arms around her, stroking her wet hair and soothing her as he would a child.

Gradually her sobs faded into gasps of thanks. He brushed them away and kissed the top of her hair, then her forehead. When she looked at him questioningly, he hesitated an instant, dropped his gaze to her trembling lips, and kissed her as he'd longed to do from, he now believed, the very first moment he set eyes on her.

"Is something wrong?" Lucy said loudly, entering the open door of the bedroom with Thornton following. Harry mentally cursed their timing as Audrey, with a start of guilt, broke from him and struggled to rise to her feet. Lucy's eyes darted wildly from one to the other. "We wondered why you were running, Harry, but it appears we've only interrupted something private." Mouth parted in shock, she stepped back, as if to find shelter with her brother.

"No, you don't understand," Audrey said, quick to dispel the evidence of the siblings' eyes. She was preserving her deception to the last, he saw. Harry stood, wishing she had let it end. "The—the railing gave way outside, and I managed to grab onto one of the balusters as I fell. I tried to climb back up but there was nothing to brace my feet against, and every movement threatened to break off the remaining wood. Harry saved me."

"Never say so," Thornton commented in a wondering voice, moving past her to the balcony. He crouched at the edge and surveyed the damage. "Oh, my God." He turned stricken eyes to Audrey. "You're a fortunate young woman."

"Let me see," Lucy said, brushing past them, then halted. "No, I can't go out, it's raining. But I can look from here. Oh, horrors!" She glanced at Audrey. "That must have been frightening. I don't know how you held on in this rain. Look how soaked you are, and Harry, too! You should both get into dry clothes and go to sleep. That's the best thing for a shock."

Ignoring her, the baron joined Thornton, who appeared mesmerized by the tangle of wood leaning from the platform. Harry ran his hand along the section of railing which remained intact, scanning for a cause of the collapse. It could not be dry rot, surely. He tried to keep the house in repair, though it was an endless work in a building of this size.

A five- or six-foot section of railing and balusters lay on the ground far below, aligned almost as perfectly as if a gate had broken off. Stubs of wood remained implanted in the balcony at his feet, tops sliced off evenly except for a scattering of splinters in the portion closest to the bedroom. The remaining ends of the handrail were also cleanly cut. Someone had sawn the fallen section to within a hair's breadth of complete severance, leaving only enough intact to make it appear normal to a young woman taking the evening air and innocently propping her arms against the rail. Harry's hands shook with rage.

Thornton's gaze met his with a knowing look. He had seen it too.

Or had been responsible. Darkness gathered at the back of Harry's eyes.

"I climbed up here a week or two ago and the banister was fine," Thornton said.

Harry glared. "Why did you do that?"

"It was a game he and I used to play," Audrey said hastily. She had slipped soundlessly beside him. His eyes softened immediately. He had nearly lost her, this sweet breath of a woman. Wanting to enfold her in an embrace, he settled for sliding his fingers down her arm.

"Go back inside," he urged. "It's nasty out here."

"That I already know, but I can't be more wet than I already am," she answered. "What happened to the railing? Was it cut?"

He could not understand how she could speak so matter-of-factly. His first impulse was to lie, to reassure her. But it was best she knew her danger. "It appears so."

Lucy grabbed a pillow and, holding it over her head, leaned outward. "What are you talking about out there? Why don't you come inside?"

It seemed a good idea; there was nothing more to be learned. He pulled Audrey into the dry, keeping his stare carefully away from the gown which had plastered itself becomingly to the contours of her body. As Thornton closed the French doors behind them, Bertha opened Marianne's door across the hall and entered the bedroom.

"Milady wants to know what all the noise is about," she said timidly.

"You may tell her someone has made another attempt on her daughter's life," Harry said. No point in softening the truth. No matter who had done tonight's deed, he held Marianne responsible.

"Mercy!" the maid cried.

Lucy said to Harry, "Now you've frightened Bertha. Don't you think you're being too dramatic? I doubt she would have died if she'd fallen; it's only two floors high, and anyone so reckless as to push against a railing can expect what happens, if you ask me."

Bertha barely glanced in Lucy's direction. "The balcony fell?" she asked the baron, her hands cupping her mouth and nose in dismay.

"It was no accident. Someone cut through the wood."

"No!" the servant moaned. Her teary eyes fastened on Audrey. "Oh, no, no, Miss Roxanne!"

Though the strength of the maid's emotions echoed his own, Harry could not help being a little surprised at the extremity of Bertha's reaction. But then he didn't know her well; she kept close to his aunt. She was a gentle soul, that was certain, to be able to endure Marianne's requirements.

"Please don't worry," Audrey said, touching her hand. "I wasn't hurt. Harry rescued me in time."

This appeared to sever Bertha's last control. "So brave!" she wailed, then drew up her apron to wipe her eyes and ran toward the servants' stair, her fading steps echoing down the corridor.

Audrey looked at Harry, but he had no answers for the display.

"Such a fuss over a little thing," Lucy said after a few second's silence. And then with more enthusiasm, "I suppose I'd better see to Aunt Marianne as she'll be wondering why everyone has abandoned her except me." She bustled importantly across the hall.

"Are you certain you're all right?" Thornton asked Audrey. "Perhaps I should fetch the physician."

"No, don't," she said, then shivered. "I'm fine."

Harry felt her strength ebbing as if it were his own. Before she fell he supported her to a chair, Thornton rushing to her other side and hovering unnecessarily. Harry sent him a look that should have scattered lions, but Thorn crouched at Audrey's side, his arm resting on the back of her chair.

"I'm very worried about you," he said. "I can't understand why these things are happening."

"I appreciate your con-concern," Audrey said, her teeth chattering.

The baron whisked the counterpane off her bed and wrapped it around her shoulders. "Yes, you sound very convincing, Thornton," he said, tucking the ends over her feet. "Of course, had you involved yourself with this disaster, there would be no better way to dispel suspicion than act solicitous."

"You can't believe I had anything to do with her accident," he said, his face going white with anger.

"It was no accident and you know it."

"Yes," he said softly. "Yes, you're right."

The room fell quiet as Harry accounted himself confused by Thornton's manner.

"I should like to go to bed," Audrey said suddenly.

Both men immediately rose and begged her pardon for their thoughtlessness. "You shouldn't be alone," Harry added.

"No, you shouldn't," Thornton chimed, irritating him beyond bearing. Audrey did not need two protectors, especially when he couldn't trust the other one.

"I'll fetch Lyddie to stay with you tonight," Harry said.

The bedchambers were equipped with bells which connected with the kitchen and the butler's pantry, but never the servants' sleeping quarters. A progressive-thinking ancestor had decreed that private time was needed for all classes, and that a bell available for use twenty-four hours a day would be too tempting for the more privileged.

Harry had reached the door before he realized Thornton remained with Audrey. "Why don't you come with me," he said, making it a command and not a suggestion.

"Perhaps she shouldn't be alone just now," Thornton returned with equal strength.

"I'd accompany you both if I thought my legs would work," Audrey said, her lips quirking.

So she found them amusing, did she? Harry sent her a slow, intimate smile, relieved that her good spirits were returning. Perhaps he was being excessively cautious, but he dared not risk her again. He crossed the room and hefted her in his arms, coverlet dropping to the floor.

"Harry!" she cried. "This—this isn't necessary!" She looked pointedly over her shoulder at Thornton, who was following them down the corridor.

"It is for me," he murmured, finding to his delight that her damp dress allowed him to feel the warmth of her body, the smooth flesh of her back and legs, almost as if there were no cloth separating skin from skin. Her eyes lowered dreamily, and he realized for the first time that his shirt lay partway open over his chest and that the remaining linen was soaked to transparency. Was she sharing his fantasy? he wondered. He flushed with desire.

"I'm too heavy," she said faintly, settling her head against his shoulder as he climbed the servants' stair. "You'll strain yourself."

"You weigh no more than my heart," he told her, lost in the blue depths of her eyes.

"How it cheers me to see cousins who care so deeply

for each other," Thornton said, bringing him back to sharp reality. "You are a revelation to me, truly. I shall have to be nicer to my sister after this."

They had reached the top of the stairs, and Audrey, blushing and asserting she could walk, slid from the baron's arms. Regretfully he watched as she linked one arm in his, then reached for Thornton.

"Now you must help me, too," she said, trying gamely for a light tone as he obligingly offered his escort. "You can't expect Harry to do all the work."

"No, certainly not," Thornton said. "I think you've almost killed him as it is."

The three of them continued to the far wing, which contained the female servants' rooms. Unlike the staff quarters in many other fine homes, the corridor was nearly as wide as the gentlefolk's below, the bedchambers as spacious. However, each room, excepting the butler's, was shared. The higher servants were housed in pairs, the lower servants divided into groups of threes and fours. Although nearly all of the doors were closed, a chorus of snores could be heard. Not all of the women had taken to their beds, and laughter and chatter rumbled behind some of the walls.

Near the end of the hall, where he knew Lyddie and Bertha shared a room, the door stood open. Hearing raised voices, Harry exchanged a glance with Audrey and increased his pace. When the threesome arrived at the threshold, Lyddie, who was facing them, halted in mid-sentence, her eyes widening in terror. Bertha, hands flapping her apron like wings, turned reflexively and gawked.

"You told them!" Lyddie shouted, shaking so that her hair began to fall from the mobcap she wore. She wore a thick, white nightdress topped by an ancient plaid robe, and as she raised her fist in the air both sets of sleeves rolled backward to expose wiry forearms. "You betrayed me!"

"No, I never," Bertha said breathlessly. "Hush, child. Hush!"

"Don't deny it, for he's come after me!"

Harry supposed she meant himself, as she was pointing a stubby finger at him. The emotions in the room were filling him with a heavy sense of unreality, spiced with the discomfort of madness.

He knew very little about Lyddie, he thought abruptly, although in Audrey's first days at Far Winds he'd felt confident enough in the maid to engage her to report on the young lady's activities. The servant had never discovered anything worthwhile, and he had let the matter drop.

It now occurred that not only did he know hardly anything about the maid, but that most of the servants were largely unknown to him. The presence of so many strangers beneath his roof suddenly seemed foolhardy in the extreme.

"What's wrong, Lyddie?" Audrey asked, moving toward her with compassion. With a dark certainty rising, Harry seized her arm before she went further into the room. She stared at him oddly but yielded. "No one has been talking about you, we were only going to ask you to stay the night with me."

Bertha declared, "No, no, she can't do that, Miss Roxanne."

"Yes, I can," Lyddie said, her voice reverting to her normal husky tones. "You told me to hush, Bertha, but now *you* can hush. This has nothing to do with you."

"Oh, yes it does. You know it does!"

"What's all this commotion about?" Harry demanded of Bertha, who appeared the more level-headed of the two, although not by much, but at least her expression did not raise the small hairs at the back of his neck. "What has she done?"

"Oh, milord—" Bertha began.

"Nothing too important, milord," Lyddie interrupted, her

lids lowering humbly. "I didn't have time to put clean sheets on Miss Roxanne's bed, that's all, and I was afraid she'd be angry. I'll go change them now."

"You won't." The older servant, tears falling, blocked the way. "She's not well, milord. Let her rest this evening, I beg you."

"Tell me the truth," he demanded.

Thornton said, "No one would have greater access to a lady's room than her maid."

"She didn't mean it," Bertha cried. "I know she wouldn't want milady's sweet daughter hurt."

"Traitor!" Lyddie accused hoarsely, retreating to a night table in the corner, her hands behind her back. "I did it all for you, and now you've betrayed me!"

Pushing Audrey behind him, Harry strode to the maid. "Are you responsible for what happened to Roxanne's balcony?" He grabbed the upper portion of her arms. "Do you realize what you've done? She could have been killed or maimed!"

"Why is everyone yelling?" Lucy said from the doorway. "Oh, Bertha. Lady Marianne sent me to get you."

In that moment of distraction, Lyddie jerked a large knife from the drawer behind her and slashed Harry's arm. He fell back in shocked reflex and pain. She ran past, the blade waving threateningly. She meant to hurt Audrey; he saw that instantly. Whatever her plan was, no matter that it was over, she still intended to harm her.

In the instant he leapt for the madwoman, he saw with relief that Thornton was shielding Audrey. Harry grabbed Lyddie around the waist and brought her to the floor. Even then the maid struggled, her cries of rage and insanity frightening him as much as the darting knife which he dodged, then finally wrested from her hands.

Audrey flew to his side as the others gathered round. "You're bleeding," she whispered, then snatched a towel from the bedside table and wrapped it round his arm. Although he was vaguely aware that Thornton took charge of restraining the maid while Lucy fired questions and Bertha sobbed as if her heart were breaking, his true universe was contained in Audrey's worried and loving eyes.

Thank God she is safe.

"She was always a good girl until now," Bertha said. "Please don't think bad of her if you can help it."

It was past midnight, but no one thought of sleep. At least Audrey could not, and the faces surrounding her in Lady Marianne's bedchamber looked far from drowsy, the lady least of all, although she lay comfortably propped on her pillows. The surgeon had tended Harry's wound, which thankfully he declared would not be serious if kept clean and inactive for a few days. The magistrate had driven off with Lyddie only moments before. Now Harry, Thorn, Lucy and she had joined the lady to hear Bertha's story one final time from beginning to end, Marianne declaring she needed their help in deciding how she must plead for Lyddie's punishment.

Audrey thought their gathering seemed like a trial of sorts. She had the feeling that Bertha was being judged as well, and her heart went out to the plump little maid facing them in a straight-backed chair. She hoped desperately that none of this had been her fault, for then it would mean she had two enemies among the servants, servants whom she had liked and trusted. It was too distressing to think her judgment had been so faulty or that anyone could hate her to a murderous degree.

Harry was seated beside Audrey in a wing chair, and she sought and found his gaze. His smile reassured her, its tenderness raising hopes she knew she should suppress despite what had passed between them this night.

He had saved her life. He had kissed her and treated her as lovingly as she could ever dream, but they were only friends. She must keep reminding herself of that. The aristocracy was different. They treated acquaintances with more familiarity than a provincial young woman like herself expected. She was not sophisticated enough. It meant nothing. They were only friends.

Nevertheless, feeling his eyes wandering over her warmed her soul. She dared to think the impossible.

Bertha had recovered her self-control, although seeing her companion restrained and screaming epithets could not have been easy. Audrey's mind reeled from their discovery. Lyddie had been an excellent servant. If the maid hated her so much she wanted her dead, how had she hidden her emotions? Audrey simply could not take it in.

"Think of where she came from," Bertha was saying, hands tugging her handkerchief. "Ten children in her family and no da to care for them, their mother drowning in drink. Lyddie started working before she was six years old, hauling water for a laundry woman. When she came here she was raw as a sheaf of grain. I took pity on her." She glanced at Lady Marianne. "I never had any children to love, and she was lost as a motherless child. Lyddie took to my instruction so eager and well. Smart she was, too. I taught her to read and write in the evenings. You saw how fast she rose through the ranks, milady. You knew she was special."

The maid's features were arched with an implicit appeal. Lady Marianne glanced at Audrey, then her nephew, her mixed feelings apparent. "I know you thought she was, and I believed you."

Bertha wriggled in her chair. "The higher she went, the bigger her dreams grew." She raised the handkerchief and turned her head to blow her nose. "One day she found out what you were planning to give me, milady, if you passed on before I did, and perish *that* thought. She got it in her mind we would retire together in a little cottage by the sea. I shouldn't have encouraged her, I see that now. But it made her so happy when little else did." She set her eyes on Audrey. "And then your daughter came back."

"We still don't know she is Roxanne," Lucy said. "I've been thinking that Nathan might have said she was and saved himself the trouble of going to Bournemouth. He's getting married, and I wouldn't be surprised if he spent that time with his betrothed."

Audrey breathed in shock that Lucy guessed so well. A quick look at Marianne cautioned her to keep quiet.

"You're not to speak so about Nathan Turner," Marianne said. "He's never given me reason not to trust him."

"My pardon," Lucy said sullenly.

"That's what Lyddie thought at first," Bertha said. "That Miss Roxanne wasn't the real one. That's when she sent that note with the arrows."

"That's a polite way to phrase her actions," Harry said.

"Thank you, milord, I try to be," Bertha replied, misunderstanding. "I don't like you to think that I knew about what she was going to do. She didn't tell me 'twas done until it was over, and I gave her a strong tongue lashing, I will say that."

Audrey said in a wondering voice, "She was the only person I told that day that I was going to visit the nurse, and I never once thought of her. In fact, she was the one who suggested I visit Naddie."

"Well, she didn't like the idea of serving an imposter, that's what she told me. She was afraid that when you got discovered out, Lady Marianne might think she was part of the trick and give her the sack. Anyway, when Turner came back with the proof that Miss Roxanne was Lady Marianne's daughter real and true, she calmed down. Until she heard gossip about how milady was planning to change her will."

"What gossip?" Lucy asked.

Bertha kept her eyes fixed on the lady. "When she thought I was to get nothing, she just went to pieces. I told her it didn't matter, that we would always have a nice home here, so long as we could work. And I reminded her that the Hastings don't throw their old ones away, that you take care of them somehow. But it didn't do any good. All she talked about night and day was that we'd lost our cottage and the sweet life by the sea. She hadn't ever even seen the ocean, milady! I tried to tell her how it roars and roars and the wind rips the hair right off your head, but she wouldn't listen."

"Are you cutting Bertha from the will, Aunt Marianne?" Lucy asked.

Marianne's attention did not waver from her maid. "Did she tell you what she'd planned, Bertha?"

"Oh no, milady, no," the maid said. "It was a complete shock to me tonight. What she did was madness. Had I known I would have stopped her."

There was silence for a moment as the lady regarded her servant with fierce concentration. Lucy stirred as if to speak again, but Thorn restrained her by touching her hand.

"I believe Bertha's surprise was genuine," Harry said.

Bertha bowed her head. "I don't hope for your pardon, milady. I have no excuses, for it was my fault the girl got such big ideas in her head. I'll have my bags packed by morning. What I hate most of all is losing your good opinion of me. Please don't send me away believing I had anything to do with what passed this night. I hope I've never done anything in my years of service that would make you doubt that."

Marianne smoothed a wrinkle from her spotless sheets.

"Roxanne, what is your opinion? You're the one who was put at risk. Should I forgive my servant of twenty years?"

"I see nothing to forgive," Audrey said. "She's blameless."

"Not absolutely blameless perhaps, but I believe her error was one of judgment, not intent. Bertha, you may go now, and I expect you at the usual time tomorrow morning."

The servant's face creased into a relieved smile, and she pressed the lady's hand to her lips. "Thank you, milady. Thank you."

"Oh, go on with you, Bertha. And I'll recommend that the magistrate send Lyddie to the madhouse rather than gaol, since her actions were not those of a rational being, I think."

Bertha murmured further words of appreciation, curtseyed, and left the room.

In the silence which followed, Audrey saw approval in the baron's eyes and felt a glow spreading through her flesh. After sending her a soft smile, Harry turned his attention to Marianne.

"You were too soft on Lyddie, Aunt," he said. "She had the presence of mind to perceive she was losing something, then she put a devious and wretched plan into motion that she hoped would restore that bequest."

"I'm doing her no favor in asking for the madhouse," Marianne said. "But Bertha will feel better."

"That was good of you," Lucy said. "You are always good, Aunt Marianne. Now what is this about changing your will? You're leaving out the servants, are you?"

Marianne contemplated Lucy for a heavy interval, then fixed her eyes upon Harry. Speaking with deliberation, she said, "I had not intended to speak until the ball, but since rumors are flying about, I see no reason to delay." She turned to Audrey and extended one hand, which the younger lady took in hers. "Especially after what happened tonight, when I nearly lost my beloved daughter."

Harry moved suddenly, the sounds of protest beginning. Marianne held up a peremptory hand. She looked at Lucy and Thorn and gave a dry laugh, as if to allay their suspicions. "Harry knows what I'm going to say, as I've told him already, but he doesn't want me spoiling the surprise for Roxanne. However, with gossip running, she will know soon anyway."

With a smile so doting that Audrey almost believed she could be the lady's daughter after all, Marianne continued, "In earlier years I thought my child had advantages enough without needing the entire funds of my mother's estate, and thus I planned to divide it among a few individuals as well as Roxanne, giving her half. As you know, you were among those individuals who would have divided the remainder. But circumstances have changed."

Lucy quietly began to moan.

"Harry has developed the estate to the extent that he has no need of my bequest. And Lucy and Thorn, you have always enjoyed the bounty of his and my labor, and we will continue to provide a home for you. But my daughter has lost seven years, seven valuable years of education, refinement, and the comforts of life to which she was born. These years can never be replaced. Consequently, her prospects of making a suitable match may have been irreparably damaged. That is why I've decided to change my will in favor of Roxanne entirely. I have already spoken to my solicitor, and he's drafting the document now. The public announcement will be made at the ball."

Marianne's final words were almost drowned entirely by the increasing volume of Lucy's cries. "You can't, you can't!"

"Oh, but I can," the lady said, her eyes both bright and watchful.

Thorn appeared pale as chalk, but he attempted to calm his sister. She batted his hands away and stood in a fury.

"Don't tell me to be quiet! Are you going to let this— this *person* inherit everything, Thorn? Are you? You know she's an imposter. She simply must be!"

"And why is that?" Marianne asked sharply. "Why are you so certain?"

Thorn went to his sister and placed an arm firmly around her shoulders. "She's distraught and doesn't know what she's saying."

"I know exactly what I'm saying." Lucy pointed a shaking finger at Audrey. "Whoever that woman is, she's not Roxanne!"

Fourteen

Apologizing profusely, Thornton hurried Lucy from the room looking hollow-eyed as a consumptive. And with good reason, Harry fumed, his irate thoughts returning to his aunt. He had not forgotten how helpful Thornton had been in assisting Audrey and himself this night, and though Harry could have managed without him, he didn't appreciate seeing the man and his sister tortured by the threat of loss of their future. And all because of his aunt's plotting, which he was beginning to suspect was delusional, if not evil.

"What are you doing?" he demanded of her.

"I don't know what you mean," she said coolly, releasing Audrey's hand and folding her fingers over her coverlet. "The two of you had better retire. It's late, and we all need our sleep."

"We can sleep later. Why are you perpetuating your game? It's over. You've found the villain."

"We've found one villain," Marianne said, matching his tone. "We haven't found the one who stole Roxanne away. Lyddie's actions were for her own reasons. She wasn't even working at Far Winds when my daughter disappeared."

"Yes, I've thought of that. Thus far your machinations have managed only to create danger for Miss Lassiter. She could have been killed tonight because of your scheming, yet you are no closer to finding Roxanne. When will you accept that all your preparations haven't worked, Aunt Marianne? What will it take you to stop—must I be the one?"

"Who says it won't work? Did you see Lucy's reaction? Did you hear how certain she sounded that this young woman is not Roxanne?"

"The desperation of the disinherited, Aunt. You know I have no patience for the Browns, but you've raised them with certain expectations. You can't imagine they will accept this change gracefully, false though it is. As a point in fact, any one of your beneficiaries could begin to view Miss Lassiter as the major impediment to their future security and act accordingly. We've already seen that happen without revealing a morsel of information. Don't you realize that you're creating murderous impulses in people where none existed before?"

Speaking quickly, Audrey said, "May I say something, since this concerns me as well?"

Harry saw a warrior spark in her eye, and he felt a blend of admiration and worry. In spite of his initial resistance to her—a resistance which he now lay at his aunt's door as its source—she had struck him from the beginning as a woman full of life, one who would never bore or vex him with inanities as so many young females seemed to do. And she never had. But that same freshness of personality had its daring edge or she would not be here. Tonight he had nearly lost her because of it.

That he could both love and fear a quality in someone perplexed him. His life had been very simple before Audrey Lassiter arrived at Far Winds, he now realized with something like nostalgia.

"Lady Marianne asked me to stay through the ball," Audrey said, "and I'm still willing to do that. If someone has anything to confess, surely he or she will do so by then."

"Good girl," Marianne said. "You see, Harry? She's willing. She knows that's what I'm paying her for, after all."

Audrey shifted uncomfortably and flushed. Believing she was embarrassed at this reminder of her hired role, Harry looked aside. His aunt had taught him much about herself during the past few weeks, and what he continued to learn was adding fuel to the flames.

"I should tell you—" Audrey began.

"She understands she must see it through to the finish to receive what I've promised her, don't you, child?" Marianne pressed. Harry could sense his aunt's eyes drilling him, and he refused to meet them.

"I'm not impersonating Roxanne for financial reasons any longer," Audrey said.

The lady regarded her. "Don't overplay your heroism, my dear. We're willing to believe you've caught yourself up in your part to a nice turn, but don't try to pretend that's your primary reason for being here."

When Audrey stiffened at his side, Harry's gaze returned to her. "I meant what I said. I have begun this work, whether it is doomed to failure or not, and I intend to finish it." Shards of blue ice were directed at his aunt, and he found himself fascinated as well as thrilled by Audrey's display of spirit. "But I won't accept payment."

"What do you mean, you won't accept payment?" Marianne queried in a hard voice.

"When I accepted Nathan Turner's offer, I did so to provide for my family, even though it felt very wrong to me. Now that my sister is to be wed, I no longer have that worry. To accept so great an amount . . . I simply can't do it."

Harry's pulse raced. Even though she must sense his

steady gaze, Audrey kept her profile to him. Could she understand what her words meant to him?

And should he trust them? niggled a detestable voice in his brain. She was very intelligent and could not fail to realize her action would relax his worries that she was mercenary. Was she releasing one fortune in order to attract an even greater one?

The hook was dangling, the bait more attractive than he could bear. But he was not quite as empty-headed as a fish, he reminded himself.

Marianne brought one of her decorative pillows to her lap and dug her fingers into the lace. "Oh? And what happens to you, Miss Lassiter? Are you expecting your sister to support you now, or are you dreaming a handsome prince will come to your rescue?"

At this bald echoing of his own worries, Harry made a sound of disgust and stood, pulling Audrey to her feet with him. "That's enough, Aunt. This young lady has made you an offer of unbelievable generosity, and you've insulted her. I'll attribute your rudeness to your state of mind. We've all had a shock tonight, and Miss Lassiter most of all. I'll bid you good night."

And so saying, he led Audrey from the room, although she looked back uncertainly at Marianne, who maintained a chilly silence. Once Marianne's bedroom and sitting room doors were closed behind them, Harry exhaled between his teeth.

"I apologize for her," he said. *And myself,* he added silently.

Audrey lifted her gaze to his. He almost wished she wouldn't, because she appeared so trusting and guileless. *Hooked,* he taunted himself.

"I think she's trying to protect you," she said in wondering tones. "She believes I'm maneuvering myself to . . ." Knowledge came into her eyes. "You—you can't think that as well, that I . . ." Her cheeks reddened.

He saw that she was too chagrined to put voice to her line of thought, and so was he. Opting to play the innocent, he said, "All I can think is how grateful I am you weren't grievously hurt tonight. Are you certain you won't allow the surgeon to examine you? I can send a footman."

"And disturb his sleep again? I refused when he came to tend to your wound, which is much more serious than my little scratches, and I doubt he'd thank me if I changed my mind now. I'll use the balm for my hands that your aunt had prepared for me, and that will heal me soon enough."

"Good. Well, then. You must be exhausted."

Harry told himself to say good night, but he couldn't leave her, not yet. Truth was, he longed to surround her with his arms and kiss her thoroughly. But he had already done that tonight, hadn't he? Had cradled her in his lap and showered her with kisses in his thankfulness that he hadn't lost her. And then carried her upstairs with heated imaginings plain as words in his eyes. No wonder she was looking at him in confusion.

"I am tired, as I'm sure you are," she mumbled, and drifted closer to her door.

"Well, then," he said, repeating himself and feeling bereft as well as idiotic. Why couldn't he let his misgivings go and accept this darling lady? If she would have him, that was. As immediately as the thought crept into his mind, he saw, as if drawn in a portrait before him, the features of another woman he once believed he loved and had trusted as he would his own life. His heart hardened with the image. "Well, good night."

"Sleep well," she said, looking as downcast as he felt while she opened her door. And then, with one hand on the knob, she turned back to him. "Harry . . ."

"Yes?" He returned to her eagerly, his feet ready to do her bidding if his mind was not.

"You rushed me a little tonight," she said.

"I did?"

"When we were in Lady Marianne's room."

"Oh." Disappointment colored his tone. Back to his aunt. But what did he expect, that she would persuade him to let down his guard when only he could do that?

"I was going to tell her something more."

"Were you?"

"Yes, now that I'm not accepting her payment. I didn't have the chance to let her know her what I want to do with my life."

How was it possible that a pair of eyes could contain so much of one's soul? he wondered. And how could someone look testy and at the same time so charming?

"And what is that?" He was speaking mechanically, only listening to her words with half an ear. When standing so near that he could smell the sweet, damp, heathery scent of her hair, he could hardly be expected to do otherwise.

"I'm going to be a governess," she said determinedly, as if he would dispute her.

"Are you?" he said, scanning her face and hair.

"Yes," she said firmly. "I plan to dedicate my life to teaching. I can think of no more worthy goal than training children with love and kindness, can you?"

"Quite so," he answered, his fingers itching to explore the firm softness of her cheeks.

"If she asks again, you may tell her I said that."

Somehow in the past seconds, her voice had grown sharp, he realized, and Harry came to the sudden awareness that all was not well.

"And please," Audrey continued, pronouncing each word with biting distinctness, "please let her know particularly that I'm *not* waiting to be rescued by a handsome prince with gold in his pockets!"

And with that, she swirled into her room and slammed the door.

On the next day, after a belated breakfast of cold toast and scalding hot tea, Audrey stood stoically before the rear window as Mrs. Prate made the final alterations to her ball gown. The French doors leading to the balcony had been swathed in drapery and cordoned off that morning by her new lady's maid, Felicia, a tall woman with frizzy white hair who had appeared nervous with her sudden elevation from parlor maid and was now cleaning the glassed front of the doll case with grunts of effort. Repairs would begin on the broken rail after the ball, the maid had told her.

While the seamstress knelt before her like a frowning supplicant, Audrey looked at the grounds overlooking the park with eyes that felt stiff as rocks in her head. She had not slept, but at least she had not cried into her pillow. Her tears were all gone now, dried at the font. Lord Harry, appealing wretch that he was, would not wrest those from her again.

She felt a prickling behind her lids and blinked rapidly so as not to make a liar of herself.

He loved her. She knew he loved her, or he would not have told her so. Nor would he have trembled as he held her after rescuing her last night, trembled so much that she didn't know where her own relief ended and his began. Not to mention his sensual caresses and the touch of his lips on hers. He *must* love her, perhaps almost as much as she loved him.

Oh, how maddening he was. He was his own—no, *their* own, worst enemy.

She understood how his horrible experience with Carradice had turned him against women at a young age. But he was a man now, and he should realize she was a different person entirely. Had he continued to be angry with her for her part in his aunt's deception, it would perhaps be understandable, if childish, of him. But he'd recovered from that, only to decide that she wanted him for his fortune. If it was not one thing, it was another. One could not help believing he made up reasons to prevent himself from giving way to love.

"I think you've lost a few pounds since my last measuring," Mrs. Prate said in disapproval as she pinched the seams at Audrey's hips. "I can't be expected to fit you properly if you keep changing weight."

Audrey murmured her apologies and turned meekly when the seamstress bid her move closer to the light. The sky was darkening outside, the gathering of clouds mirroring her own hopelessness. She had known all along she was flying too high.

A surge of pride helped balance her gloom. At least she'd been able to tell Harry her hopes for a governessing position. Perhaps he would write her a recommendation, she thought, sinking back into misery.

"There," Mrs. Prate said. "The pins are set, and you can take off the gown, but be careful not to stick yourself. Don't gain weight, either. Now I've got to see to Miss Brown's, if she's awake yet. Some people sleep their lives away."

"Oh, Miss Lucy's not asleep," Felicia said, coming to stand beside them, her surprised-looking gray eyes darting back and forth between her mistress and the seamstress. Audrey felt very small between the two towering women, rather like a child. "I saw her setting out at dawn carrying a rope."

"A rope?" Audrey could not believe she had heard her properly.

"Yes, miss. She was headed across the road, like she meant to go for a walk. When they was little, she and her brother used to go off exploring those caves, so I wondered if that was what she was about. Well, you remember, Miss Roxanne. You went, too."

"Oh, yes," she said vaguely.

"Well, I never," Mrs. Prate said. "As if I didn't have enough to do without waiting for her."

Audrey's suspicions were at the ready. Although Marianne had hurt and angered her last evening, Audrey agreed with her on one issue: Lucy *had* seemed uncannily certain that she was not Roxanne. That the girl would do something so uncharacteristic as to go hiking at daybreak with a rope seemed more than strange. But what any of it could have to do with Roxanne's disappearance, she could not imagine. Surely Lucy had not kept her hidden in a cave all these years.

Her speculations were interrupted by the entrance of Bertha after a polite knock. Lady Marianne wanted to see her, she said. Tasting dread, Audrey finished her toilette with Felicia's anxious assistance. Moments later, wearing a soft cream gown, she entered Marianne's room. Whatever she felt for the lady, she could not fault her generosity in providing beautiful clothes. She tried to take heart in that thought as Marianne waved her to a chair without giving her more than a glance.

Today the older woman lay almost prone in her bed, and her skin looked waxy, her lips bloodless. Audrey viewed her with alarm.

"Do I look ill?" the lady asked, acknowledging her concern with a satisfied gleam.

"You're lovely as always, but—"

"But I look like death, or so I hope." With a glance to make sure the sitting room door was closed, she plumped another pillow and pushed it beneath her head. "I've powdered until my pores are suffocating in service to the cause."

"Oh, in that case, you look terrible."

"Good." One side of Marianne's lips lifted in a grudging smile, a smile that disappeared as quickly as it came. "Now. We need to discuss that nonsense you spoke last night."

Audrey did not pretend ignorance. "Lady Marianne, I don't intend to take your ten thousand pounds. I truly meant what I said."

"Then you're breaking our arrangement."

"I don't understand how you can say that, when I've made it plain I intend to stay until the ball as you asked."

"Don't be huffy with me, miss. I'm not fooled by your sudden selflessness. You intend to entice my nephew with your grand gesture. Well, know this. I'll not have him tied to an adventuress. He deserves better."

Audrey moved to her feet. Struggling to keep her dignity despite the rage throbbing through her veins, she said, "You haven't known me long, Lady Marianne, but you should know me better than that. I've told your nephew what I plan, which is to be a governess. I'm not trying to trick him into anything."

"Governess," she said scornfully. "Very well played, young woman. Very well, indeed. I know what's afoot here. You're using your sister's marriage to release you from the vulgarities of accepting money from me. Then you make him think you're above material concerns and put his chivalry into motion by declaring your intention to entrust your own welfare into the hands of strangers. Well, what if I told you I planned to sack Nathan Turner if you don't fulfill your part of our bargain? How will he support your family then?"

Seconds passed in which Audrey could hear the beating of her heart in her ears. "You can't," she said hoarsely.

"You don't think so? Harry will prevent me, is that what you believe? It's true that he owns Far Winds and can usurp my decisions in such matters. But no one can push me from my position here. Harry wouldn't dare. He knows what I've given this estate, both in monies as well as my life's blood. More importantly, he understands how much this estate has taken from me."

She closed her eyes for a moment, placing a hand over her heart as if to calm it. "Even to my own son, whose death presented my nephew with all he owns," she said quietly. Then, growing fierce again, her stare skewering Audrey, she continued, "Yes, Harry realizes well what he owes me, and he won't contradict my wishes. Even if he does, I have ways that will make Nathan so uncomfortable he'll have no choice but to leave."

"You would do that to Nathan, after all these years?" Audrey asked in hushed tones, aghast at the extent to which this woman would go to have her own way. "I've heard you say again and again that he's your most trusted servant."

Marianne breathed as if to speak, hesitated, then said, "I don't suggest you put it to the test."

It was not possible, Audrey thought, lowering her eyes. No one could be so vindictive, least of all Lady Marianne. Naturally the older woman was strong-willed; but she had shown her kindness many times. Why was she so prejudiced against her?

"How you must hate me," she said, the words flowing unbidden from her pain. She wished she hadn't said them, for it made her sound weak, and Marianne would pounce upon vulnerability like a tiger at the kill.

Instead, the older woman surprised her by responding, "I don't hate you, child. I've grown rather fond of you over the course of your stay here, and would be more fond if I didn't know what ambitions you've developed for my nephew."

"But I haven't—"

"Don't throw lies at me. I've seen how you look at him, and your adoration is as plain as if you wrote your feelings on your forehead."

It is? Audrey thought in misery.

"No, I have nothing against you other than that. You must understand I'm concerned only for Harry's future."

"Don't you want him to be happy?" she asked in a small voice.

Marianne lifted her brows. "Of course I do. That's why you must leave. I remember the passions of youth, and I know they run strong and fast. And brief, alas. Don't flatter yourself into thinking he will be happy only with you, my dear. He must make a strong alliance which will be good for Far Winds. Only *then* will he be truly content, for once the fever in his blood has calmed—and it will, child, it will—he'll return to his true source of joy, which is this estate."

A glimmer of suspicion had begun to tug at Audrey's mind during this speech, a shimmering belief that blazed into full conviction. "You want Harry and Roxanne to wed!"

Shock came into Marianne's eyes, then was quickly covered with an impassive expression. But Audrey had seen it, had seen the confirmation of the woman's most dearly guarded secret.

"Of course," Audrey said. "Now I understand why you've chosen this moment in time to plan such an elaborate attempt of recovery. Your daughter is of a marriageable age, and you've known that Harry must take a bride sometime. This is your last desperate chance to keep Far Winds in your own family's line."

"I've searched for Roxanne ever since she disappeared,"

Marianne said vehemently. "I want my daughter back for *herself* as any mother would."

"I don't doubt that for a moment, but your first love is this estate. I pity you."

"Don't condescend to me, you young—"

"If you do find Roxanne, and Harry wishes to marry her and makes all of your dreams come true, then you have my congratulations," Audrey said curtly as she moved to the door. "You may revel in your wealth and trees and rose gardens and this great pile of bricks until you're all in your dotages with walking canes, and I'll not stop you. But I won't take your money, no matter what you threaten." *Especially now.*

When Audrey entered the salon in the moments preceding luncheon, Harry stood politely, as did Nathan and Thornton, but neither of them felt their hearts drop to their boots as his did. At least he hoped not. If either man experienced the same rush of feeling at the sight of Miss Lassiter as Harry, he had by heaven better keep it to himself.

He watched her carefully as she scanned the inhabitants of the room from inches inside the threshold, her eyes snagging on him, away, then returning with a flash of something like resentment. She was still angry, then. He could not blame her. Their last interchange had displayed her understanding of his fears that she might be an opportunist. He did not believe she was, at least not in the sense that Marianne suggested, and he must make her understand somehow. But the manner in which she was viewing him and the other gentlemen did not make him hopeful that such an opportunity would present itself soon.

"Excuse me," she said, moving away. "I've only now

thought that I need to look up some information in the library."

"Perhaps I can be of help," Thornton said. "I'm a mine of information on trivial subjects. Do you need to know the major exports of India? The population of Spain? You have only to ask."

"No, nothing like that," she said, a chuckle in her voice. "It was our family history I'd like to study. Harry, could you show me the records? You must keep books of some sort."

"Of course," he said gladly, nearly pushing Nathan from his path in his effort to get to her.

"Ah, well, passed over again." Thornton sighed behind them as Harry led her down the hall.

She whispered as they walked, "Are you and Nathan planning to shadow my every move even now that Lyddie is gone? Please tell me you do not."

"Sorry, but the answer is yes. Until I'm certain you're safe."

They had arrived at the library, and he led her into the intimate room with its mahogany shelves of books, a small fireplace, a scattering of isolated chairs, and a round table and chairs set in the center. It was a private room, one which he used as a retreat when Lucy and Thornton wearied his patience, but he had visited it seldom since Miss Lassiter's arrival. As he went to peruse the shelves, Audrey sat at the table.

"Please don't trouble yourself," she said. "I'm not truly interested in your geneology, I only wanted to speak with you alone."

This pleased him more than it should have, for her expression did not suggest she intended a loving exchange but something more distressful. Now that he took his seat beside her and saw her more closely, he realized she appeared deeply distraught.

"Audrey, what's wrong?"

She extended her fingers toward him on the table, as if she meant to take his hand but didn't dare. He had no such reservations and covered her fingers beneath his, hoping to give comfort. Her skin shocked him with its coolness.

"Harry, you . . . you have a degree of fondness for me, do you not?"

"More than fond," he said, gratified that she had opened the very subject he wished to broach. "Last night, I believe you misunderstood me. I don't have the notion that you're"—Suddenly he found it difficult to speak about this, especially as her eyes sharpened with a doleful look of cynicism, but he *must* explain himself—"that is to say, I disagree with Marianne when she called you . . ."

"An adventuress?"

"That word and your name should never be breathed in the same sentence."

Her skepticism deepened. "What word would *you* use, then?"

"Adorable," he said honestly. "Winsome. Charming . . ."

She shook her head impatiently. "I'm not looking for compliments you don't mean. We both know you're determined to judge all women on the basis of one experience, and I don't say that to belittle its importance in your life. That—that *female* was beyond shocking in her behavior, and I hope she is wretched and—and *hot* in Australia, hot as blazes. But you've given her the final victory, my lord, and for that you must accept your portion of the blame. She has conquered your spirit, your trust, your hope for goodness in human character. You have let her win, Harry."

For a very long interval, silence reigned in the small room. He felt a deep coldness spreading from his head downward. His gaze drifted blindly to the open doorway. By degrees he became aware of the clock ticking on the mantel, of Tidwell passing in the hall on his way to attend one of his duties, of his hand releasing Audrey's to fall to his lap.

"But I've not come here to speak about that," she said, oblivious to his pain or not caring about it. "I find it necessary to ask a favor of you."

"A favor," he repeated through numb lips.

She leaned toward him earnestly, as if trying to call back his attention. As if she had ever once lost it. "Promise me, Harry, that you won't dismiss Nathan, no matter what your aunt desires. Please?"

"What?" He could not process her words. She was the only person he knew who could delight, startle, infuriate, and stun his brain into mash, all within a matter of seconds.

"Your aunt has threatened to give him the sack if I don't accept her wages, and I won't accept them. I won't. No matter what anyone says or does. But that's no reason to punish him or my sister."

"Hold a moment. You're telling me that Marianne—why would she speak of cutting off Nathan if—oh." Years of observing his aunt's mind at work told him the rest. She thought Audrey's refusal of her ten thousand pounds would make the girl more attractive in his eyes, and she was willing to stoop to coercion to force her to accept the original agreement. "I confess I'm appalled at what you're telling me. I knew my aunt was desperate, but I didn't know her thinking could sink so low."

"I'm surprised as well. She has many strange thoughts." Audrey's expression made him wonder what else his relative had inflicted upon the girl, but she appeared unwilling to say more, even when he sent her his most probing look.

"Rest assured that this is one idea she won't bring to fruition," he said. "You don't have to worry."

She thanked him gravely and pushed back her chair. Had

Tidwell not arrived to announce luncheon, he would have begged that she remain. It was just as well, he supposed.

You have let her win, Harry. The simple words growled in the background of his mind with the force of rumbling thunder. Could Audrey have any idea how angry her statement made him?

Angry with whom, he could not say.

Ever correct no matter what his feelings, he offered his arm to the young lady and escorted her toward the dining alcove. Thornton and Nathan joined them in the hall, Thornton eyeing the stairs with a questioning look as they passed.

"I don't suppose anyone's seen Lucy," he said idly upon entering the morning room. "It's not like her to away without telling anyone."

As the baron pulled Audrey's chair for her, she exclaimed, "Felicia told me she saw her crossing the road at dawn. I'd forgotten until now. She missed her fitting with Mrs. Prate."

Thornton's steps faltered. "Missed a fitting appointment? Now you've frightened me."

Despite the lightness of his tone, Harry gave Thornton a keen look. His features were as smooth as ever, yet color had ebbed from his cheeks.

"She was carrying a rope, Felicia said," Audrey added. "You don't think Lucy meant to go climbing alone, do you? The maid said something about caves."

"One never knows with Lucy," Thornton said, taking his seat. A fraction later, he said, "But perhaps I'd better look for her in case."

He hurried from the room, the attempt to downplay his concern fooling no one.

"Lucy never misses a meal," Harry mumbled.

Tidwell began to serve plates of field greens and tomatoes mixed with a creamed dill sauce. The baron glanced at the vegetables without registering them, traveling back in memory to a similar luncheon years ago when Roxanne had failed to appear. There had been mild curiosity at first, then concern, and later, panic-stricken searches. And nothing had ever been the same again.

"I'm going to help Thornton," he announced, rising.

"I'll come with you," Audrey said, his worry reflecting in her face.

"No," he said firmly. "You remain with Nathan."

And though he sent her a look meant to paralyze the best-intentioned helpfulness, he beat a hasty retreat when he saw the flash of rebellion in her blue, blue eyes.

Fifteen

As Audrey contemplated the gentlemen's sudden departure, she accepted Tidwell's offer of a roll without awareness, then stared at the crusty concoction—one thing they could not do at Far Winds was bake, at least not to Rebecca's standards—without appetite. There could be no doubting both of the men were disturbed about Lucy's uncharacteristic behavior. She felt a sense of urgency building that the lowering clouds outside did not help. The dining alcove had fallen into the shadow of late evening, though it was only past noon. Tidwell was beginning to light the candles.

"I'm grateful for an opportunity to speak with you," Nathan Turner said. She was startled; she'd almost forgotten he remained seated opposite her. "I've wanted to tell you more about my courtship of my dear betrothed." He glanced meaningfully at Tidwell. "Since you've expressed an interest in Rebecca in the past, Miss Roxanne."

For the passing of several seconds, she stared at him without comprehension, then said, "I assure you, Nathan, there's nothing I'd rather do, but some other time. I've been struck with an excruciating headache and need to lie down."

The steward murmured sympathetically and scooted to

his feet as she slipped from the room. Remembering to walk at a pace indicative of great pain, she climbed the steps slowly until leaving his line of sight, then hastened upward and down the corridor, descended the servants' stair, and exited the rear entrance with a smile and casual wave for the kitchen servants which she hoped would dispel suspicion. Careful to circle the side of the house opposite the morning room, she crossed the avenue and ventured into the wood.

She moved as quickly as possible, hoping to catch a glimpse of Harry or Thorn. If she did not soon do so, she would return to the house rather than endure the humiliation of becoming lost.

She had never walked here before, as the tended grounds of Far Winds had thus far offered enough diversion. From tidbits of conversations over the past weeks, she knew the baron owned much of this undeveloped land and that sections of it were reserved for future plantings and others allowed to lie as nature willed. The Hastings forebears, like most Englishmen, treasured land above all else, and there could never be enough of it. Audrey understood the need, for it was bred into her bones. Yet as she struggled through the undergrowth and lifted her hem to cross fallen logs, she could not help thinking that some families carried that desire to excess while others could not even afford to purchase four walls and a roof to keep them warm in winter.

Her pique soon diminished as the woods thinned and gave way to gentle hills which delighted the eye. From the seclusion of the last stand of trees, she scanned all that lay before her. Oaks, elms, chestnuts, ash, and pine dotted the landscape in pleasing arrays. From this elevation she could see a section of the Hogs-back, the eight-mile-long ridge road which led from Guildford to Farnham. She also spotted cottages in the far distance, and sheep grazing in a meadow. But of Harry, Thorn or Lucy, she saw no sign.

She resolved to climb the nearest hillock, and then if that revealed nothing, she would turn back. The clouds looked ready to burst at any moment, and she heard thunder rolling.

The journey took longer than expected. By the time she made the ascent, humidity had fattened her curls, and perspiration was prickling down the small of her back like tiny insects. She almost wished it would rain. And then a flash of green descending over the next hill caught her eye, and she felt a flood of renewed energy. Harry had been wearing a green jacket that brought out the color of his eyes to a heartbreaking extent. She could not help noticing that morning in the library, even as he fired her temper with his immovable ideas about women, painting everyone in the world with the same brush. She could do the same; she could turn herself against him by imagining he was boorish as Burl Ingerstand or heartless as the carpenter Will Whitson, but she had not. Truly, it became difficult to remain understanding of Lord Harry Hastings. Nevertheless, she trotted forward.

When Audrey crested the rise a few moments later, she was breathless and overheated and temporarily forgot the necessity of remaining hidden. Thus it was Harry who first spied her from a couple of hundred feet away, his anger evident as he knelt beside a small aperture gaping into a barren, rocky hillock. That he did not want to be seen by anyone or anything within was plain, and, when she shook her head at his motions to go back, he furiously signaled her to be quiet, one forefinger transversing his lips.

Crouching as she ran, Audrey skittered to his side, her eyes question marks.

"What are you doing here?" he mouthed, scarcely making a sound. "You were ordered to remain at Far Winds."

"I don't always do as I'm told," she whispered.

His eyebrows flexed downward. "So I've noticed."

"Have you found Lucy?"

"She's inside. Thornton went in a moment ago."

"Then why—"

"Listen."

She fell quiet and leaned closer. In the stillness, she could hear the faint sound of voices within, most certainly Lucy's and Thorn's, and in her relief she started to move forward. Harry threw out an arm to stop her. Perplexed, she settled back and waited.

A period of silence followed, through which she gradually discerned sobbing. Again she looked at the baron, her concern forcing him to make an explanation.

"I was far enough behind not to be noticed by Thornton," he said, his impatience thickening his voice to a heavy whisper, "and as he seemed to have a particular destination in mind, I decided to remain unobserved. It all seemed peculiar to me. I suppose this was one of their old haunts, though. Then I heard Lucy, and he was arguing—"

He grabbed her arm as the voices renewed inside.

"This is the most ridiculous thing you've ever done," Thorn said. "You could have been killed."

"I had to know," Lucy whined, her voice echoing eerily from the depths, making Audrey shiver. "I've wondered all these years. Can't you hurry?"

"Unlike you, I don't have the advantage of a rope," Thorn said, his words coming in short gasps. "And if I had a rope, I would have tied a better knot around that rock and not pulled it in behind me. I'm going slowly because if I fall and break a leg, we'll both rot in this hole." Silence. "Why didn't you simply ask?"

"Because I was afraid."

"Afraid of what—that your fears would prove true?"

"Yes," she said, sobbing. "Or that you'd be angry at me for thinking it. And then you might hate me or leave as our mother did."

"Oh, Lucy," he said tiredly. "Sometimes—"

There was a sliding noise, then a short, feminine shriek. Harry and Audrey exchanged glances of alarm and moved immediately to crawl through the entrance. After several feet the opening yawned to a curious kind of anteroom from which several tunnels led. At this point, Audrey was able to stand to her full height, and she eyed the limestone walls with trepidation. A faint illumination from outside scattered enough light to see how dark the tunnels looked, impenetrably dark, and behind one of them were the siblings they must evidently rescue. The baron pointed briefly to a series of names carved in rounded, childish script into one of the walls: Roxanne, Lucy, Thorn.

"I'm all right, I'm all right," Thorn said, his voice sounding thankfully near, somewhere behind the aperture to their right. "Though I need to rest a moment before climbing back up. I hope I have enough energy to pull you when I do. Haven't you been gaining weight again?"

"I most certainly have not!"

"Hold on, Thornton," Harry said. "I'm here to help."

A surprised quiet fell, then Thorn said, "Thank God."

Although relieved that Thorn had not been injured badly, Audrey felt her most primitive fears rising to the surface in this enclosed space; and when the baron maneuvered her behind him, she did not object. She had never been in a cave and expected anything to happen. The woeful, moaning spirit of Roxanne would not surprise her, nor would a gnarled, bearded troll. She was certain there would be spiders.

Harry had already begun his crawl into the dark. He had not bothered to caution her to remain behind, and she thought this a trifle unfeeling of him. She knelt to follow, sparing a moment's sorrow for the certain ruin of her gown.

Fortunately it was only a short passage before they could stand again, and she was thankful that a shaft of light shone through the rocks above, enough so that they could stop short of a formidable slope that angled into the ground, then fell away like a well. Imitating Harry, she peered over the edge on hands and knees to see the upturned faces of the Browns far below. Had Lucy willingly climbed into this hole? Audrey felt a tremor of admiration and censure for her foolhardiness. Nothing could induce her to descend into such a pit.

"I see you brought Roxanne with you," Lucy said.

"She brought herself," Harry answered. Rather unkindly, Audrey thought.

A sprinkle of dirt crumbled beneath Audrey's white-knuckled fists, and Lucy sheltered her eyes with both hands as she looked upward. "I suppose I'd better apologize for doubting you, Roxanne."

Thorn began to wind the rope which lay at his feet. "Apologies later. Pray focus your thoughts on getting out of here first."

"You needn't bother anyway, Lucy; you've already apologized," Audrey said.

"No, but I mean it from the heart this time." Lucy gave a strained attempt at laughter. "I came down here expecting to find your bones, if you can imagine that!"

Audrey sent Harry a dumbfounded look. "Did you say *bones?*" she squeaked.

"Yes, years ago I thought—"

"Hush, Lucy, and stand back," Thornton interrupted. "Harry, my sister climbed down with a rope which held out long enough to keep her from breaking her neck. I'm going to try and send it up to you."

Holding onto one end, Thorn threw the coils upward, but the rope snagged on the angled part of the hole and slid back. After two similar attempts, he judged the feat impossible and declared his intention of climbing.

"There's no point in risking it; the walls are too steep

where you are," Harry said. "I'll go to the drop-off and you can try again." And before Audrey could object, the baron turned and began his descent.

Lucy and Thorn had gone this way moments before, she assured herself, her heart pounding in fear for him, but Lucy had the assistance of a rope, and Thorn was an experienced climber and even he had fallen partway. Accidents happened, and people could be killed crossing a road.

As the moments passed, however, though she continued to feel tension in every pore, Harry moved with confidence and a steady strength that inspired hope. In less time than she would have dreamed possible, he reached the edge of the slope and, boots planted firmly into the wall and one hand clinging to a rock jutting from the earth, he instructed Thorn to throw the rope. Harry caught it in one effort, wound the end around one hand, and ascended.

When he attained his feet, Audrey flung her arms around his neck and kissed his cheek, then stepped back in embarrassment. "That was the bravest thing I've ever seen," she explained immediately, lest he think she was throwing herself at him. Which of course she had, only not in a bad sense.

Although he raised one eyebrow ironically, the baron looked pleased. "You haven't seen a great deal in life, have you, my dear?"

My dear. She tried not to read too much into his choice of the soft words, for he probably used them with everyone from the maids to his horse, but she couldn't deny liking the sound, no matter how irritating he was in his inability to trust her. And the tender way his eyes were moving across her face, the gentle manner in which he wiped a smudge from her cheek with his handkerchief—she liked that, too.

Sounds of grumbling could be heard from below. "Anytime you want to throw the rope, Harry, we're ready," Thorn called.

The baron jumped into action. After Thorn tied his end around Lucy's waist, Harry began to pull. Over his objections, Audrey did her best to help, but after an instant she realized she was only getting in the way in the cramped space and retreated to the role of encourager. For her part, Lucy scrabbled to gain footholds to support her weight. After an excruciating effort by both, the girl finally attained the top. She sat limply for a few seconds but did not appear traumatized by her ordeal, merely out of breath. Several times she started to speak but could not. Audrey watched her sympathetically, imagining the thousand and one things she would wish to say after tempting death and being rescued so dramatically.

At last Lucy seemed to recover. "Did either of you bring anything to eat?" she asked. "I only had a piece of toast for breakfast, and that was hours and hours ago."

Unfortunately they had not brought food, and Harry turned to Thorn's rescue. His ascent came much easier. The baron had only to anchor the rope around a boulder while the younger man climbed. Once he arrived on safe ground, he grasped the baron's hand in thanks and clapped him on the shoulder.

The enclosed space was far too small for four adults, and they quickly returned through the tunnel to the antechamber. Although it was only a short, stooping walk from here to the outdoors, the sound of a raging downpour outside prompted a unanimous decision to tarry.

Harry spread his handkerchief atop a rock and offered the seat to Audrey. Knowing that her gown was past saving, she accepted his gallantry with a weary smile. He sat beside her, legs stretched before him, while Lucy and Thorn huddled near the opening. With the flow of rain making furious, lonely music and with relief plain on every face, their presence in the ancient room might be companionable, were it not so curious.

"I'm sorry to have caused such trouble," Lucy said, and Audrey marveled at how lively she sounded after her disaster. "I know it must seem strange to you that I came here. Well, Roxanne, you might not think it strange, since we used to climb constantly as children. If you can remember, that is. Do you see how our names are still engraved on the wall? But I'm so relieved to know you're still alive, even if it does mean I'll lose every penny. As long as I know the inheritance is going to you—the real you—it's all right."

The young lady grimaced and flexed her hands outward. "To be perfectly honest, it's not all right, because a dowry is essential if I'm ever to get married. I came close to a betrothal with Robert Lynley, well not close precisely, but he seemed quite taken with me, didn't he, Thorn?"

"He didn't run in the opposite direction when he saw you, if that's what you mean," Thorn said noncommitally.

Lucy pulled a face at him. "Roxanne, do your remember Robert? He had red hair and freckles as a boy, and he has red hair and freckles as a man. But Sylvia Ainsworth stole him away, I'm certain because of the size of her fortune. So you see, I shall probably never get married unless"—she grinned at the baron—"someone like Harry comes along with his purse already full. Oh, I have so much to tell you, Roxanne, now that I know it is you! You cannot imagine how relieved I am."

Thorn said, "Lucy, calm yourself, will you? Your voice is like a rapier gouging holes through my head."

She giggled. "Sweet brother, how I must apologize to you for thinking as I did, but I was afraid to ask, afraid of what I'd discover. I should have trusted you, and I did for years, except for that one niggle of doubt which I've kept to myself. But when Aunt Marianne announced last night that she intends to change her will, all my old worries came to the front, and I thought, *I must look and be certain, once and for all.* I should have known you wouldn't leave anyone to die, least of all our little Roxanne!"

Audrey's glance shifted from Lucy to Thorn, who looked uncommonly pale in the dim light. Her palms grew moist. She felt herself on the edge of a great discovery but was afraid to hope.

After a beat of silence, Harry said carefully, "Lucy, what are you talking about?"

"Pay her no mind," Thorn said, his lips scarcely moving, his voice flat. "She seldom makes sense, and I've found that if I simply nod now and then it's sufficient."

"Oh, Thorn," Lucy said, and slapped his knee playfully. Her neck arched and swiveled as she viewed the anteroom with a fond expression. "I haven't been here since the day Roxanne disappeared." She glanced at Audrey. "Have you remembered yet?"

Unconsciously holding her breath, Audrey shook her head. Lucy continued, "No, I suppose not. I hope I never hit my head and forget everything. It must be dreadful knowing nothing."

When the girl fell into a reverie, Audrey exchanged a glance with the baron. His eyes were sharp with speculation, as she knew hers must be. Softly she asked, "What happened that day, Lucy?"

"What? Oh, yes, sorry. I was thinking that if this rain doesn't end soon I shall simply die with hunger. I would give my left eye for a currant bun." She curled an errant strand of hair behind one ear. "We were playing a hide-and-seek game, only the two of us. Thorn wouldn't participate. He thought he was too old, and I suppose now he was. But neither of us thought so then. Anyway, Roxanne, after playing a few rounds, you wanted to move the game outside. That's when you caught sight of Thorn as he was crossing the avenue. We knew he intended to go exploring because you'd told us you were, didn't you, Thorn? Only you said we couldn't go with you this time, that you were becoming tired of nursemaiding babies. Remember that, brother? You made me so angry I wanted to claw out your eyes."

When he perceived an answer was expected, Thorn said, "Being so much older, I knew I was responsible for the two of you when we were together. Both of you were becoming more adventurous. More dangerous to yourselves. I suppose I resented the responsibility."

"Never apologize, I don't hold it against you now," Lucy said. "But you can see how natural it was that Roxanne decided we would follow you secretly. When you came to the cave, we gave you time enough to climb into one of the inner tunnels, then we ran into this outer part, where we are now. We knew you intended to descend into the pit, because you were fascinated by it. Roxanne was, too."

She waved a hand expressively in Audrey's direction. "You always enjoyed the outdoors far more than I. And since Thorn had forbidden us to go into that inner chamber because it wasn't safe, that fascination grew. You were determined to have your turn at the rope. We crawled into one of the side tunnels"—she peered at the inner walls of the cavern—"I think it was this one on the right. Whichever one, it went nowhere and smelt fusty and seemed more fitting for a pair of mice than a couple of young females. We waited there for a long time, hoping that Thorn would finish and we could descend. In those days you kept a rope tied to that boulder in there, do you remember, Thorn?"

"Yes," he said, the word squeezing through his teeth.

"We sat folded into that tunnel for what seemed forever to me. I became tired and bored, but not you, Roxanne. Perhaps at thirteen I was getting too old for this sort of thing too. I begged you to give up your plan and promised we'd come back another day when Thorn wasn't there. You refused and said you intended to go further into the cave and follow Thorn into the pit at that very moment. I wouldn't do that, because my brother was capable of nagging at me for days, whereas he always treated you better. We argued, but neither one of us was willing to give way. Finally, to my everlasting shame, I went home and left you there. It was the last time I saw you."

Beside Audrey, Harry had grown very still, his body tense. "And what is it you believed happened?" he asked.

"I didn't know, but I was certain Thorn did." Her eyes rounded sadly as she contemplated Audrey. "I thought you must have followed him as you threatened, and that you probably fell into the pit. And when Thorn returned alone and never said anything, I was afraid you'd been killed." Her gaze darted between Harry and Audrey, her expression appealing. "You must understand, we were children. We had no one to care for us other than Aunt Marianne. If something had happened while you were in my care, Roxanne, I'm sure I wouldn't have told anyone for fear of being thrown out."

Thornton rested his forearms on his knees. Without meeting his sister's eyes, he asked, "And that's what you thought I did? Left Roxanne alone and untended in the dark?"

"Don't be angry with me, Thorn," she pled. "To me such actions were understandable. The pit is no lonelier than a grave, after all. I never once imagined you had hurt her, don't think that. But once Roxanne was dead, accidentally dead I mean, what good could be served in telling anyone?"

"What good?" Harry asked sharply. "You could have spared Marianne the seven years of hell she's endured since, never knowing what happened to her daughter."

"He would have risked us both if he had," Lucy declared.

"Besides, I did suggest to the search members that she might have gone to the cave by herself, and I know people looked here and every square inch of Far Winds. And miles beyond, for that matter. Even I came back the next day and crawled through to the pit. I might have tried the descent, but when I saw Thorn's rope was missing, I couldn't. That's when I started to reason to myself that the men must have taken it away after looking for her. And since she wasn't found, she must not be there." She shook her head. "Still, that silly idea would not go away. If only I'd searched before now, I could have rested my mind."

Lucy sighed and stretched her arms. "But we're arguing a moot point, Harry," she said with contentment. "It doesn't matter what Thorn might or might not have done; Roxanne didn't fall into the pit because she's with us again and has told us what she remembers about the gypsies and everything, and now at last I can believe her."

Audrey had been watching Thorn steadily over the past seconds, but she could not discern what he was thinking, for his head was bowed, his eyes hidden. "What *did* happen that day in the cave?"

"Perhaps one day you'll be able to tell us," he said after a moment, his ravaged gaze rising to meet hers. Softly he added, "Roxanne."

With that look, she felt a chill of certainty that something horrible had happened to the little girl, and that Thorn knew, whether by intent or accident, what had occurred. Disappointment and sadness crushed her. Without wishing to, she had grown to feel a grudging affection for Thorn, thinking of him almost as a brother. That he was the kind of person who could do such a thing trembled her soul. She swept an agonized glance toward Harry, but his eyes were fixed immovably upon the other man as if he were regarding a new and revolting creature.

Thorn did not miss their shocked censure. Smiling

grimly and rising to his feet, he said, "Thank you, Lucy, for your candid reflections. You've accomplished much with them, planting suspicions where none existed before."

"But I don't understand," she said, clearly upset. "Nothing happened to Roxanne!"

"Don't trouble your head with it, my sister," Thorn said, and walked into the rain.

When the deluge slackened to a drizzle about a half-hour later, Harry led the ladies back to Far Winds, one on each arm. The heavy downpour had beaten portions of the earth into mud, and more than once Lucy slipped on the return journey. She had fallen into a distracted quiet, as had they all.

While they walked, he experienced the growing conviction that his world was escalating into a frenzied, mad place. Now he struggled to join the splintered pieces of the last weeks together. He could live without many things, but logic and order were not among them.

Since he came to live at Far Winds, life had settled into a predictable and safe routine. The death of his uncle and the disappearance of Roxanne had devastated that placidity, but those events were spread over spans of time to allow recovery. All families had their tragedies. But nothing in his history had prepared him for the jarring pace of the past weeks, when it seemed each day brought a new and unwelcome revelation.

He glanced at the fair, elfin lady at his right. Well, not all unwelcome. But the turbulence had begun with her.

No, to be precise, it had started with his aunt, but he hadn't known that then. How striking to think that mere weeks ago Audrey had entered his life, that he'd begun what he thought was a noble effort to reveal her as an imposter, only to learn Marianne had deceived them all.

That was the worst of it, to find himself at odds with his aunt, to learn that even she was not the rock he'd always imagined.

And every day that passed, every mind-shaking day, he'd fought his slide into love for Miss Lassiter despite a morass of distrust. Then to see her life threatened not once, but twice—how unjust that was; how unnecessarily this honorable, bewitching creature had been endangered by his aunt's contrivances. He believed that last night's blood-chilling run from his room to hers, when he knew at any second Audrey could fall to her death, would haunt him until his final moment.

And now today's disclosure. To discover his aunt might have been correct after all, that someone from Far Winds had known about Roxanne's disappearance and perhaps played a part in it, and that the someone must be Thornton—the suspicion stunned him. He had not held his almost-cousin in high regard, but that was because of the young man's dandy nature, his ineffectual life and negligent disregard for the running of the estate which supported him. Never had Harry dreamed him capable of this, of hiding a child's disappearance, of perhaps even hiding her death, and then maintaining his silence for seven years.

Apparently no one was as he or she seemed.

His carefully crafted belief that people were predictable and obvious when it came to character was crumbling around his ears. But behind every flaw he could, for the first time, perceive reasons that spurred actions, from the simplest to the most complex.

As soon as the three of them arrived at the house, the ladies retreated to their rooms and Harry went to Thornton's chamber, determined to discover the entire truth. The young man's room was empty. Disgusted but not surprised, Harry washed and changed before speaking to his aunt. She deserved to know this latest development, but he dared not think how it would affect her.

He was struggling with his cravat when someone knocked. When he answered, Lucy, carelessly dressed in a fresh gown, rushed into his room waving a piece of paper.

"Oh, Harry, Thorn's gone," she said, her voice trembling. "I knew something was wrong when he spoke the way he did in the cave, but I don't understand what's made him so upset. He left me this note. What do you think it means?"

Taking the missive from her hands, Harry read, *I'll be gone for a little while, sister. Don't worry. Must sort out some things, but I'll return.*

She watched him anxiously. "Is he in trouble? I feel something's terribly wrong."

"I don't know, Lucy. Perhaps he'll explain when he returns." Harry wondered if any of them would ever see him again, but he hadn't the heart to voice his doubts to her.

"Do you think something occurred that last day with Roxanne, and he's afraid she'll remember now? No, that couldn't be so; he never said anything. How could he not tell me? But if he did, if something did happen to her, do you think Aunt Marianne . . ."

Gazing into her frantic eyes, Harry was surprised at the flow of compassion he felt for this young woman who had so often annoyed him in the past. She was worried again that she would lose her home. How many countless times had that thought crossed her mind during her life here? It staggered him to think what it would be like to have no resources, to know you were dependent upon the goodwill of others for the very food in your stomach.

"No matter what happened between Thornton and Roxanne, you'll always have a place at Far Winds, Lucy," he said gently. "You don't need Marianne's support for that. You will have mine."

Her eyes filled with tears, and for a troubled moment he feared she might have misunderstood his words, read more into them than he'd meant. But once again he was wrong. "Oh, thank you, Harry," she said, looking radiant. "Truly you've always been good to me."

No, I haven't, he thought. *But I hope to be better now.*

As Lucy departed, he felt a stabbing need to see Audrey, more overwhelming than the deepest hunger. But first he must deal with Marianne. He finished tying his cravat and walked to the lady's chamber.

It took him only a few moments to sketch in their activities of the morning, and as he had expected, Marianne accepted the news with extreme agitation.

"Gone? Where is he? What has he done, Harry? What has Thornton done with my child?"

"Steady, Aunt. We don't know anything for certain. I can send out search parties if you wish."

She breathed deeply, calming herself. "No, no, he said he'd come back. If he hasn't returned by tomorrow night, that's when we'll begin. I don't want to start rumors flying by having our men roaming the countryside the day before the ball, and truly we can't spare them. There is too much to be done."

She was still worrying about the ball. "The important matter is to end Miss Lassiter's role. I believe you have what you wanted, and it's more than I expected you to gain. At the very least you have Lucy's report."

"But I need more, much more." She pressed her fingers to her eyes, and Harry noticed with shock how frail and skeletal the backs of her hands were looking, how prominent the veins. "She can't have fallen to her death. Please, God, don't let it be that; I have hoped and prayed for so many years that she is alive." She blinked, sweeping away tears. "I want my daughter." Her voice sank. "Even if it is only her bones, I want her home."

Easing himself onto the side of her bed, Harry covered her fingers with his. "I know you do. As I live, we'll find Thornton and make him tell us all he can. In the meantime, you should cancel the ball."

She freed one hand and lifted a handkerchief from her bedside table. Dabbing at her eyes and nose, she whispered, "Not yet. Everyone is expecting the celebration to be the highlight of the season. We'll carry on as planned."

The baron found his patience stretching. "Is this your need for perfection again, to do what is expected? Are you afraid of making people talk because of a canceled gathering? How much more will you have to explain when you send out word that you've played a hoax on the entire village?" He was not reaching her, he could see that. In frustration, he released her fingers. "I have reasons why I don't want Audrey Lassiter identified formally as Roxanne."

She regarded him steadily. "And I can guess what those reasons are." With a sigh, she tossed back her counterpane, slid from the bed, and tread slowly to the french doors. "I had greater plans for you, Harry, but I don't entirely disapprove. You would not believe how she talks to me sometimes, but she has made me think."

"She has made me think as well." He smiled.

Marianne turned back to him, impassioned. "Allow me to maintain the fiction one more night, Harry. Perhaps Thorn will come back, or Lucy will remember something else. Maybe she hasn't told all she knows. It's possible Thorn didn't see Roxanne at all, and that someone else entirely is involved in her disappearance. The threat of losing the inheritance might still force that person to confess. I've been more crafty than you thought, you've admitted as much. We've learned a great amount, haven't we, things we might never have known if I hadn't hired Miss Lassiter.

Grant me this one concession, Harry. Only one more night, dear. Please."

In the face of such pain, he could only do one thing. He kissed her forehead in reluctant acquiescence.

Sixteen

Throughout that afternoon and evening, Audrey longed to have a few moments alone with Harry to discuss the events at the cave, but that time did not offer itself.

Nathan remained a glowering presence until after supper, when he took himself off with a muttered comment about seeing to the wheat since certain parties could not be expected to do as they said anyway. Although she had apologized for eluding him that morning, Audrey feared her future brother-in-law no longer trusted her. No one seemed to, she thought in the salon after he'd gone, eyeing the baron woefully as he leafed through a newspaper. It seemed unfair and harsh of everyone when she had only the best of intentions no matter what she did.

Lucy's concern over her brother's disappearance made speculations impossible. She clung to Harry with the dependence of a newborn kitten, and though Audrey found her irritating, she was too pathetic to reprimand or even to escape. Audrey endured as long as she could, but by ten o'clock she announced she was going to bed.

Harry surprised her by declaring that he meant to do the same, then encouraged Lucy to retire as well. Tomorrow was the ball, he reminded them. They would all need their rest.

Moments later, closing her bedroom door behind her, Audrey reflected it was a reminder she didn't need. The ball loomed before her like a march to the guillotine. Not only was she debuting as someone she wasn't, it marked the end of her stay at Far Winds.

How Marianne intended to explain the ruse to everyone after she left, she had no idea. She wondered if Marianne herself did. But that, at least, would not be her problem. She would be on her way back to Saint Duxbury, where she anticipated helping her sister with her wedding and planning her own future. Her enviable future as a governess.

She would not cry. There was more than enough self-pity in the world already.

A knock sounded at the door, and she went to it smoothing back her restless hair—a hopeless task, as the curly mop always did what it wanted. Just like everyone and everything else she knew.

"Harry!" she squeaked.

He immediately shushed her by placing one hand over her mouth, then stepped inside the door with his other arm surrounding her. His eyes swept her face, the bed, the room, the bed, back to her. He retreated.

"Meet me in the rose garden," he whispered. "Ten minutes." And he was gone.

She hadn't needed ten minutes, only one, but she dawdled lest he think her overly anxious. When she entered the open gates of the garden, she saw him by the fountain, the moonlight frosting his auburn hair with silver. She caught her breath at his tall, masculine grace, his noble, pleasing features, and the enchantment of their surroundings. Moisture from the rain had waxed leaves and hedges to a dark shine and clung to rose petals like soft crystals. The statuary gleamed pale and ethereal under the moon's web. Even time appeared influenced by lunar witcheries as she glided toward him with a preternatural slowness, like walking in a dream.

His eyes rested on her with a strange light as he thanked her for meeting him. "I suppose you're wondering why," he said in the husky tones she loved, the voice so unlike his quarreling one, or commanding one, or . . . She was lost in his eyes.

"I imagined you wanted to talk about what happened today with Thorn," she whispered, not wanting to break the spell. "Where do you think he's gone?"

The baron shook his head. "I don't care where he's gone. I want to talk about you. About us."

Audrey swallowed with enormous difficulty, her gaze never leaving his. "You do?"

"Yes." In her distraction in getting here, she had carelessly left a ribbon untied at the collar of her gown, and he bent closely to do the honors. Could he see her heart throbbing through her bodice? she wondered, her mouth going dry. He gave the bow a final tug, straightened, and said, "I wanted to thank you."

Disappointment nearly knocked her off her feet. "I can't imagine why." Her voice had returned to normal, she noticed.

"First of all, I'm grateful to you for helping me to see that no one is perfect."

She blinked and wished she had refused his invitation. "You're too kind, truly you are."

His lips quirked upward. "Secondly, you've helped me understand that I'm the least perfect of all."

At this moment she did not care to dispute him, and so remained silent.

"You've also led me to realize that most people are good and don't intend evil, no matter how their actions appear," he continued.

"I never dreamed my actions would seem so evil to you," she said with growing heat.

"Not yours, you beautiful vixen, but everyone's."

"Oh," she replied softly.

"Most of all, I want to thank you for making me open my heart again." He placed a hand over his chest and patted, smiling sadly. "This one right here. Open for trade. Ready for experience. Ready for joy. For grief. For wonder. For life." His voice lowered to a whisper. "Ready for love. Because of you."

"Be-because of *me?*"

"No one else, my beloved," he said, folding her into his arms with a grin. "And you'd better not tramp over that heart, because it's uncommonly tender at this moment. In fact, it will need all your care and guardianship for a long, long time . . . say a lifetime?"

"Harry," she sobbed into his shoulder, "Are you asking me to—are you—"

"Must I kneel in a puddle to make it plain? I want to marry you, Audrey. I want to spend the rest of my life with you."

"Oh, thank you, Harry," she wept. "But I cannot. Your aunt—I have nothing—I'm no one—"

He covered her mouth with his. After a long, blissful, delicious moment, he released her. "Do you love me?"

"More than anything in God's creation," she vowed.

"That's all we need, my love," he said, and drew her close again. She sank toward him in complete surrender. Her thoughts were a dizzying blur of happiness. She had come to Far Winds to earn a living for her family. Instead, she had found her life.

For most of the following day, Harry absented himself from the house, telling Audrey at breakfast that he meant to look for Thorn at nearby inns and taverns on the slim chance he had not strayed far from home. After Harry left, time passed slowly for her, but the hours were wrapped in a golden, glowing haze.

She did not know if anyone had ever been so happy or so full of dreams as she was. She felt blessed beyond every woman alive. He loved her. The baron had conquered his past and found a way to love her. Audrey believed she could endure anything now.

Harry returned in time for a light repast before the festivities began. He'd had no luck in locating Thornton, but he didn't seem discouraged by it. While they nibbled on grapes and slices of cold ham and chicken in the alcove with Lucy, his eyes locked with Audrey's again and again. His glances were warm reminders of his love, which must remain silent for now. They had agreed to wait until after the ball to make the announcement to his family, when there would be more time for everyone to adjust. Audrey knew Marianne would be upset and didn't look forward to the scene.

And then it was time to dress for the ball. After her bath, Audrey submitted to Felicia's assistance in her preparations. The gown Mrs. Prate had crafted was suitable for a princess, she thought. Indeed, she would never have requested anything so royal, but Marianne had insisted on the gold brocade material. As the stiff, shimmering fabric slid over her petticoats, Audrey had to admit the ball dress was the most beautiful thing she had ever seen. It matched her hair almost exactly, and the golden, diamond-studded tiara that Marianne loaned her made the image in the mirror sparkle.

No, she decided, smiling. It wasn't finery which made her sparkle, but knowing the baron loved her.

As she descended moments later, she found him awaiting her at the foot of the stairs. The light in his eyes reflected back everything she wished for in life.

"You are a vision," he said as she placed her hand on his arm.

"So are you," she responded. He stood impossibly elegant and tall in a black jacket and trousers, a silver brocade waistcoat, and a crisp linen shirt. "No one will look at me or any lady at the ball. All eyes will be drawn to you."

"Careful, miss," he said in an intimate voice. "You'll make me proud and vain."

"That's my intention for the next sixty years, so you had best prepare yourself, my lord."

"Then I am the most fortunate of men."

Further such exchanges were impossible as Lucy approached wearing a lovely white gown overlaid with silver netting, a diamond tiara resting upon her head.

"I wish Thorn were here," she said mournfully. Harry commiserated and offered his other arm. The three of them joined Marianne in the salon; she had been brought downstairs in her chair only moments before. Her patrician beauty was enhanced by a garnet damask gown, and she looked at Audrey with distant approval before asking Tidwell to wheel her to the ballroom where the receiving line would be held. Harry followed with the young ladies.

Audrey had only briefly seen the ballroom during her stay at Far Winds, as that airy chamber was located on the first floor of the east wing, a portion of the house seldom used. Everything certainly looked in order now. The servants had polished the wooden floor to a sheen, and the woodwork, ivory walls, and blue velvet draperies had been cleaned. Long windows on three sides of the room showed glimpses of the darkening landscape outside, and rows of chairs for nondancers were aligned before them. In one corner a string ensemble tuned their instruments to the violin. The wall to the immediate right of the entrance supported a raised platform with steps leading off either end, and it was here they stationed themselves to greet their guests.

Before many moments passed, the company began to arrive. Throughout the next half-hour, Audrey felt her cheeks growing pinker as she became increasingly aware of their sharp interest in her. Of course she'd known this avidity was coming, for everyone had heard about the young woman purported to be Marianne's daughter. The lie had never grown easier, however; and now that she was to become Harry's wife, she wondered if her neighbors would ever forgive her deception. She grew more and more uneasy.

Finally, the music began, and Harry danced the first selection, an old-fashioned minuet, with her. She was thankful her mother had taught Rebecca and herself several dances in the privacy of the vicarage, or she would have been completely lost. Even so, every time he touched her, concentration flew away. She would have to mind her steps or he would cry off for shame of possessing a clumsy wife.

Since so many were curious about her, Audrey's dance card filled quickly. Before every selection was filled, however, she searched the room for a gentleman wearing a kerchief. She found the short, stocky fellow speaking to an older man near the doorway.

"Forgive me, sir," she said to him, steadying her gaze upon his startled eyes so as not to stare at the black kerchief which covered his mouth and chin. "I've just learned you are Captain Berkbile, and I've heard so much about your exploits at the Peninsula. Would you think it terribly bold of me to reserve the next dance for you?"

The man glanced at his companion, then stiffened his back. "I should be honored," he said with a bow, and led her to the floor.

The hours passed. Audrey danced with many gentlemen,

but whenever conversation turned to her identity, she artfully changed the subject.

Finally the moment she dreaded most came. Marianne planned to make her announcement before the guests broke away for supper, which would be served in the formal dining room and courtyard. As the clock struck eleven, she signaled that Audrey, Harry, and Lucy should join her on the dais. Audrey breathed deeply and took her place between Marianne and the baron.

Tidwell called the guests to order, then wheeled Marianne to the forefront.

"My friends and neighbors," she began, "I'm happy my health allows me to visit with you tonight."

"We're pleased, too!" shouted someone in the crowd, and there were convivial murmurs of agreement.

"Thank you all," Marianne said. "I know many of you have been speculating about this ball, the first I've given in so very many years, and now I will answer all of your questions with—"

"Hold a moment," said a strong voice from the doorway. Audrey met Harry's surprised eyes, then turned to the door. The guests stirred as if a strong wind had passed over them, and they murmured and whispered with excitement.

"Thorn," Lucy said, sounding relieved.

"Before you speak, Aunt Marianne, I have someone I'd like you to see," he said.

Thorn was finely clothed, the cut of his black evening garments contrasting pleasingly with his golden hair, and he turned to collect something—Audrey could not see what because he was in the way. And then she *did* see, and her heart jumped so violently she thought it might leap from her breast.

The room fell into a stunned silence, except for the glide of wheels rolling across the oaken floor.

Thorn was pushing an ivory wheelchair in which sat a

slight young woman. She was a lovely girl, her skin the peachy porcelain so esteemed in their country, and her ash-blond curls were caught up becomingly in a pink ribbon that matched her satin gown. Tiny slippers peeked prettily from her hem, but they seemed only to draw one's gaze to the imprint of gaunt, wasted legs beneath her skirt. Her eyes, a startling blue, were fixed with relentless intensity upon Marianne.

Beside Audrey, the lady struggled to her feet, groaned, tried to speak. Harry moved instantly to support her. Audrey drew nearer to them, and Lucy, one hand to her chest, paced forward, her body trembling from her tiara to her silver slippers.

"Roxanne?" Lucy breathed. Her eyes flickered to Audrey, returned to the invalid. And then she repeated wonderingly, "Roxanne?"

"Hello, Lucy," the girl said, her gaze never leaving Marianne. "Hello, Mother. I've come home."

The older lady's face crumpled, smoothed, crumpled again as she moved down the steps. Harry tightened his arm about her waist, keeping her upright. She came within a yard of the chair and seemed unable to go further.

"Is it truly you?" she asked in a wavering voice. "Are you my daughter?"

Her query, spoken so pitiably and with such a long history of suffering, pierced Audrey to the core. For a moment she was unable to bear the emotional intensity and closed her eyes. When she opened them, Marianne had crossed the remaining distance and was crouched before the chair, her hands braced on its side rails. The guests maintained a breathless quiet, though several were sniffing, and someone blew his nose.

"Don't you recognize me?" the girl asked, the cast of her features solemn but otherwise unreadable. Audrey had the sensation of great emotions tightly leashed. "Perhaps you prefer not to, since I am in this chair."

The lady lifted one trembling hand to the invalid's cheek. "It *is* you," she said, and slowly gathered the young woman into her arms. "My Roxanne. Oh, my darling child. Oh, thank God, thank God. You are home."

She had been correct all along, Harry thought moments later when the family retired to the salon and closed the doors to bar the curious. His aunt's scheme had yielded Roxanne. If he lived a hundred years, he would never recover from the shock. Perhaps there was something to be said for a mother's intuition after all.

Marianne had ordered her guests to resume their entertainment, and the lilt of a waltz and excited voices could be heard through the walls. But inside the salon, hardly a dry eye was to be seen. Even Thornton pressed a handkerchief to his face intermittently, and Harry felt a suspicious stinging behind his lids. He had not wept since his mother's death, and he told himself not to do so now. Audrey was streaming enough for both of them, and someone had to remain strong.

Only Roxanne appeared unmoved. He did not wish to think it, but the coldness behind her eyes made further identification unnecessary. Beyond a doubt, this was the Roxanne he remembered, and he fought a rising tide of dislike that he knew was as uncharitable as it was immature.

"Where have you been all these years, my child?" Marianne was asking. With sudden anger she turned on Thornton. "If you're behind this, if you have kept my daughter from me—"

"Don't," Roxanne interrupted, her vibrant voice amazing

Harry in its similarity to Marianne's. "He didn't keep me from you. *I* kept me from you."

The lady stared. "I don't understand."

"Of course you don't. You never did." Her glance found Harry. "You haven't changed much. Still playing the sycophant to my mother? I'm certain you remain her favorite." Before he could respond, her gaze moved on to Audrey. "And this is my impersonator, I gather. You look nothing like me."

No, she didn't, Harry thought, his old feelings for Roxanne reopening like festering wounds. *Audrey is an angel, whereas you are a shrew.* But she had been missing for seven years and was crippled, so he kept his feelings to himself.

"Hurry and tell us what happened to you," Lucy demanded. "Now that I see you I don't know why I thought for one minute that she"—Lucy pointed to Audrey accusingly—"could be you. And why haven't you dismissed the imposter, Aunt Marianne? We don't know who she is! And how is it you were able to walk to this room unaided—have you recovered? I don't understand anything!"

Marianne said, "I'll explain once Roxanne is done speaking." She was seated beside the wheelchair, and now she reached for her daughter's hand. "Tell me why you wanted to disappear. Make me understand. Didn't you realize your absence would devastate me?"

"Why should I think that, when you had your son again?"

"What are you talking about?"

"I was barely able to remember Joseph before he died, but afterward you elevated him to sainthood. Every day of my life you compared me to him, and I was always found wanting. When Harry came to live with us, he became Joseph to you. Everything Harry did was perfect. Everything I did was not. I was afraid of him, did you know

that, Mother? You should. I told you often enough that I
thought he might murder me. I've learned since that I was
wrong, but you did nothing to soothe my fears. You said I
was being ridiculous."

Harry reminded himself that Roxanne was only seventeen and had doubtless suffered great pain, which can un-
hinge the hardiest mind. Nevertheless, the childishness of
her resentments staggered him.

Marianne appeared to take no umbrage. "I'm sorry I
didn't realize what importance you were giving those
events." Tenderly she touched her child's hair. "Naturally I
wanted Harry to feel at home, for he had been through
much. But no one could ever take your place or Joseph's,
and I never meant you to think he had." Slowly, Marianne's
fingers dropped to Roxanne's knee. "What happened to
your legs, dearest?"

The girl's eyes narrowed. "I knew that would be the first
thing you'd want to know. Why is Lady Hastings's daughter
crippled? The image of perfection is gone, isn't it, Mother?
I knew you would be ashamed of me. That's why I told
Thorn I never wanted to go back. If you thought I was
imperfect before, what would you think of me now?"

She leaned toward Marianne. "I never intended to return
to Far Winds today or any day. But you left me no choice.
Suspicion had fallen on Thorn, and I couldn't allow you
to send him off to gaol. We don't care about the inheritance,
Mother. You may leave it to whomever you wish, for Thorn
keeps his mother and me in fine style—"

"Thorn supports you?" Harry could not help saying.

Lucy cried, "You and his—*my*—mother? Thorn, have
you seen our mother and didn't tell me?"

"I couldn't," Thorn said. "When Roxanne fell into the
pit—"

Audrey exclaimed, "So she did fall!"

"Stop!" Marianne held her hands to her temples. "Start at the beginning, Roxanne."

The girl's lips pressed into a humorless smile. "Very well. On my last day here, unbeknownst to Thorn, I followed him to a cave we'd explored several times. He planned to descend into a deep hole we'd found, and I wanted to as well. But he said it was too dangerous for me." She gave Thorn a soft look. "He was correct, but I was stubborn. While he was nearing the bottom, I arrived and began to lower myself down the rope. He begged me to go back. I tried, for I quickly found it more difficult than I'd imagined. But then I slipped and fell all the way to the bottom."

"Dear God," Marianne breathed. To Thornton she said, "You should have told me at once. How could you not do so? How could you be so cruel?"

"He wasn't being cruel," Roxanne said. "He was merely a boy, and he felt responsible for Lucy. If you had thrown him out for his negligence toward me, what would he have done? How could he watch out for his sister? And you would have, don't say otherwise, Mother, even though he didn't deserve it. Besides, I wouldn't allow him to take me to you. Not like I was."

She stared at her hands, her voice growing calm. "He carried me on his back out of the cave, borrowed a horse from the stable and took me to his mother. She nursed me in her little rooms in London, and there I felt more love and acceptance than I ever knew at Far Winds. When I begged her to allow me to stay, she was willing but couldn't support me. That's when Thorn began to send her most of his allowance, the allowance you give him, Mother. Do you appreciate the irony? And that's how we lived for several years, with his funds and the small amounts Cherise earned sewing. She said it seemed a fair exchange." Her gaze lifted to Marianne's. "She was raising your daughter while you raised hers."

Eyes sparking, Marianne said, "She did it for revenge."

"My mother," Lucy said. "You're talking about living with my mother, Roxanne, and I didn't even know she was alive."

Thorn looked at her with compassion. "Our mother never lost contact with us. When Father died and left us destitute, she had no choice but to come here. Aunt Marianne was willing to take the three of us in, but Mother knew she blamed her for Father's descent. She couldn't tolerate her censure, and so she departed, hoping to earn enough to have us join her again. When she left, Aunt Marianne forbid her to have further communication with us, but she kept in contact with me secretly. You were too young to keep quiet, Lucy. I would have told you later, but after Roxanne's accident, I couldn't. I'm sorry, Sister."

"Why wouldn't you allow them to communicate with their mother?" Audrey asked the lady.

With the briefest of glances at her, Marianne said, "I felt her influence would be unfavorable. My brother didn't drink to excess or gamble until he married Cherise."

Harry felt Audrey's hand creep into his. He closed his fingers over hers and gave her an encouraging look despite his own dismay at his aunt's behavior.

Lucy's eyes shone with hurt. "Thorn, I don't understand why you didn't take me to live with Mother."

"Because the allowances would be cut off," Marianne stated baldly.

"That's exactly it," Thorn admitted. "And until recently I couldn't afford the loss of that income. But now we can, at least for a while."

"Thorn has become quite a hand with the cards," Roxanne said. "He's recently won a tidy sum that will support us for some time, so you may return with us if you wish, Lucy."

"Roxanne, do you mean to say you intend to leave again?" Marianne queried. "I forbid it!"

"You cannot forbid me anything, Mother. As of last evening, I'm a married lady and under my husband's protection." Roxanne smiled up at Thornton. "May I introduce you to your new son-in-law? I have wanted to marry him since I was a child."

Harry's fingers tightened around Audrey's. As Marianne sank into her chair, Thorn placed a hand on his wife's shoulder and gave the older woman a look of cool amusement.

"Always be careful what you wish for, my dear," he said.

Epilogue

On the second Saturday in October, Audrey was seated at her dressing table adjusting her veil when the baron opened the door without knocking, walked three paces into the room, then apologized profusely.

"You know you aren't supposed to see the bride before the wedding," she chided.

"Too late for that," he said, bending her backward for a passionate kiss. When his embrace went on too long, she fought him laughingly.

"Harry, Harry! What will Rebecca think?"

"Rebecca?" He released her, looked innocently around his bedroom, then pretended shock at the sight of the young lady standing in white before his cheval mirror. "Oh, you meant *that* bride. Then it's perfectly all right that I see her, since I'm not the groom."

"Oh, what nonsense," she said, her glance caressing him.

"Now you've hurt my feelings." He appealed to Rebecca. "Do you hear how she speaks to me after only six weeks of marriage? What will she be like in a year, I ask you?"

"More insufferable than ever, I imagine," Rebecca said, her eyes glowing as she looked back and forth between them.

Audrey observed their banter with joy overflowing in her

heart. How her sister had blossomed in the past weeks at
Far Winds. The love of a fine man, the safety of her own
home, the knowledge that their father's care was secure—
what wonders these simple things had accomplished in Rebecca's life. What wonders they'd accomplished in Audrey's,
too.

She went to her sister, lifted her veil and kissed her
cheek. Rebecca had taken to wearing her hair down, and
the scar lay almost hidden behind a fall of lustrous brown
hair. She was bothered less by it now, Audrey thought.
Nathan had told her it made her look more interesting than
the average beauty.

"Now let me think, why did I come in here?" Harry
said. "Oh, yes. To fetch the two of you. Nathan is tearing
out his hair worrying that Rebecca will come to her senses
and cry off while there's still time. So if the ravishing at-
tendant can be persuaded to proceed, and if Rebecca hasn't
changed her mind, I shall escort the lovely bride to her
father's side."

Giggling, Rebecca declared she had no better use of her
time than to marry Nathan. Audrey gathered her spray of
flowers and, giving the couple behind her a fond smile, she
walked forward.

Below the balcony, the hall was filled with rows of servants and a few neighbors who knew the steward well, all
of them looking up at the small wedding party. Nathan and
the Reverend Foggerton stood at the bottom step, and their
father waited in his chair to give Rebecca away.

Since Audrey's wedding had also taken place on the elegant stair of the manor, the scene reminded her sweetly of
her own ceremony, despite the difference in wedding
guests—Marianne, Thorn, Roxanne, Lucy and Cherise had
been present then, but could not return so quickly to Far
Winds for Rebecca's marriage.

At her appearance, the string quartet at the far end of

the balcony began the processional march. She descended slowly, continuing to think of her own wedding and the events of the past months.

Marianne had insisted upon giving Audrey the ten thousand pounds she'd promised for her impersonation. After a number of refusals, Audrey had finally given way and accepted the gift in the guise of a wedding present. With Harry's permission, she was using most of it to enlarge Nathan's farmhouse to better accommodate her father, who declared he was too old to adapt to a fancy house like Far Winds.

The relationship between Marianne and Roxanne remained turbulent, but at least communication was taking place. When Roxanne continued to refuse to stay at Far Winds, the lady had used a portion of her fortune to purchase a town house in London, and she lived there now with her daughter and Thorn. Although Audrey found Roxanne's prickly personality difficult, her restoration of the girl's forgotten diary had softened the way to a budding friendship. She and Harry planned to visit them in London during the Season.

Lucy had gone to stay with her mother and dwelled within walking distance of her brother. In the more lively atmosphere of the City (Lucy wrote) she had made a number of acquaintances, and several gentlemen had called upon her. Audrey believed Lucy's increasing warmth toward herself stemmed from her alliance with the baron more than anything, but she was pleased to accept any signs of peace in his complicated, troubled family.

By comparison, her own relatives seemed the epitome of all that was normal. She could not be happier that Rebecca and her father would be living nearby.

The marriage party had reached their designated places, and the vicar began the service. Her beloved baron, having given Rebecca into the care of her father, was standing to

Nathan's right. Within a moment their sire had performed his part of the ceremony, and when Tidwell wheeled him backward, Audrey moved closer to Rebecca. From this angle she could observe her beautiful sister, a beatific Nathan, and her incomparable husband.

As blissful as the moment was, she could not wait until the wedding party departed. It would be the first time she and Harry would have Far Winds to themselves. But not for long, she thought, unconsciously cradling her stomach with one hand and gazing downward, a secret smile curving her lips. Not if her suspicions were true. She raised her eyes to find Harry watching her, his expression warm and a shade speculative. With a pert, playful look, she returned her attention to the vicar.

After the ceremony ended, the wedding party was applauded and cheered as they led the way to the dining room and a light repast within. Rebecca greeted her well-wishers with shy, darting smiles while Nathan beamed at everyone.

When Harry's arm slid around her waist, Audrey leaned backward with a contented sigh. "She's so happy," she said. "Rebecca is in love."

"No more so than her sister, I hope."

"That wouldn't be possible," she assured him.

He pulled her closer. "I'm glad to hear it. Lately you've been looking as if something's on your mind. I've been afraid you're keeping something from me."

"A woman should have *some* secrets," she teased. "Although I might be persuaded to tell, if the proper methods were used."

"Methods of persuasion, is it?" he asked huskily.

Despite the company around them, Audrey could not resist sending him a sensuous glance. An answering fire sparked in his eyes.

"Fortunately, my husband, you know them all," she whispered.

BOOK YOUR PLACE ON OUR WEBSITE AND MAKE THE READING CONNECTION!

We've created a customized website just for our very special readers, where you can get the inside scoop on everything that's going on with Zebra, Pinnacle and Kensington books.

When you come online, you'll have the exciting opportunity to:

- View covers of upcoming books
- Read sample chapters
- Learn about our future publishing schedule (listed by publication month *and author*)
- Find out when your favorite authors will be visiting a city near you
- Search for and order backlist books from our online catalog
- Check out author bios and background information
- Send e-mail to your favorite authors
- Meet the Kensington staff online
- Join us in weekly chats with authors, readers and other guests
- Get writing guidelines
- AND MUCH MORE!

**Visit our website at
http://www.zebrabooks.com**

Celebrate Romance With Two of Today's Hottest Authors

Meagan McKinney

__In the Dark	$6.99US/$8.99CAN	0-8217-6341-5
__The Fortune Hunter	$6.50US/$8.00CAN	0-8217-6037-8
__Gentle from the Night	$5.99US/$7.50CAN	0-8217-5803-9
__A Man to Slay Dragons	$5.99US/$6.99CAN	0-8217-5345-2
__My Wicked Enchantress	$5.99US/$7.50CAN	0-8217-5661-3
__No Choice But Surrender	$5.99US/$7.50CAN	0-8217-5859-4

Meryl Sawyer

__Thunder Island	$6.99US/$8.99CAN	0-8217-6378-4
__Half Moon Bay	$6.50US/$8.00CAN	0-8217-6144-7
__The Hideaway	$5.99US/$7.50CAN	0-8217-5780-6
__Tempting Fate	$6.50US/$8.00CAN	0-8217-5858-6
__Unforgettable	$6.50US/$8.00CAN	0-8217-5564-1

Call toll free **1-888-345-BOOK** to order by phone, use this coupon to order by mail, or order online at **www.kensingtonbooks.com**.

Name _____

Address _____

City _____ State _____ Zip _____

Please send me the books I have checked above.

I am enclosing	$_____
Plus postage and handling*	$_____
Sales tax (in New York and Tennessee only)	$_____
Total amount enclosed	$_____

*Add $2.50 for the first book and $.50 for each additional book.

Send check or money order (no cash or CODs) to:

Kensington Publishing Corp., Dept. C.O., 850 Third Avenue, New York, NY 10022

Prices and numbers subject to change without notice.

All orders subject to availability.

Visit our website at **www.kensingtonbooks.com**.